W9-DAQ-989

THE FAMILY PLOT

A Novel

MEGAN COLLINS

THORNDIKE PRESS
A part of Gale, a Cengage Company

GALE
A Cengage Company

LIBRARY OF CONGRESS CIP DATA ON FILE.
CATALOGUING IN PUBLICATION FOR THIS BOOK
IS AVAILABLE FROM THE LIBRARY OF CONGRESS.

ISBN-13: 978-1-4328-9329-3 (hardcover alk. paper)

Published in 2021 by arrangement with Atria Books, a Division of Simon & Schuster, Inc.

Printed in Mexico
Print Number: 01   Print Year: 2022

For the murderinos

For the murderings

ONE

My parents named me Dahlia, after the Black Dahlia — that actress whose body was cleaved in half, left in grass as sharp as scalpels, a permanent smile sliced onto her face — and when I first learned her story at four years old, I assumed a knife would one day carve me up. My namesake was part of me, my future doomed by her violent death. That meant my oldest brother, Charlie, who had escaped the Lindbergh baby's fate by living past age two, would still be abducted someday. My sister, Tate, would follow in her own namesake's footsteps, become a movie star, then become a body in a pool of blood. And my twin brother, Andy, named for Lizzie Borden's father — I was sure his head was destined for the ax.

It didn't take me long to shed that belief, to understand that our names were just one of the many ways we honored victims of murder. But even after I stopped expecting us all to be killed, Andy insisted our family was "unnatural," that the way we were raised wasn't right.

I still don't know where he got that idea; back then, the life we lived in our drafty, secluded mansion was the only kind of life we knew.

Now, I'm standing in front of it, the home he ran away from on our sixteenth birthday — two years before we were scheduled to get our inheritance ("Leaving Money," as Charlie called it), and three before I left myself, having waited there, certain my twin would return, for as long as I could. I used to sit at the bottom of the stairs, gaze pinned to the door, hoping he'd walk through it again, tell me all my missing him was for nothing.

I was the only one who missed him. Mom read his note — *The only way out is to never come back* — and swallowed hard. "Your brother's chosen his own path," she said, swiping at her tears as if that was the end of it. Dad stomped around the house for a while, grumbling about the hunting trip Andy had skipped out on. "He's a coward, that twin of yours," Dad told me, as if Andy belonged to me alone. And then there was Charlie and Tate, who were visiting when we found the note. They'd come all this way

8

for our sixteenth birthday, but they left without helping me look for him, Charlie claiming he had an audition, Tate trailing after him like always. Which left just me, alone in my anguish for years after that, lighting the candles with Mom and Dad, saying the Honoring prayer that I've since learned they created themselves.

Dad died the other day. That's why I've come back. And I'm hoping this will be the thing that brings Andy back, too. Maybe he's already inside, listening for my footsteps. Maybe I can stop my internet searches. Every week, I look for my brother on Facebook and Twitter and Instagram. Greta, who runs the café beneath my tiny apartment, has taught me all the tricks on social media, but still, my searches come back each time with nothing.

Today, I took the long way up from the ferry, watching the rocky shore recede below me as I climbed higher toward the center of Blackburn Island, where our house looms stony and colorless in front of the woods. For minutes now, I've been staring at those skeletal trees, remembering how Andy used to whack at them, how he'd pick up his ax whenever something flared inside him — and how almost anything could set him off: Dad quizzing him about hunting rifles;

9

Mom teaching us about Ted Bundy's victims; Tate sketching her namesake, Sharon. For all the hours Andy and I spent locked to each other's hips — hiding in the credenza to jump out at Mom; distracting our groundskeeper with leaf pile forts — I never understood why he'd spring out of the house sometimes and pick up the ax that leaned against the shed. And when he told me, over and over, that our family was unnatural, that we needed the outside world, needed to trust people beyond each other, I didn't understand that, either.

The November wind is icy on the back of my neck, pushing me closer to the front door. Dead leaves skitter around my feet as if welcoming me home.

It's been seven years since I last stepped foot on this porch, even though when I left at nineteen I didn't go far. My apartment on the mainland is a quarter mile from the ferry, easy access should Andy ever return, but when I first moved there, Greta acted like I was from a distant, mythical place. *I can't believe you grew up on Blackburn Island,* she said. *I'm obsessed with the Blackburn Killer. I have every article that's ever mentioned him, and I spend hours a day on message boards, discussing all the theories. Oh my god, did you know any of the victims?*

10

I could recite their names in my sleep. Not just the victims of our island's serial killer, who murdered seven women over two decades and was never caught, but the ones from quiet neighborhoods, the ones on city streets. We honored them each year on the anniversaries of their deaths. We uttered their names as we stood in a circle, lighting each other's slim white candles. Then we whispered the prayer — *we can't restore your life, but we strive to restore your memory with this breath* — before blowing out the flames. When I told Greta I didn't know the victims personally, but that they were part of our Honoring calendar, her forehead wrinkled with confusion, and I wondered for the first time if Andy had been right, that there was something unnatural about us.

But is he here now, sitting on the stairs, watching the door from inside as I force myself to turn its knob and finally push it open?

I blink until my eyes adjust. The light outside was dazzling and real, but in here it's dimmer than dusk. The foyer, I see now, is vacant and cavernous; the staircase holds nobody up. The chandelier sways a little, as if something has nudged it, and I have to focus on breathing until the pang of being wrong subsides.

"Look who finally showed up. Tate and I have been here since yesterday."

I turn toward Charlie's voice. Through the wide archway to the right, I see him sitting in the living room, in curtained, lampless dark. I can just make out the glass of amber liquid in his hand. He sips it now, barely ten a.m., before he stands and approaches, burgundy-sweatered and lanky as ever.

"What, you're not a hugger?" he asks with a wink.

He embraces me before I can answer. When he lets go, he takes my bag off my shoulder and slings it over his own, the weight of it tipping him farther than his typical sideways slouch.

"You look good, Dolls," he says. "What's it been — nine years?"

I blink at him like he's another dark room I have to get used to. How can he not know it's been ten years, four months, and three days since we last saw each other? It's easy to remember. You just take the time it's been since we last saw Andy and subtract one day. I suppose, though, that Charlie's tried to see me before now. He's sent me texts over the years, inviting me to his shows — the off-Broadway ones and the *really* off-Broadway ones — but I've never gone. I knew I wouldn't be able to stomach it, watching him pretend to be somebody else. To me, he'll always be the man who read Andy's note — *The only way out is to never come back* — and returned right away to New York. Greta likes to remind me that Charlie was twenty-six at the time, someone with a life already separate from us, but what she doesn't get is that when I talk about Charlie, or Tate, or my parents, I'm not looking for perspective; I'm looking for her to agree that all of them failed my twin.

Now, I tell Charlie exactly how long it's been, and he eyes me strangely before sipping his drink again.

"Where's everyone else?" I ask.

"Tate's playing dutiful daughter to the grieving widow upstairs. And Dad — well, he's in the morgue still, waiting for his Honoring tomorrow."

I skip past the image of our father, cold in a drawer somewhere. "Is that really what we're calling it?" I ask. "An Honoring?"

Charlie's mouth tilts in amusement. "What else would we call it?"

I shrug. "Dad wasn't murdered. It doesn't seem like the Honoring rules would apply."

"Well." He leans in conspiratorially, bourbon on his breath. "The way I hear it, Dad's heart was a real bastard about it. Took him out in two seconds flat. Pushed him facedown in his venison stew." He demonstrates by pitching his head toward the mouth of his glass. "Mom had to wipe the meat off his cheeks before the paramedics came. It's poetic, really. Dad hunted so many deer in his lifetime, and in the end, he died on top of one. Seems almost . . . intentional, doesn't it? Like his heart knew what he'd been up to and murdered him for it."

He's smirking. And his words are wobbly. Tate's warned me about this, through her frequent emails I rarely return. She's said that Charlie's a disturbing drunk.

"That's quite a welcome," I tell him. "Thanks."

He shrugs like it's no problem. Like it isn't appalling, describing our father's death that way. But I don't feel it like the kick in the gut I know I should. I didn't feel much of anything when I learned of Dad's heart attack. Just sort of an: *Oh. Okay.* I was at the café, looking for traces of Andy in Detroit (I've been working my way through all the major cities again), and Greta overheard me on the phone. She brought me hot chocolate with extra whipped cream and said she was *so, so sorry, god, that's awful, Dahlia.* But actually, the news of Dad's death was, to me, just news. An inevitable update on the time line of my life.

14

I get why Charlie's acting out, why he's smirky and buzzed. It's a front, I'm sure, for the pain roiling inside him. Charlie actually knew Dad, in ways that I — and I suspect Tate — never did. Dad paid attention to Charlie the same way he paid attention to Andy. All those shooting lessons over the years, those whispered conversations while scoping the woods for the flick of a tail. *I don't know what to do with girls,* Dad confessed once, when I asked why it was only boys who got to go on hunting trips. It's not that I wanted to hunt; I just hated the idea of Andy experiencing something without me. But hearing Dad admit that was a relief. I didn't know what to do with him, either, this man with few words and fewer smiles; with no involvement in our education, not even to watch the murder documentaries Mom showed us; with nothing more than nods of acknowledgment whenever he passed me, as if I were an employee like our groundskeeper, Fritz. I got permission, then, to love Dad less. To not even worry about loving him at all. Which was fine with me. It left more space for Andy.

"Come on," Charlie says. He sets his glass on the credenza, gestures with his chin toward the staircase. "Mom's been waiting for you."

As I follow him up, I glance behind me, still always checking for Andy.

"Don't be rude, Dahlia, say hi to Grandma and Grandpa," Charlie says, throwing me another smirk over his shoulder. And that's fine, if he needs to make this all a joke, but the photos of Mom's parents that line the staircase wall are anything but funny. I know the faces in those frames aren't ghosts — ghosts don't have weddings, don't smoke cigarettes, don't kiss with smiling lips — but they started this, didn't they? Our haunted childhoods. Our haunted lives. And maybe this is what Andy meant when he said our family was unnatural. Because Mom crowded our walls with her murdered parents.

It is unusual, our origin story: Mom moved here at twenty-one, to her family's summer house, immediately after home invaders killed her parents at their Connecticut estate; she married Daniel Lighthouse, an orphan himself, who — for someone who didn't *know what to do with* girls — captivated Mom right away; and Dad indulged her eccentricities, encouraged them even, and did not protest as she turned the mansion into something like a mausoleum.

Before we reach the top of the stairs, I

16

hear footsteps on the landing, and then a gasp. It's Tate, pushing Charlie to the side, rushing to meet me.

"Dahlia!" she says. "What the hell? You're all grown-up!"

She laughs like I'm playing a joke on her, like I'll unzip my skin and emerge as the girl I was the last time she saw me. Then she pulls me into a hug so fierce I almost lose my footing.

"Careful, Tate," Charlie says. "Let's not kill our sister, shall we? Mom hardly has any room left in her shrine." He smiles at our grandparents on the wall, as if they're in on the joke.

It's weird, though — these hugs they've both given me, as if we Lighthouse children were a happy foursome of siblings, not divided into pairs by the difference in our ages, by the fact that Andy and I could read each other's minds, and that Tate just worshiped Charlie. She ignores him now, stepping back to examine me again, and she's as striking as ever, wavy blond hair piled on top of her head, wayward curls framing her face. She's wearing a turquoise sweater over a pair of magenta jeans, and she's the first bright thing I've seen since entering this house. That's part of her "brand" now, brightness. When she photographs herself with her dioramas on Instagram, she's always in pink or aqua or yellow. It's contradictory to her depictions of the Blackburn Killer's crime scenes — the dark rocky shores, the obsidian water, those dead women, who, even in their miniature ice-blue dresses, look like shadows flung upon the rocks — but it works somehow.

I wonder if Andy is one of Tate's fifty-seven thousand followers. I wonder if he ever scrolls through the feed of @die_orama, feeling exposed by our sister's art.

The *New York Post* profiled her last year, and Greta taped those pages to the café wall, insisting I was related to "true-crime royalty." When I read the article, I held my breath, unsure how much Tate had shared with the *Post* about our way of life. Greta's the only one I've told about the possibly "unnatural" things from our childhood, details she's both devoured and savored: the library in the back hall, which we dubbed "the victim room," its bookshelves crowded with newspapers reporting on murders; Mom's homeschooling curriculum that required us to write our own "murder reports," in which we presented our theories of unsolved cases in neat five-paragraph essays. (This detail is Greta's favorite; *You were just like me,* she says, *a citizen detec-*

tive! At first, I thought she invented that term, until she told me about the network of people online who lose hours each day investigating cases.)

The article didn't mention murder reports, but Tate explained that she felt a kinship with the Blackburn Killer's victims, given that he'd been active on the island while she lived there. More than that, she believed that by re-creating the bodies, right down to the rope marks on the women's necks, the *B* branded on their ankles, she was returning the focus to the seven people whose lives were cut short, instead of the intrigue of "whatever sick fuck" did the cutting.

In her Instagram posts, Tate never writes how we grew up honoring those seven women on the anniversaries of their deaths, accumulating dates as the years went by, as the killer kept strangling, kept branding, kept dressing his victims in identical ice-blue gowns, and dumping their bodies in shallow water. But whenever I see Tate's dioramas — those intricate, lifelike, bite-size crime scenes — I can't help but feel like she's sharing family secrets.

"You're *so* grown-up," Tate tells me again. She turns so she appears in profile and tilts her chin up. "And what about me? How do

19

I look? How's" — she pauses to give a mock grimace — "thirty-five treating me?"

"You look great," I say. But she knows that. In the selfies she posts between dioramas, her followers shower her with praise: *Girl, you're gorgeous; I'd kill for your hair.* They love her style, her dioramas, her captions about each victim — and they love Blackburn, too. The *Post* profile, which quoted people who'd learned of Blackburn through @die_orama, explained that Tate has essentially transformed it into a tourist destination, that the shores where all those women were found are now a draw, not a deterrent. "It's exhilarating," one person said, "standing on land where a real serial killer dumped his bodies."

It's been a decade since the Blackburn Killer last struck, but people on the island still dead bolt their doors — a precaution we never needed. It seemed that no one, not even a serial killer, wanted to slip inside our house. "Murder Mansion," the islanders called it.

"Dahlia. You came."

It's Mom at the top of the stairs this time.

"Of course I came," I say.

She's dressed the same as always — sweats and slippers — but she's paler than I've ever seen her, skin like a crumpled piece of paper someone's tried to smooth back out.

Mom wraps me in her arms, leaning down to rest her chin on my shoulder. "I'm so glad you're here," she says on a sigh.

Charlie, above us, fidgets with the strap of my bag. "Yes, what a lovely family reunion," he says. "Right where everyone hoped it would take place: on the stairs."

Tate smacks his arm. Mom exhales into my neck, breath heavy with loss. As she hugs me tighter, I feel how potently she's missing Dad. She was like a moth with him, drawn to a light I could never see. When he entered a room, her eyes flew to his face; when he recounted a recent hunting trip, she leaned forward, fluttery with anticipation. He didn't have to say much — usually didn't — and maybe it's because he said so little that she hung on every word, grateful and stunned that he'd spoken to her at all.

"I'm sorry," I say to her.

"About what?" she asks.

"Global warming?" Charlie can't help but quip. "The wage gap? All your fault, Dolls."

Tate smacks him again.

"About Dad," I say.

Mom pulls back to put her hands on either side of my face. Her eyes are puffy and red, cupped by dark pouches. "Don't be sorry about Dad, he didn't suffer at all.

21

It was a quick, natural death. Shocking, and horrible, but the best there is in the end." She strokes my cheek. "Now, if you're going to be sorry about anything . . ."

"Oh, Mom, not again," Tate says.

"What?" I ask.

"She's been guilt-tripping us," Charlie says.

"No." Mom shakes her head. "No guilt trip."

"She's mad," he continues, "that we've stayed away for so long."

"I'm not mad," Mom insists. "I've just missed you, that's all."

Tate puts her arm around Mom's shoulder. "Do I or do I not call you three times a week?" she asks. "And do I or do I not send you all the treats you can only get in Manhattan? You said you loved those chocolates from Moretti's."

"I did love those chocolates," Mom agrees. "I just love you all more."

"Aw. That's sweet," Charlie says, but there's something tart in his tone. "But like we told you yesterday, which I'm sure Dahlia would agree with —" He looks at me meaningfully, urging me to mimic his nod. "We've had to make our way. And that requires distance. Time. I've been gone as long as I lived here, and I'm *still* adjusting to the world."

Mom swivels to face Charlie, her jaw quivering. "I always meant," she says, "to prepare you for that. For the outside world. That's what everything was for."

She extends her arm toward a photo on the wall, one where her parents laugh at some party, each with a cigarette between their fingers, and she caresses the frame slowly. It's a haunted gesture, as if she's trying to touch the past, trying to save her parents from their future.

"What Charlie means," Tate says, cutting him a glance, "is just — there's so much life out there, you know? I had no idea how much! The world is huge with it."

Mom's fingers drop from the frame. Her shoulders slump.

"And in a way," Tate adds, squeezing Mom closer, "I appreciate it more, I think, because of everything you taught us. Don't you agree, Dahlia?"

Tate's eyes lock onto mine, and they're so blue, so hypnotic, that I find myself nodding. But then I remember Mom's response to Andy's runaway note — *Your brother's chosen his own path* — and I don't know why I'm bothering to comfort her. She's never cared before if we stayed away, and I still haven't forgiven her for that, for giving

23

Andy up so easily.

The fact is, we all had our reasons for never coming back. Charlie claimed he needed to stay close to the city, be ready at the drop of a hat for whatever new role might open up. And because Charlie didn't return to Blackburn, Tate didn't either. *Codependent,* Greta tsked when I told her how they've lived together in the same Manhattan walk-up ever since they both got their inheritance. And me, I lasted only three years in the house without Andy, done with dodging the shadows that piled up like dust bunnies in every corner. But what about him? He left without telling me why, without even saying goodbye, and I've had to live all these years in the not knowing, which is a lonely, comfortless place.

I know he was troubled by things I wasn't. I know he took his ax to the trees in the woods — not to cut them down, but to wound them, scar them, to make them carry something on their bark he couldn't hold inside him anymore. I know his emotions ran hot and hard; he was quick to anger, frustration. But what was it that made him run? I don't believe — I've never believed — that our "unnatural" life was enough of a reason. I haven't forgiven our family for letting him go, and I haven't forgiven him, either, for going.

"I'm just glad you're here now," Mom says to us. "The circumstances are dreadful, of course, but I'm happy to have all my children back home."

All?

Did she really just say all?

"Did you —"

But I'm cut off by a shout bursting through the back door.

"Mrs. Lighthouse! Mrs. Lighthouse!"

The urgency in Fritz's voice prickles the hair on the back of my neck.

He limps into the foyer, quick as a man nearing eighty can. His right leg — the bad one — drags a little, and his long, milky hair is streaked with dirt.

Mom rushes down the stairs to meet him. "What is it?" she asks.

Charlie, Tate, and I clomp down as well, and when Fritz spots me, he does a double take. "You came," he says, breathy from running, from shouting.

"Of course I came," I say, for the second time. "What's going on?"

"It's . . . Outside, I . . ."

He trails off, prompting Charlie to roll his eyes. "What is it? Is everything *o-kay*?" And I remember this now — how Charlie used to speak to Fritz as if he were dumb.

"No. N-n-no," Fritz stammers, his focus still on Mom. "I was in the woods out back, digging up Mr. Lighthouse's plot, and —"

"We're burying him *here*?" Charlie asks Mom.

"Of course. They'll transport him when we're ready."

"But — Isn't that a bit . . . ghoulish?" Charlie asks. And it's a strange question, given our lives.

Mom's shoulders roll back as if he's offended her. "Not at all. That's where my parents are buried. It's the family plot. We put in stones for your father and me."

"Um, guys?" Tate says. She gestures to Fritz, whose eyes are wide, seemingly all pupil.

"I don't know what . . ." our groundskeeper starts. "Or-or *how,* but somebody's already . . ."

"Already what? Spit it out!" Charlie booms, plucking his bourbon off the credenza.

Fritz swallows then, throat bobbing in his neck like all those actors in the crime scene reenactments we saw, their fear looking hard and bulbous inside them. It makes me swallow, too, makes me rub at the hair still rising on the back of my neck. But when Fritz speaks again, his voice doesn't waver.

"Somebody's already buried in Mr. Lighthouse's plot. And I think —" Fritz shifts his gaze to me. "I think it's Andy."

Two

"When was the last time you spoke to your brother?"

A detective is here. He's sitting across from me in the living room, and he's got a notepad and a pen and a sympathetic smile I don't need. Before this, people in white jumpsuits were shuffling back and forth between a van in the driveway and the woods in our backyard. They took samples from the bones, or something like that. Because it's mostly just bones; it isn't Andy.

"It's not my brother in that grave," I tell the detective.

"I hope you're right," he says. "And we're working right now to identify the remains. Dental records, DNA. But in the meantime, your groundskeeper seemed sure it was Andy. Do you have any idea why that might be?"

"You questioned him, didn't you?"

"I did. But I'd like to hear what you think."

I squeeze my mug of hours-old tea. "It's the ax. You talked to my siblings, so I'm sure they told you: Andy used to hack at the trees in our backyard."

"He'd chop them down?"

"No, not chop. More like . . . chip. He'd chip away at them, when he was stressed or angry. It was a coping mechanism."

He leans forward, repositions his pen. "Coping mechanism for what?"

"For . . . I don't know. He'd get mad sometimes. But I guess — well, Fritz said — there was an ax in the . . . that that's what . . ."

"The body was buried with an ax," he finishes for me, "and the skull has fractures consistent with the blade of that ax, leading us to believe, at this point, that the person whose remains are in that grave was killed by the ax they were buried with. And the ax in question appears to belong to your brother. Apparently he carved his name into the handle?"

Andy had bitten his lip as he engraved it, slicing out the *A*, the *N*, struggling with the curve in the *D*. The skin around his eyes, which crinkled so easily, had crimped with concentration.

"That's right," I say. "But if the murder weapon was Andy's ax, wouldn't the assumption be that Andy was the killer — not the one killed?"

"You think your brother murdered someone?"

"Of course not. I'm just saying: it's not my brother in that grave. My family told you he ran away, right? Ten years ago. Anyone could have used the ax after that. But not on him. He was already gone."

"So you've spoken to him in the last decade?"

"Yes, I — Well, no. Not exactly."

"Not exactly?"

The curtain behind him sways, a tiny shiver of movement. And even though the living room doors are closed and the windows are locked, I know it's just a draft. I don't think for a moment that it might be Andy's ghost.

"No," I say. "I haven't spoken to him."

I've learned that outsiders don't understand the link between Andy and me. I tried explaining it to Greta once, but even she just scrunched up her nose. *You mean, like, telepathy?* she asked. And I stopped right there, didn't bother to describe the time I was lying in bed, something like two a.m., rereading a book on the Black Dahlia. I had a flashlight under the covers, hand over my mouth as I got to the part about the cuts across her face, and I heard my door squeak open. I popped my head out from under the blankets to find Andy, who'd felt my horror in his sleep and had been wakened by it like an alarm. He whispered at me then to put the book away, allow my namesake to rest for once.

We knew things about each other, Andy and I, without ever having to utter a word. So if my brother were dead, I would feel it. I would know.

"What makes you think he ran away?" the detective asks.

I tap my fingernail against the mug. "He left a note. My mom told you that already."

He nods, flipping back a few pages in his notebook. *"The only way out is to never come back,"* he reads. "What did he mean by that?"

I tap some more, and he looks at my finger, which instantly stops me.

"What did my family say it meant?" I ask.

"Your sister said to ask you. That you were closest with Andy."

"I *am* closest with Andy," I correct him — because, really, past tense? It's just bones in a hole in the ground, and Andy's out there, in Vegas maybe, where people spend

31

thousands each night on the hope for a brighter tomorrow, where any shadows are chased away by flashing, exuberant lights. I bet no one talks about murder out there. I bet he loves it.

"He wanted something different," I tell the detective, "from the way we were raised."

"And how were you raised, exactly?"

I stare at him. "I think you know."

With all the commotion before — the people in white jumpsuits; Fritz tracking dirt into the house, throwing condolences around as if he had any way of knowing it was Andy in that grave — I didn't recognize the detective at first. He seemed a few years older than me, and he looked like anybody: thin, average height, dark hair that swooped at the top, like a cat had been licking him. But when we started this "interview," he introduced himself to me again — Elijah Kraft — and I almost laughed. *You're Chief Kraft's son,* I said, and he had the decency, at least, to look a little sheepish. *He's not the chief anymore,* he told me. *My father's in a nursing home. For dementia.* I think I was supposed to feel sorry for him. But was Edmond Kraft sorry? Did he ever think of it all — his obsession with us back then; his slinking around our property, always with

32

the intention to catch us in some dark, criminal act — and feel even a tinge of remorse? I doubt it. Chief Kraft was like everyone else: suspicious of us, monitoring us, believing himself entitled to his intrusions.

"I know the rumors," Elijah says.

"Ones your father probably started."

"I know they call this place Murder Mansion."

"They're idiots," I say.

"I know your family worships the dead."

And at this, I actually do laugh.

"No?" Elijah asks, jotting something down. "Is that incorrect?"

"We *honor* the dead," I tell him. "Specifically, victims of murder."

Which Andy isn't. He isn't.

"And what does that mean exactly?" Elijah asks. "To honor them?"

I glance at the living room doors, slid together, shut tight. It feels so odd, to talk about this with a stranger, especially Chief Kraft's son. I can picture Mom, listening at the door, bristling as I speak. But this man is a detective, he's seen bones in our backyard, and I know what he's thinking.

"On the anniversaries of their murders," I say, "we would light candles for them. Say their name, say a prayer. The idea was to

33

meditate on their death — but more important, their life."

"A prayer to whom?" he asks, eyes stuck to whatever he's writing. "You said you didn't worship them, but prayer is a means of worship, right?"

His pen races across the page, moving too much for the little I've said. "A prayer on their behalf," I reply.

"To God?"

"No, not to God. To . . . I don't know."

My siblings and I never took the Honorings as seriously as our parents did. Charlie made faces as we lit the candles, shimmied his shoulders as we chanted the words, and the rest of us smothered our smiles so Mom wouldn't see. It was never the murders we were mocking, or the victims themselves — we respected every story we learned. It was just the "silly, incessant ritual" of it all, as Charlie once said, the idea that candles and a sentence could do anything for the dead.

"You don't know," Elijah repeats.

"God wasn't part of our homeschool curriculum."

Now he looks at me. His eyes, shadowed by dark brows, narrow. "I've heard it referred to as 'the murder curriculum.' Is it true that's all you learned about? Murder?"

"We learned about mur-*ders*," I correct him.

"And that was your whole education? Just . . . murder?"

"Mur-*ders*," I say again, because there's a world of difference. "We learned plenty of other things, too. I know math up to trigonometry. I know supernovas and black holes. I know the Gettysburg Address. I just also know Rachel Nickell."

Forty-nine stab wounds; killed in broad daylight; her two-year-old son covered in her blood.

"And she is?" Elijah prompts.

I remember Mom's reenactment. This was something she did to illustrate the brutality of a crime — and to protect us against it. She believed that if we witnessed the horrors that others had experienced, we'd recognize the same danger if it ever came our way. For Rachel Nickell's reenactment, she wore an outfit of all white, and jabbed herself with a red marker, scribbling on her shirt to indicate blood. Forty-nine times she struck herself. Forty-nine times I flinched.

"She was murdered," I say.

He bites the inside of his cheek, but it feels like he's biting his tongue. "I see." He looks at his notebook again. "So you say Andy left ten years ago, when the two of you were sixteen."

"The night of our sixteenth birthday. Yes."

"And what was he like that day? The last time you saw him."

"He was fine," I say. "Our siblings had come back for the first time since they'd left home. It'd been eight years since we'd seen Charlie, seven since Tate. So he was excited."

Excited is not the right word, but I'm certain that the real ones — *moody, jittery* — would only keep the detective jotting in his notebook. I remember it well, though: the way Andy's leg shook beneath the table like a jackhammer. I remember, later, Charlie staring at us from across the candles as we said the prayers for our namesakes. He seemed astonished by us, almost unsettled, like he'd only now remembered we existed. I glanced at Andy to see if he'd noticed our brother's stare, but he was scowling at his candle as if he could blow out its flame with only his gaze.

He'd been stormy for days, spending more time with the trees, his ax. Whenever I asked him what was wrong, he snapped away from me like a startled animal. *Nothing, I'm just tired, I haven't been sleeping well* — and he did have bags beneath his eyes, dark as bruises. On our birthday, he went to bed soon after the Honoring, grumbling about Tate and Charlie, how they scurried away together into one of their rooms before the smoke from the candles had even cleared. He'd been planning to ask them about "out," he said. That's what he called it. Out.

"Excited," Elijah echoes. "So excited he ran away that night? So excited he said, *The only way out is to never come back?*"

I fidget with my mug. "We were very sheltered growing up. We really only left the island a handful of times. And I think Andy saw Charlie and Tate that night, back from a big city, and got inspired to leave early. Be out in the world like them."

That's what I've been telling myself, for all these years. But inspired or not, Andy broke something that night when he left. I always pictured our connection like a silver cord between us, a taut wire, but when he wrote that note, snuck into the darkness to wait for the ferry, he might as well have cut it in two. Hacked it apart with his ax.

"Inspired to leave early," Elijah mumbles, reading back his notes. "Earlier than what?"

"Eighteen. When we were supposed to leave."

His expression darkens. "You were forced to leave at eighteen?"

"No, not forced, just — Our siblings did

37

it first, when they each gained control of their trust funds. And Andy and I planned to do the same."

The trust fund is how I manage the way I do — jobless, hunched over my laptop, scouring photos of any crowd on social media, looking for crinkly eyes, for the cowlick on the back of Andy's head.

Elijah nods, writing down my answer.

"And once someone in your family left home," he says, "they just . . . never returned? Until now, anyway?" He pauses. "I was sorry to hear about your father."

But he doesn't sound sorry. He sounds suspicious. His gaze creeps around my head to the wall behind me, where Honoring candles are stacked like skinny firewood on the shelves.

"Like I said," I tell him, "Charlie and Tate came back one time."

"That's right. On the night before you noticed Andy was gone. Ten years ago. Why did they come back on that night in particular?"

I shrug. I've never known what was special to them about our sixteenth birthday. It wasn't the rite of passage to us that it was to others. We weren't gifted cars, like kids in movies.

"Was there something specific" — he tilts

38

forward — "that all of you were staying away from?" He lowers his voice. "Did your parents ever hurt you?"

"What? No!"

"Then why didn't any of you come back?"

"I don't know! I don't know about Charlie and Tate, other than Tate doesn't do anything without Charlie and Charlie wanted to stay in New York. But me, I just — my brother ran away — and I waited for him until I was nineteen, until I finally took him for his word, what he said in the note about never coming back. And I wasn't as close with the rest of my family as I was with him."

That's an understatement. The truth is, it felt pointless to get close to them. Mom was always dying in front of us, each reenactment more convincing than the last, so I began to think of her as only half there. Dad was there even less, lacing his boots to head out hunting, barely registering my presence, even as we stood in the same circle for Honorings. Charlie and Tate were a unit, indifferent and impenetrable to Andy and me — which was fine, because Andy and I were a unit, too, and as long as I had him, I knew I was valued, complete.

Andy gave me the best of everything. If we split a sandwich, he handed me the big-

39

ger half. If he grabbed two glasses from the cabinet, he offered me the one without water spots. If we sat on the porch steps, he gestured for me to take the seat in the sun. I'd say to him, *You deserve the best thing, too, you know,* and he'd reply, *No I don't. Not like you.*

"So if he wasn't here," I say to Elijah around the lump in my throat, "if he wasn't going to *be* here — then I didn't see the need to be here either."

Elijah scribbles, then turns the page, scribbles again. "And what about your groundskeeper, John Fritz," he says, eyes on the words he writes even as he speaks. "Did he ever hurt you?"

"Fritz?" I spit out. "Why would Fritz ever hurt me? I've known him my whole life."

He snaps his head up. "People we've known our whole lives can still hurt us. Some might argue they can hurt us more."

"More than what?"

He glances at the page. "A stranger."

He pulls in his lower lip, chewing it for a moment. Through the doors, I hear some-one's footsteps. They get close, get silent, and then they move away.

Elijah clears his throat. "It appears a crime's been committed. You understand that, right?"

My mind leaps to Andy's namesake, all those Borden crime scene photos. The couch with a back like three cresting waves. Andrew's head against the pillow as if he'd merely been napping.

But the blood. The split skull. The implication of an ax.

It isn't Andy, lying out there. He's in Jacksonville or Lansing, or some city I haven't covered yet in my latest round of searches, but he isn't — he has not been — *here.*

"I understand," I say. "But I don't know who was killed out there. And I don't know who killed them either. And you can't possibly think . . . Fritz?"

Fritz who rested his arm on the handle of a rake, watching us laugh in our leaf piles. Fritz who swept more leaves together, telling us, *Go ahead, dive in.* Fritz with a pronounced limp, from an injury he doesn't talk about. Fritz who picks up every caterpillar he finds, strokes its back, wishes it *good luck in the cocoon.*

"We're going to be investigating all possibilities," Elijah says.

"Okay. So does that include the Blackburn Killer? Because Fritz isn't a murderer. But we've got one, don't we? On this island? One your dad failed to find."

41

Elijah squints at me. We both know it isn't fair to put that on Chief Kraft. The Blackburn Killer was masterfully elusive, his kills sporadic enough to seem almost random. Two years went by between the first two murders, four between the final two, and the month always varied; the first woman was killed in September, and the last, nineteen years later, in July.

The police never found his DNA, either. When he dragged the bodies into shallow water, he made sure of that. By the time they washed back onto shore — a different stretch of shore each time — the salty ocean had licked them clean. And another thing: the nails of the women were always immaculate, not a single foreign cell stuck beneath them.

In one of Greta's breathless monologues about the Blackburn Killer, she told me how the police focused on the blue dresses for a while, tried to find who designed them, where they'd been purchased, but that was a dead end, too, as if the gowns, gauzy and cold, had been stitched from the ocean itself. Even the branding iron, with which the Blackburn Killer marked the women's ankles, led police nowhere. *Experts said the curve of the B was "crude and rudimentary,"* Greta explained, *so they think it was made*

42

by the killer himself.

"Surely you know," Elijah says, "that the death in question is nothing like the deaths of those women. They were discovered on the shore, for one thing. This person was buried." He pauses. "On your property."

I tighten my grip on the mug.

"But as I said," he continues, "we'll be investigating all possibilities."

On the table beside him, his phone rings. He frowns at its screen.

"Excuse me, I need to take this."

As he slides apart the living room doors, the darkness of the foyer gapes like the mouth of a cave. Strange that nobody's turned on the chandelier, that the eight p.m. sky seems brighter than the inside of our house. Elijah steps outside to answer his phone, and I feel my way along the walls, following the voices coming from the kitchen.

The swinging door is closed, but when I open it, there's finally light — a little, at least, from the bulb above the stove. Tate and Charlie sit at the counter, legs dangling from stools, palms circling mugs. Mom paces back and forth between the sink and the oven.

"Is Detective Good Boy done with you?" Charlie slurs, and I don't think it's tea in his mug.

"He got a call."

"From the bone people?" Tate asks, her spine straightening.

"Is *that* what we're calling them?" Charlie says. "I'm fine with it if we are. Did you see that one guy, the really tall one? He can *bone* me whenever he wants."

"Charles!" Mom says, voice like a whip.

"Sorry, Mom. Sorry. Not my fault — it's *the city*. It's made me so crass."

"It's made you an *ass,*" Tate mumbles, and Charlie slaps his hand over his heart, pretending to reel from a stab.

"Stop," Tate whines. She puts her elbows on the counter, massaging her temples. "You're acting like we're hanging out at a bar or something, when really —"

"Oh," Charlie cuts her off, looking around as if taking in his surroundings for the first time. "This isn't a bar? No wonder the service sucks."

"— when *really,*" Tate continues, "we're waiting to hear if it was our brother out there."

"It wasn't Andy," I say.

Charlie turns so sharply I almost jump.

"Is that what Kraft said?" he asks.

"No. I just know. He's not dead."

Mom makes it over to me in two quick

44

strides. "You've spoken to him, haven't you — your brother?" She picks up my hand, stroking the back of it with a firm, insistent touch. "In these last ten years, you've heard from him, right? And maybe you didn't tell me because he needed more time away, but . . . you know where he is, don't you?"

Her eyes are frantic, flicking like a too-fast metronome.

"I . . ." I start to say, but the kitchen door swings open behind me, and I look back to find Elijah Kraft. In one hand, he holds his cell phone, and in the other, dangling at his side, is the notepad where he's been writing down our lives.

Mom's grip on my hand tightens. Tate and Charlie perk up on their stools.

"Is there news?" Tate asks, just as Mom says, "What is it?"

Elijah glances at his feet, and when he looks up, he looks around — at the clock that's always broken, at the Honoring calendar pinned to the wall, at the butcher block and all its knives.

"I'm afraid," he begins — and right away, it's like someone turns down the volume, "that we've been able to confirm it."

And this, as he continues, comes to me as only a whisper: "The remains in that grave, they belong to . . ."

45

And this — like a blade thrusting toward me — comes to me in silence (but I'd know the shape of his name anywhere; I can see it on Elijah's lips): "Andy."

Mom screams. I see her mouth split open, her face go red, but I don't hear it. I don't hear anything at all.

THREE

On our thirteenth birthday, Andy carved his name into the wall beneath my bedroom window. Even then, he was thinking of leaving.

We should go, he said, concentrating on the knife. *We're old enough now to figure things out on our own.*

But I didn't feel old enough. We'd only just reached the age at which Mary Phagan was raped and strangled, her body found in the basement of the pencil factory where she worked. We were only just as old as Lisa Ann Millican had been when she was abducted by a disturbed couple, who, among other horrors, injected her with drain cleaner. At thirteen, I was still scared to venture too far beyond our door. It wasn't until I was nineteen, living without Andy for three years already, that it became scarier to walk the halls of a house where I could only trail after his ghost.

I didn't know, then, that "ghost" was not a metaphor. That whatever slip of energy that made him *him* had already detached from his skin, or that his skin itself was a disintegrating thing, a feast for grubs and worms. But how could I not have known? For ten years, I've watched for him, searched for him, worn out the letters of his name on my laptop keys — certain that he was out there, his heart still beating in sync with mine. I always thought that, if he died, I'd feel it, like a coffin snapping shut on my own body. But all this time, I've been breathing just fine; all this time, I've been wrong.

I'm sitting on my old beanbag chair, the twin to one in Andy's room, and as I shift, I brace myself for pain. I had no idea how demanding grief is of the body. My eyes feel like they've been used as punching bags. I'm thirstier than I can ever remember being, but there's a hundred-pound weight in my stomach, my chest, my throat, and I don't know if I can make it to the kitchen for water. I hear footsteps down there, heavy ones that seem to shake the walls. For a moment, I think they must be Dad's, but then I pause, and I remember. And though his loss is not the one that's crushing me now, I wince about it anyway. It's a terrible thing, forgetting someone is dead.

I should check on Mom. Even though she never looked for Andy, the way she gripped my hand last night, the way hope bled from her mouth as she insisted I knew where he's been — that meant something to me. It meant she lost a piece of herself when she let him go, and all these years she's been wishing he'd bring it back. But now she's lost even more: Andy, for good, and her husband, too — a man she always seemed in awe of, a man whose mild attention was enough to make her blush.

As I stand up, I find I'm still in yesterday's clothes: oversize sweater, dark gray leggings. My bag is in the corner of my room, but I don't care enough to reach inside it and dig for another outfit. I step into the hall, legs shaky and sore, but I barely make it ten feet before Charlie, holding a large box, rounds a corner and crashes into me.

"Dolls," he says as I stumble back. He sets the box on the floor and stands there, one shoulder lower than the other, dragged down by his usual slouch. I can smell the alcohol wafting off him, but it smells old, the residue of whatever was in his mug last night.

"What are you —" I try to ask, but he

leaps forward, engulfing me in a hug so tight I gasp.

"You must be dying," he says. "God, if anything ever happened to Tate, I'd just . . . I know she's not my twin, but still. It always felt like it was me and her, and you and Andy, and now it's just . . . you."

I can't breathe; my lungs feel pinned to my ribs. Then Charlie takes a step back, gripping my shoulders and shaking me in a way that jumpstarts my breath.

"You're going to get through this," he says. He scans the hallway. "We all are. I'm making sure of that."

I look at the box near my feet. "What is this?"

"It's from the attic. Our old murder reports. We're going to include them in the memorial."

"In . . . Dad's memorial?"

"Dad's *and* Andy's. We're doing a joint one, I've decided."

And there it is again, that pinned-lung feeling. Memorials are for saying goodbye, but I've only just discovered Andy's gone. Really gone, I mean, not a runaway, not anonymous in some city — but gone. In the ground.

"But not only that!" Charlie adds. "We're going to make it a museum of sorts. The

Lighthouse Memorial Museum." He splays his hands in the air, palms out, spreading them farther apart with each word, as if he's seeing the name lit up on some theater marquee.

I manage a syllable: "What?"

He drops his hands. "The vultures are circling. The rest of the islanders — they know something's happened. I got up early this morning, went for a walk into town to clear my head, and a mother accosted me with her baby. 'Is it true?' she asked. '*Two* Lighthouses are dead?' I don't even know how she knew who I was. Maybe she's asking everyone. But the way she said our name . . . It was like we're these dangerous, blood-sucking freaks, living in Murder Mansion, plotting our next move. But I've played Biff in *Death of a Salesman,* Dolls!"

He shakes his head, indignant. "My instinct was to get away from her," he adds, "just like we always did."

Mom encouraged us to steer clear of the islanders. She said they wouldn't understand our way of life, and with their murmurs of "Murder Mansion," their gazes that followed us whenever we left the house, it was clear she was right.

"But look where that division got us," Charlie says. "Andy was axed to death!"

51

"You think one of the islanders did it?" I ask, even though *axed to death* makes the hallway spin around me.

Charlie stares at me, his eyes opaque. Unreadable. "Yes," he says. "Someone on this island did it."

"The Blackburn Killer?"

Charlie hesitates before he shakes his head again, this time like a dog shaking off rain. "They don't — Nobody knows, Dahlia. But my point is: I'm not hiding anymore. *We're* not hiding anymore. The idea came to me this morning like a lightning strike. In five days, we're going to open our doors to everyone, for one day only — limited viewings draw the best crowds — and we're going to let them witness it all. I'm collecting artifacts — papers, candles, items from the victim room — anything that tells the story of who we've been. It's time for everyone to see we're not some freaks on top of the hill. We're *people.* We were brought up differently, sure, but we're human beings, for fuck's sake."

He picks up the box and stomps toward the stairs — as if that's the end of it. As if it's his decision alone as to who can enter our house or snoop through our things.

"Wait." I follow him downstairs. Our footsteps rattle the frames along the staircase, and I glance at Mom's parents — smiling in birthday hats, blowing smoke rings at each other in lieu of a kiss, oblivious to the guns that were coming for their heads.

Charlie carries his box to the living room, dumping it on a stack of others teetering on top of the coffee table. "Find anything, Tate?" he asks, and now I see our sister crouched in the corner, rummaging through the bottom shelf of a cabinet. She's pointedly *not* in yesterday's clothes. Her sweater is a too-cheerful yellow, and her hair, freshly showered, cascades down her back in glossy waves.

"Sort of," she says, words muffled. She jolts when she sees me. Clamped between her teeth is a paintbrush, but she yanks it out to say my name, her lips an unnatural red.

"How are you doing?" she asks, walking toward me, arms outstretched — and again, what is with these hugs? Doesn't she remember how, as kids, she literally shooed me and Andy — *Shoo, little ones, shoo!* — whenever we'd ask what she and Charlie were whispering about? Doesn't she remember how, the last time I saw her, she read Andy's note like it might accuse her of something, her eyes squinty with caution but not concern?

53

As she pulls me in, the end of her paint-brush stabs my shoulder blade. "Oops," she says. "I've been gathering supplies." She turns back to Charlie but keeps her hand on my arm. "There's not much here; I'll have to go into town. I can pick up whatever you need while I'm there."

"So you're on board," I say, "with this . . . Lighthouse Museum thing?"

"Lighthouse *Memorial* Museum," Charlie pipes in. "But we can shorten it to LMM, if that's easier for everyone."

"I'm on board in the sense that Charlie will do what Charlie wants to do," Tate says. "It's not *my* preferred way to memorialize our family, but I respect the intention behind it."

"But you're actively helping with it?" I say, nodding at the paintbrush in her hand.

"Oh!" She looks at the brush like she forgot she was holding it. "No. This is for my own project. A new diorama."

My mouth drops open. "You're making one *now*?"

"I have to. It's all — It's too much other-wise. I need to process. And this is how I do that. If I can remake Andy's body, I can —"

"Wait," I stop her. "You're doing a di-orama of *Andy*?"

"Of course," she says, standing straighter.

54

"He was murdered, Dahlia. He was . . . All this time, he's been there." She points toward the back of the house. "I need to make sense of that. Don't you?"

"Not to fifty-seven thousand strangers I don't!" I whip toward Charlie. "Not to an island full of people who've always thought we were monsters."

"That's not what my Instagram is about," Tate says, her voice overlapping Charlie's.

"That's the whole point!" he bellows, stabbing a triumphant finger into the air. "They won't think of us as monsters after this."

I gape at them both, each so adamant that theirs is the correct way to mourn. But Andy would hate it all: the spectacle of it, how *unnatural* it feels. He'd grab my wrist, pierce me with an urgent stare, tell me for the hundredth time that we should leave.

If I'd listened to him, would he be alive right now? Would I have run away with him one night, stood by his side on the ferry as we watched the ocean throw itself against the rocks? Maybe we would have made it out there, together, Leaving Money be damned. Maybe we'd mimic our siblings' choices: live in the same apartment, cheer each other on as we followed our separate dreams. But my only dream has been to find my twin, so now what do I do?

"You better get a move on," Charlie says to Tate, "if you want to be done in time."

Tate nods, brushing past me with a sad, pitying glance, and heads for the stairs.

"Done in time for what?" I ask.

Charlie opens the box on top of his stack, pulls out some papers, and answers me as he reads. "For the museum. The diorama will be a *very* popular exhibit."

"She's going to display it?" I seethe. I'm about to keep going, tell our brother that his and Tate's grief is shredding their sanity, but Charlie raises his head sharply, sniffs a few times, and squints at the foyer behind me.

"What's that?" he asks.

I turn to see that the air is blurred. Smoke billows past the living room, rising up the stairs.

"Something's burning," Charlie declares — and I smell it, too, as soon as he says it.

"Kitchen!" I blurt, but he's already on his way there. I lift the collar of my sweater to cover my mouth as I follow.

When we burst through the swinging door, we find Mom waving a cloth toward the oven, coughing into her arm. It's a strange sight; I've never known her to burn anything. Dad did most of the cooking, but on his hunting days, Mom made dinner so

56

he could eat as soon as he got back. On those nights, roasts were medium rare at best, potatoes difficult to cut. *Undercooked,* Charlie would grumble, and Dad would hiss at him to be grateful, prompting an appreciative twinkle in Mom's eyes.

"What is this?" Charlie asks.

"It's cookies!" Mom says, shoving her arm into the smoke to pull a pan of thin black discs from the oven. She drops it onto the stove as if it's burned her through her mitt.

The three of us stare at these supposed cookies: charred skins, overlapping edges.

"Please don't tell me these are for the LMM," Charlie says.

"LMM?" Mom asks.

"That's what we're calling the Lighthouse Memorial Museum," he replies. "It was Dahlia's idea." He winks at me.

I wait for Mom to protest his plans for the memorial. She was the one who made us live this way — shuttered and shut in, protected from people like the ones who killed her parents, our boundaries shrinking smaller each time the Blackburn Killer struck. I can't imagine her welcoming islanders into our home, offering them dessert as they gawk at our grief. But she only sighs.

"The cookies were for you kids," she says.

"These are chocolate chip. Tate's favorite."

I bite back my bitterness. Is Mom aware that Tate is going to minimize Andy's death to an eight-by-ten display? Does she know that, right now, the daughter she's baking cookies for is "gathering supplies" to turn him into an exhibit? A post?

"And then I'm going to make snicker-doodles for Dahlia, and peanut butter for you, Charlie. And then who knows what else — sugar, or oatmeal raisin, or, oh! My mother used to make these raspberry almond cookies that would melt in your mouth. Except — we'd need jam, raspberry jam, and I don't know if . . ."

She trails off as she darts toward the pantry. Charlie crosses his arms, amused, and I look closer at Mom. Grains of brown sugar freckle her cheek; clumps of flour whiten her hair.

"You don't need to make us cookies," I say. "It seems like a lot of trouble."

"Don't be silly," Mom replies. "I just . . . I got distracted down the hall for a minute. Forgot to keep watch." She laughs, high and girlish. "I can handle cookies, Dahlia. Cookies are easy."

Except I've never seen her bake them before. Or anything else for that matter.

"Odd that the smoke detectors didn't go

58

off," Mom muses, shoving aside boxes of pasta, cans of beans. "I'll have to call someone about that." She swallows, and it's the first moment since we've walked in that she seems even remotely sad. "I suppose that's something Daniel would have done."

Her voice hitches on Dad's name. Her face crumples, and in the creases of her skin, there's the weight of what she's lost. My eyes sting with tears, but before my vision can blur, the moment is over. Mom smiles so wide it scares me.

"First!" she chirps. "We'll need these cookies. I'll have to redo the chocolate chip, start again from scratch."

As she dives back into the pantry, I can only stare. This bustling, beaming version of my mother is so unlike the one I know. That mother smiled thinly, when she smiled at all. That mother couldn't make it up or down the stairs without stopping to gape, for minutes sometimes, at her parents, no doubt remembering their gruesome end.

Now, Mom mumbles as she runs her hands over rows of spices, canisters of sugar and flour. Then she spins around.

"We're out of baking powder!" she cries. "I'll need to go into town to get some."

She reaches back to untie the waist of her apron and pulls it over her head, revealing the same sweats from yesterday.

"Tate's going," I say. "Why don't you let her pick it up for you? I can tell her to —"

"No!" Mom shouts, and it shocks me, honestly, to hear her raise her voice. "I'm perfectly capable. I can get the baking powder. I can call about the smoke detectors. I can make my children's favorite cookies!"

By the last syllable, she's shrill as a teakettle. And now she's twirling toward the door and shoving it open. Charlie and I watch the door swing hard in her wake.

"Well," Charlie says. "That was . . . a thing that just happened."

He picks up a burnt cookie from the pan on the stove, sniffs it, inspects it, and taps it against the counter. Black crumbs flake off the cookie's surface.

"I think she forgot the chocolate chips," he says. Then he looks at me. "Well. Now that we know the house isn't burning down, I better get back to work. The LMM won't curate itself."

"Charlie," I say, "don't you think it's a bad idea to —"

"Uh, uh, uh," he interrupts, wagging a finger in the air. "Criticisms of the LMM will only be received *after* the LMM. Just like any other show. At that point, you can publish a full-page review in the *Blackburn Gazette* for all I care."

He spins around with exaggerated grace, and then he leaves me alone.

They've all gone crazy. Charlie, Tate, Mom. They want to display Andy, exploit him — or bury their heads in a bowl of flour — so why should I stay here a minute longer? This memorial, this museum, won't be about him. There's no way I'll stand there, in a room of gossip guzzlers, and tell them how he carved his name all over this house. How he always stubbed his toe on the fourth floorboard from the top of the stairs. How I thought that was the funniest thing.

My phone chirps with a text, muffled by the pocket of my sweater. When I pull it out, I see Greta's name, and I close my eyes before I read her message, aching with nostalgia.

I want to go back. Back just a couple days, to the little apartment that always smells of cinnamon. Back to Greta's knocks on my door, offering me search tips I hadn't thought of yet: *Have you checked assessor's websites?* Some nights, when she got off work, we'd set up our laptops side by side — her on her message boards, toggling between open tabs; me crossing one city off my list before moving on to the next — and I want to go back to that. Back to when I believed my twin was alive, and my biggest problem was that I couldn't find him.

Oh my god, Greta's written, I just saw your text, I can't believe it. I'm so sorry. How are you doing? What can I do?

My fingers hover above the screen, unsure what to type. I know friends are supposed to support you in times of tragedy — but friendship remains an uncomfortable fit for me, like an itchy sweater, or a too-tight turtleneck. Back when we first met, Greta glommed on to me quickly, giddy that, most times, when she referenced a cold-case murder, I actually knew what she was talking about. *It's like we share a language,* she said one time — but it's a language I grew up speaking and therefore find no beauty in, whereas Greta labors over learning it, marveling at its every sound. We're not as similar as she thinks we are. We're not like me and Andy, who didn't need language at all.

Call me when you're ready, she texts now, but I slip the phone back into my pocket.

Through the kitchen window, a flash of yellow catches my eye. It's police tape, I see when I squint, and it's fluttering in the wind. There's a mound of dirt out there —

in the woods, in the family plot — hunched like a tumor on top of the earth, and my muscles seize at the reminder: Andy didn't just die; someone killed him. They picked up his ax, lifted it over their head, and they —

Afterward, they dug a hole for him. A hole.

They dug up the plot that waited for our father, marked by a stone that always chilled me with its prematurity. *Daniel Lighthouse,* it proclaimed — or warned — right beside another that waited for Mom, *Lorraine Lighthouse,* set into the ground beside her parents' graves.

Somebody dropped Andy's body into a plot that was never meant for him. They covered him in dirt. But how did they know we wouldn't notice him back there? That we wouldn't see the freshly turned earth and wonder what had been buried? They'd have to have known our patterns: that I gave the family plot as wide a berth as I could; that Charlie and Tate would be too self-involved to stick around; that Dad took a different path for his hunts; that even Mom only went there on the Honoring day for her parents — which occurred months after Andy's disappearance.

And who would have wanted to hurt him? Elijah asked about Fritz last night, but it

63

couldn't have been him. Fritz has always been gentle, a man who gave us wildflower seeds and told us to think of them as food for fairies as we sprinkled them onto the grass. We never believed in magic or fairies, but we played along, as old as eleven or twelve the last time we did it, tossing those seeds around the edges of the yard because we knew that Fritz loved beauty, loved brightness, loved every growing thing.

Still, to bury Andy in our family plot, the killer would have had to know, first, that the plot was there at all.

I try to think of anyone, besides Fritz, I ever even saw in our woods. There was Chief Kraft, of course. He often did a sweep of our entire property before he knocked on our door for one of his "casual drop-ins," as he called them. He claimed he was keeping us safe, making sure nobody was "up to mischief" on our expansive property, but we knew the truth. In his view, we were the threat.

Then there were the islanders. They usually kept to the side of the road, where they stood and stared, gossiped and judged. But I suppose they could have snuck into our woods easily enough.

And it's that image — a person skulking between trees — that reminds me of something, *someone,* I haven't thought of in years.

There was a girl, back when we were younger, who lived on the other side of the woods with her grandfather. She was around our age, with dark curly hair and the biggest eyes that Andy and I had ever seen. Her name was Ruby Decker. But that's not what we called her.

We called her the Watcher.

We were ten the first time we noticed her. She was prowling our woods like a stray cat, gaze fastened to the back of our house, as if counting its every stone. At night, her flashlight beam bounced off branches and leaves. For years, we spied on her spying on us, using binoculars to see her more clearly through the trees. We talked about her enormous eyes, joking that they must have been surgically enlarged. The better to see us with, we guessed.

But then, when we were fifteen, Andy came inside one day and told me he'd spoken to her. She'd approached him while he was swinging his ax at a tree, and they'd talked for a while, and she was *actually kind of cool.*

Cool? I repeated. *Are you friends now or something?* I couldn't imagine that, couldn't even see the point. What use was some girl through the woods when Andy and I had each other?

He shrugged off my question. He said he'd been all riled up, but Ruby helped to calm him down. She made him laugh, he added, helped him pick a splinter from his palm.

After that day, he lost interest in spying on her. *She's just a girl,* he said, pulling my binoculars away. *She's not a spectacle.*

But we were one to her. And maybe she saw something the night Andy died. Maybe I should talk to her grandfather, ask him for Ruby's number, see if she remembers the boy who hacked at trees.

Then again, there's another option, one I think of as I hear a crash in the living room, followed by Charlie's cursing. I could leave this place, before the museum, before Tate even begins her diorama. I could ditch the smell of burnt cookies, take tonight's ferry, crawl into my bed above the café, and cry for Andy until I'm desiccated inside.

It's a tempting thought — comforting, even, in a brutal sort of way. But I already left Blackburn Island once, back when I had no idea that my brother's body was rotting in its soil. I cannot leave it again until I find out who buried him there.

All I know is how to search for Andy.

That's all I've done for years. And I could change my search terms, scour the web for the man who killed him instead. But I won't find him on the internet, will I? Chances are, I'll find Andy's murderer here. On Blackburn Island. A place that has always been filled with people who want us gone.

FOUR

I take the long way through the woods, avoiding the family plot, the fluttering yellow tape. I walk around Fritz's toolshed, set back into these trees, its ivied, dirty brick too unsightly to blemish the lawn. When I pass the wall where Andy's ax used to lean, I avert my eyes.

Clouds hang like a canopy overhead as leaves crunch beneath my feet. The wind, omnipresent on Blackburn Island, pushes me forward, and with every breath, the salt of the ocean stings my nose. Even from here, we could always smell it, always hear the rushing waves. We can't see the water from the top of this island, clogged as it is with trees, but the ocean's scent is everywhere.

Andy hated that. Hated the ocean itself. He didn't see it as wide open or freeing, but as something that kept us in. *I'd rather be landlocked,* he said. *At least then there's always somewhere else to go.* For a long time, I didn't bother searching for him in cities on the water — not until inland searches became dead ends, and I had no choice but to find hope in coastal towns. Still, I couldn't imagine him there. In our sixteen years together on this island, we hardly ever went to the shore. Part of it was Mom's rules — she kept us from places where bodies washed up — but part of it was Andy, too. I loved him enough to stay away from what he hated.

When I make it to the clearing in the woods, five minutes from our property, I see Lyle Decker's cottage, the only other house perched this high on Blackburn's hill. Compared to ours, it's a dwarf, yellow and quaint. He might not even live here anymore; whoever answers the door might have no idea who Ruby is, let alone how I can reach her.

I hear a whacking sound, off to the left, and I curve around the side of the house to find a woman, back turned — splitting wood with an ax.

My breath catches. She places another log on the stump, raises the ax above her head, and comes down hard again. *Thoomphk.*

My exhale sounds like a wheeze. When the woman turns, wiping the back of her

69

hand across her forehead, it only takes us a moment to recognize each other.

"Dahlia Lighthouse?"

Strange how easily she identifies me. She may have been the Watcher, but Ruby and I never stood within ten feet of each other, and Andy and I don't look enough alike — me with my dark hair and narrow nose; him with his sandy locks and wide mouth — to chalk it up to resemblance.

"You still live here?" I ask.

She puts the ax blade-down on the ground, holding the handle in place with a flattened palm. "Of course I do," she replies.

Her voice is huskier than I imagined it would be. With her black, doll-like curls and pouty mouth, I always thought she'd speak in a whine.

"I assume you're back because of your father," she says.

I tip my chin in half a nod.

She looks into the distance, through the woods, toward the place where our mansion would be, if she could see it from here. Her eyes are still so big, cartoonishly round, and she blinks them, hard, as she stands up straighter.

"Is the rest of your family back?" she asks, and I feel it in my stomach, the absence of Andy, cold and machete-sharp.

"Some of them," I say.

"What about Andy?"

There's something hopeful in her gaze, like she thinks that if he *had* come back, he'd be coming straight to her, a girl he hardly knew.

"Andy is dead," I tell her. "He was murdered ten years ago. With his own ax."

I could have been kinder about it. Gentler. Or, actually — no, I couldn't, because there's nothing gentle about losing Andy. The word *murder,* once so simple to say, now stings my tongue, a thing that must be spit more than spoken.

For a few moments, her face is blank. Then there's a shiver of movement, rippling her expression into one of confusion. Seconds pass in which we only stare, each of us watching, each of us watched, until her features crumple into raw devastation. Her eyes shove out tears, ones so fat I could probably see my reflection in them.

She bends over, leaning her forehead against the butt of her ax. Then she bangs her head against it. Once, twice — a beat beneath her sobs.

"Hey, don't —" I start, but she snaps into a standing position again.

"Murdered by who?" she demands.

"We . . . we don't know. Someone buried

71

him in our woods."

Her face freezes in horror. Her mouth gapes, dark and twisted, until she covers it with one hand. "I thought he just left!" she wails. "I had no idea he was killed."

I take a step away from her. She's shaking now, fingers and shoulders trembling. Her reaction is alarming in its intensity. Suspicious, too. Even though her words could be my own — *I thought he just left; I had no idea he was killed* — I don't believe that one conversation with Andy would make her feel his loss this acutely, more than ten years later.

"You didn't even know him," I say. "So what is this? What are you doing?"

I try to channel Charlie, inject my tone with superiority, haughty disdain — but as the words come out, I find it's a hand-me-down that doesn't fit.

"I knew him better than I've ever known anyone," she cries.

I can't stop myself from scoffing. "You spoke to him one time."

Her tears pause for a second as she glares at me. Then she wipes her cheeks, crying even harder. "We hung out *all* the time."

"You . . ." I squint at her. "What?"

"We'd meet up in the woods," Ruby continues, "mostly at night."

"At night?" I shake my head. At night, Andy and I lay in beds that were pressed against the shared wall between our rooms, and we both slept easier, deeper, knowing that even when we were separated, we were only inches apart.

"We'd write these notes to each other," Ruby says, sniffling. "He brought the snacks, and I brought the flashlights — so we could see our paper."

"Notes?" I can't stop echoing her words. "What kind of notes?"

She hiccups, or maybe sobs. It's hard to tell with all the noise she's making.

"I don't know," she says, "like: *You are the rabbit's foot to my petal-covered moon.* Nothing that made sense. We'd compete, sort of, to see who could make the other laugh the hardest."

Tears still dripping, she raises one hand and brings it to her chest. Then she picks at her shirt, pinching the fabric along her sternum, rubbing it between her fingers.

"Mostly we talked about getting out of here," she continues, gaze distant, voice thick. "This island has so much darkness. For Andy, it was your family, and for me —"

"My family isn't dark," I say — because the word is *unnatural.* *Unnatural* is what he

73

would have told her, if she knew him as well as she says.

"For me, it's all those women," she goes on. "I'm twenty-five now. The same age Melinda Wharton was."

Melinda Wharton. I haven't heard anyone but Greta say her name in years. But of course I think of her, every September 20. Of course I picture Mom and Dad lighting the candles, without us, saying the prayer for the first woman the Blackburn Killer ever dumped on the shore. She was a preschool teacher, killed before Andy and I were even born, when Charlie was six, Tate five. In her Instagram post about her, Tate explained that Melinda had come to the island to visit her grandmother, who later told police that Melinda left for a walk around ten p.m.

But the next time Mrs. Wharton saw her granddaughter, it was to identify her body, which had first been strangled, then left in shallow waters to wash up onto the rocks. Melinda was the only presumed victim of the Blackburn Killer who wasn't branded, wasn't dressed in an ice-blue gown. She was, however, found with a light blue scarf wrapped around her neck. This inconsistency with the next murder, two years after Melinda's — when Stephanie Kepler was found with a *B* burned into her ankle, wearing a dress different from the one she'd left her house in — kept police from connecting the murders initially. It wasn't until three years later, when Erica Shipp was discovered branded and dressed identically to Stephanie, that the term *serial killer* was used on the island at all.

It haunted me, of course, all those strangled women; whenever another washed up, there was always the question of who would be next — but unlike Ruby, it never made me want to leave. The world Mom taught us about was teeming with murderers; I believed that if I went somewhere else, I'd only live beside a different killer.

My parents could have taken us away, like the people who fled after the third or fourth woman was discovered, but Dad just grumbled about cowards, insisting that he refused to be driven away from the first place he'd ever called home. His mother had left him, a baby in a car seat, on a crowded beach in Maine, and for his entire childhood, he ping-ponged to different foster homes in New England until he finally landed on Blackburn at nineteen. For a couple years, he worked at the market in town, rented a room over someone's garage, and was about to move on to someplace bigger when he ended up meeting Mom.

She'd just returned to the island, raw with grief, after selling her parents' Connecticut estate, which she'd had to scrub clean of their blood. She'd sold their company, too — a generations-old gun manufacturer — largely because of a fact that would forever haunt her, one that, later, she would tell us only once before never speaking of it again.

The gun that killed her parents had been their very own brand.

With the Blackburn house all she had left of them, Mom willed herself to grow roots in the island's soil. She buried her mother and father in the woods, and she married the market clerk who whipped out an arm to save her from slipping on spilled milk. When she saw Dad, that first time, she actually gasped, startled by his handsomeness.

Mom did keep us closer whenever another woman was found, cinching our boundaries like a belt around a waist, and she often peeked between curtains with a distrustful eye. But since Dad so adamantly scoffed at the thought of running off scared, she never suggested moving, content to seclude herself with the startlingly handsome man who could have gone anywhere, but decided to stay on this rocky, unpretty island with her.

"Andy talked all the time about leaving,"

Ruby says now, lips quivering. "He said he'd make sure the Blackburn Killer never hurt me. I thought he meant we'd run away soon, before I was all grown-up, like those women, the victims, always were. But then later — when Andy was gone — and there were no more murders at all . . . I thought maybe he'd meant something else. Maybe he meant he'd take down the killer, stop him somehow. And then I thought maybe he actually had, and that's why he had to go so suddenly."

She swipes a hand across her nose. "But he was supposed to take me with him. Supposed to take both of us." She gestures to the space between us, including me as part of that *both*. "That's what he told me, anyway. 'You, me, and Dahlia. We've got to get out of here.'"

I have to admit: she does a good impression of him. She even hunches her shoulders, speaks out the side of her mouth. It cuts a little to see it.

"He never mentioned you," I say, "whenever he talked to *me* about leaving."

It's mean. I know it is. Her face buckles with the cruelty of it. "Oh," is all she says, and then she picks at her shirt again, more vigorously than before, like she's trying to reach past fabric and bone to soothe the heart beneath it.

I should say something. Apologize maybe. Tell her that I never learned how to share him; he was always so singularly mine. We knew each other best, loved each other most — but I didn't even know he was dead. And I had no idea about her.

Ruby takes her palm off her ax, letting it thump to the ground at her feet. The sound, the swiftness of the movement, startles me, and I'm defenseless against the images that spring up: blood on metal, metal splitting skull.

"I need some tissues," Ruby says. "You can come if you want."

Walking past me toward the house, she sniffles, and when I catch my breath, I follow.

Inside, she disappears down a hall. I look around, taking stock of a living room decked out in brown: wood paneling, pine tables, a couch and loveseat the color of mud. Very little hangs on the walls — a crooked painting of the sea; a framed photo of teenaged Ruby; and situated near a lamp, illuminated like something holy, two embroideries in circular wooden frames, each stitched with a different phrase.

Home is a place you'll never leave, says one, and beneath those words: a yellow house like the one I'm standing in.

The other has *Ruby loves Grandpa* scrawled in the center, surrounded by a wreath of purple and yellow hollyhocks.

"I made those," Ruby says. I whirl around, find her dabbing her face with a tissue. "Andy loved them."

Frowning, I return my gaze to the frames. I don't see anything there that Andy would love. He didn't care about flowers, not even our own hollyhocks, which bloomed each year in our yard. And the first phrase — *Home is a place you'll never leave* — was the opposite of what he believed.

"He only came inside once," Ruby says, stepping beside me to stare at the words' navy thread. "But when he did, I caught him admiring them, like he was in awe. Like they were works of art or —"

"Why you talkin' 'bout that boy?"

I jump at the sound of Lyle Decker's voice. He's in a wheelchair, blocking the entrance to the hall. Last time I saw him, on a rare trip into town, he towered over me, offering a grunt instead of a greeting. Now, he's hooked to an oxygen tank, tubes sticking up his nose, and there are bruises like fingerprints up and down his arms. Beneath his eyes are bags as big as pockets.

"Grandpa," Ruby says. "Something terrible happened. Andy Lighthouse —"

"That boy should've never come around here," he cuts her off. And the way he says *that boy* straightens my spine.

Ruby squares her shoulders. "Yes, I know you — Yes. But Grandpa, he . . . he died." She glances at me, and my throat stings as she continues. "He was murdered."

Lyle leans forward, stretching the plastic tube linking him to oxygen, to life.

"Then he got what he deserved," he says.

I gasp in chorus with Ruby — but she recovers quicker than me.

"Grandpa, you don't —" She puts her hand on my shoulder, and even through the fog of my shock, I feel the instinct to shrug it off. "This is Dahlia Lighthouse. Andy's *sister.*"

"I know who you are," Lyle says, eyes like arrows aimed at my face. "And I know what I said. Your brother Andy got what he deserved."

The air is sucked from the room. Lyle rasps, even with oxygen tubes.

"What —" I start, but Ruby clamps her hand on my arm and pulls me toward the door.

"That's enough, Grandpa," she says, and before I can stop her, she's guiding me outside, depositing me on the crunchy, yel-

80

low lawn, shutting the door behind her with a decisive thud.

"What did he mean by that?" I demand. "Why would he . . . how could he say that?"

Ruby puts a finger to her lips, quick and sharp. Then she walks away, waving for me to follow, until we reach her backyard.

"Look," she says, glancing at the house, "Grandpa is very protective of me. Always has been. His wife — my grandmother — left him when my mom was just a kid, and then —"

"What does that have to do with anything? He said Andy *deserved* to be murdered."

"I'm getting to that," she insists. "His wife left him when my mom was a kid, and then my *mom* left when I was a baby. She was only eighteen when she had me, and . . . well, she calls sometimes, but Grandpa doesn't like me to answer the phone, and he never lets me speak to her. He tells her if she really wants to see me, she knows where to find me." Ruby looks down, playing with the zipper on her puffy vest. "She's never come back."

"But why —"

"He raised me," she cuts me off. "And homeschooled me, just like you and Andy were. Well" — she stops herself, a smirk seeping onto her face — "not *just* like you

81

and Andy were."

I shift beneath her gaze. Did Andy tell her about Mom's curriculum? Or does she know about it the way everyone on Blackburn does: through things Chief Kraft spied when he dropped in at our house, warnings he handed out to islanders like flyers?

"Grandpa made sure I never wanted for anything," Ruby says. "And I didn't, really . . . except some company."

She pokes some dried-up grass with her foot. This patchy, narrow backyard is nothing like our lawn, where each green blade has been lovingly tended to, Fritz using scissors in the summer to shape what the mower chopped.

"But Grandpa's always been nervous about me interacting with other people. He's fine with, like, Mrs. Baker at the market, or Mr. Ford at the bike shop, but he doesn't like me hanging around people my own age. Especially boys. Or — men now, I guess."

"That's . . . controlling," I say. Which might be unfair of me. I barely even know who Mrs. Baker or Mr. Ford are, seeing as Mom rarely allowed us to go into town.

"Maybe," Ruby says. "But I get it. My grandmother left him for another man. Then my mom left with whoever my dad was. So I can't really blame him. For seeing boys — men — as the things that take the people he loves. I've spent a lot of my life trying to convince him I won't leave him, too." She shrugs. "You saw the embroidery."

"Ruby loves Grandpa," I recite dully. "Home is a place you'll never leave."

"Exactly. I made those when I was twelve, and they've been hanging there ever since. He's taken them as a promise. Which is fine. Back then, I intended them to be one."

"But you did want to leave him," I say. "With Andy."

I'm queasy at the thought: Andy and Ruby slipping off into the night while I lay in bed, believing my brother would be there, would always be there, when I woke in the morning.

"I did," Ruby says, "yeah."

She rubs her arms, her sleeves unprotected by her vest. "I was fifteen," she says. "And selfish. And I wanted a bigger, safer life than I thought this island could give me. But soon after Andy left —" Her sentence skids to a stop. "Soon after Andy *died,* Grandpa got sick. Turns out he had COPD. And that's led to heart problems. Bad ones."

She pauses, leaving space for me to respond, but I don't know what she expects from me. My brother is dead, and sick or

83

not, her grandfather just said he deserved it.

"So I gave up my dream of leaving," she says. "Grandpa's always taken good care of me, and what was I going to do? Hop on a ferry as soon as he needed my help? I'm all he has. And anyway, there hasn't been a murdered woman on this island in over a decade. I don't need to —"

"But what he *said*," I interrupt. "Why would he say that about Andy?"

"Because Andy was a boy," she replies. "He was a boy I spent time with, and Grandpa figured it was only a matter of time before he took the last girl in his life he had left to love." She swallows, her lower lip trembling. "And he was right. I would have left with your brother. I truly believed I was going to."

The wind sweeps her hair, slapping it like a gag over her mouth. She tears it away as she continues.

"Grandpa *hated* Andy. Or the concept of him, at least. So we started meeting up in secret, late at night. I told Grandpa we'd stopped hanging out altogether, but even still, he'd talk about Andy like he was this predator I'd escaped. Like he'd been sharpening his claws just for me, and I was lucky to have made it out alive."

She's too close to me now. Her breath crashes against my face, and it's as if she's been inching toward me as she speaks.

I move back a little, but she steps into the space I've created.

"It was so lonely," she adds, "having to keep my only friend a secret. And I'd been starving for companionship — from someone my own age — for a really long time."

There's a rustle in the trees, and we both turn our heads, searching for the source of the sound. I half expect Lyle Decker to wheel himself out from the woods, reveal he's been eavesdropping. But nothing moves, nothing appears. Even the wind has paused.

Ruby crosses her arms and points her magnified gaze back at me. "I guess that's why I was so fascinated by your family. All those siblings. A father *and* a mother. Even on nights when Andy and I weren't meeting up, even before we officially met, I'd sneak out and just . . . watch your house. I'd see windows light up, or darken, and I'd pretend I was inside, just another Lighthouse kid."

I picture her perched in a tree, her owly eyes observing what we thought nobody could see, and the image is enough to snap me out of her story, remind me why I crossed the woods to find her in the first place.

"Did you ever see anything?" I ask. "When you were watching us, did you see anything — anyone — who shouldn't have been there? Around the time Andy disappeared?"

Right away, she moves back. Just a fraction of a step, but I notice it anyway: this space she's put between us.

"No," she says. "I'm sorry, I — No."

A thump comes from inside the house. Ruby glances at one of the windows, and I look at it, too, its curtain swaying back and forth.

"I have to go," she says, big eyes darkening. "But listen. I know the islanders have a lot to say about you all. But for all the rumors about your family, I never saw anything strange."

She walks backward toward the house. "I know Andy thought you all were unnatural," she adds. "But I would have given *anything* to be one of you."

FIVE

I hear voices.

I'm back near the front of the mansion, about to step along the cobbled walkway to the front door, when the conversation reaches my ears.

"How do you just . . . not notice, when a body's been buried in your backyard?"

"I guess they found him in the woods. A little ways back."

"I bet they killed him themselves. Some Satanic ritual."

"They're not Satanists, though, right?"

"Tomato, to-mah-to."

I freeze, as if becoming immobile is the same as invisible. There are four of them, all women, standing on the part of our driveway that crests up from the road. That means they're trespassing, clumped together on our property, though still fifty yards from me at least. Arms crossed, they squint at the imposing stone of our home.

How easily it comes back — that old inclination to duck from the islanders' gaze. But if I duck, I move, and if I move, they'll —

"Hey!" one of them calls. "Hey, you're one of the daughters, aren't you?"

"Hey, come here a sec," another says. "We just want to know what happened."

I look at the women for one more moment, their faces indistinct from this far away, and then I turn around, hurrying toward the back entrance of the house.

On my way, I glance toward the woods, that yellow tape and mound of dirt — and that's where I see Elijah Kraft, staring down into what I can only imagine is a human-size, Andy-size hole.

Grief gushes through me like a shot of adrenaline. I'm stopped short by the raw, potent force of it.

From where he stands near the headstones, Elijah gestures for me to wait. He takes one last look at the dirt, jots something in his notepad, then weaves through the trees and out into the yard.

"Glad you turned up," he says. "Your brother told me he didn't know where you were."

For a moment, I think he means Andy, and my heart leaps into my throat. It stays there, pounding, even when I remember Charlie.

"I know this probably isn't the best time," Elijah says, "but I have some questions for you, and I —"

"You're right. It's not the best time."

Tears creep into my eyes as Elijah regards me. I bite my lip to keep them from spilling.

"I understand," he says. "But I'm trying to figure out what happened to Andy, and I could use your help. Should we head inside?" He fiddles with the lapels on his unbuttoned coat, drawing them closer against the cold. "Or if you're uncomfortable speaking around your family, I'm happy to take you down to the station instead."

"Why would I be uncomfortable speaking around my family?"

He shrugs, flipping to a fresh page in his notebook. "I'm just offering."

Even now, before I've agreed to anything, his pen is poised, reminding me of his father. Whenever Chief Kraft spoke to Dad, his notepad was always out, his pen digging into the page like a shovel stabbing at dirt. I glare at Elijah for a few seconds before I feel myself loosen. I've got no energy for resisting.

"Inside is fine," I sigh, leading him toward the back door.

As soon as we enter, I hear clinking sounds in the kitchen. I imagine bowls colliding as Mom fumbles through another attempt at cookies. At least the smoke is gone, for now.

Walking toward the center of the house, where two hallways branch off just before the foyer, I hear something scrape against the floor. Elijah and I pause, our heads tilted toward the noise, and when Charlie appears, hunched over, pushing a large box out of the living room, I clench my teeth until pain jolts through my jaw.

Charlie hasn't noticed us yet. He's frowning at an open box, hands on his hips, as if its contents have disappointed him. I wave Elijah down the hall and open the second door on the right.

Together, we enter the victim room.

"Wow," Elijah says when I close the door behind him. He moves toward the farthest wall and points to a portrait hanging there. "Is that Kitty Genovese?"

I nod. It's one of Tate's paintings, which Mom would sometimes let her do in lieu of a murder report. Tate really took to Kitty's story; the *New York Times* claimed — erroneously, it later turned out — that thirty-eight people witnessed her stabbing in Queens, but none of them did a thing. When Kitty's Honoring came around each March, Tate would bow her head, ignoring Charlie's eye rolls. *We can't restore your life, but we strive to restore your memory with this breath,* we'd chant, and after we blew out the candles, Tate would add, quietly, "I'm sorry everyone's such a coward."

"What is this room?" Elijah asks. His eyes skim over the newspapers stacked along the built-in shelves. He touches one of the bright red tabs poking out: B, it says, denoting the section where articles about Penny Bell, Kirsty Bentley, and the Boy in the Box are stored.

"It's our . . . library," I say — careful not to use the name we'd coined. "It's where we keep information about murder victims."

As he cocks a brow at me, I regret my choice of room. Even the foyer would have been preferable; Charlie's preparations would be less a distraction than the newspapers stacked fold out, one of which blares the headline "Woman Found Dead in Grade School Playground."

"Do you want to sit?" I ask, gesturing to the couch in the center of the room. He has to drag his attention away from the shelves, but then he nods, sloughing off his coat and

91

settling onto the cushions. I take a seat in the reading chair across from him.

Scribbling at the top of his notepad, Elijah peers at me. His gaze is dark and tight, eyes like buttons sewn too snugly into his face.

"So," he starts, "did Andy have any enemies?"

I almost laugh at the question — lifted, it seems, straight from a police procedural.

"Of course not," I say.

We hardly had anyone in our lives; how would we have managed to acquire any enemies?

"No one who had a grudge against him?"

I pause at his rephrasing. "Apparently Lyle Decker didn't like him. But for stupid reasons. Andy and his granddaughter were . . . friends, I guess, and Lyle didn't like her hanging out with boys."

"Okay," Elijah says, writing. "That's helpful. Anyone else?"

"People on this island have always had a grudge against my family. Like — just now, there were women in the driveway, gossiping about my brother. Calling us Satanists."

"Is that how you identify? As Satanists?"

"No!"

"Do you think one of those women might have wanted to hurt your brother?"

"What? No, I —" I narrow my eyes. "What

92

are you doing, exactly, in this investigation? Shouldn't you be checking DNA, or . . . or prints on the ax?"

Elijah clicks the top of his pen, clicks and clicks it again. "Unfortunately, all we have are Andy's remains. Any hair or skin cells, any foreign fibers, have long since decomposed. As for the ax, I'm afraid that with the time that's passed, and the moisture in the soil . . ."

He trails off, not needing to say the rest: DNA, fingerprints — all that evidence is gone.

I press my lips together, waiting for a wave of nausea to dissolve.

"I assure you we'll be doing everything we can, questioning the appropriate people. But in the meantime, I'd like to go back to Andy's note. Can you tell me again about the circumstances in which it was found?"

I swallow. I was the first one up that morning, which was unusual. It was just after eight, and the house was filled with a quiet that felt like the world was holding its breath. Dad had been sick the night before, muscling through dinner with a queasy grimace, so I figured he and Mom were sleeping in. But Andy — he should have been awake already, rummaging in the kitchen for pots and pans, making enough eggs or oatmeal for both of us to share.

The note was waiting on the credenza, folded like a tent, and later, it made sense to me that Andy would leave it there. As kids, the credenza was a place we'd crouch inside, waiting to jump out and scare Mom. It was a hideaway in which we whispered and giggled, back when Andy was still small enough to find joy in the closed-up dark.

As soon as I finished reading the note, it slipped from my fingers, and Mom told me afterward that she thought I was being murdered, from the scream I emitted.

I relay this story to Elijah.

"And the handwriting," he says. "It looked like Andy's?"

"I . . . think so? It was a long time ago, but — Wait." I lean forward, Elijah's meaning suddenly clear. "You think it wasn't his note. That's what you're getting at. Whoever . . . whoever killed him must have written it, trying to make us think he'd run away. Which we *did.* Oh my god."

How could I not have noticed? I knew Andy's handwriting as well as my own. I should have recognized a forgery. But then again, maybe I was too shocked to notice: shocked by the note altogether, shocked he would mean those words, *never come back.* Shocked he would actually go.

94

"Well, wait a minute," Elijah says. "Yes, that's one possibility we're looking into, but it's also possible that Andy *did* write the note, that he left the house that night, but was killed before he had the chance to leave the island."

I shake my head, watching it play out in my mind: someone — *not* Andy — slipping into the darkness of our house, sneaking across the foyer, leaving the note where they were certain we'd see it.

"I don't think Andy wrote it," I tell Elijah.

Because if he didn't write it, then he didn't intend to leave me behind.

"Okay, let's say for a moment it was forged," Elijah concedes. "From what you've said, it sounds like the handwriting was pretty convincing. Any idea how someone might have managed that?"

"I don't know. Isn't it *your* job to figure that out?"

"I'm just thinking: they would have needed samples of Andy's handwriting. And then of course there's the issue of —"

"The murder reports," I say.

"The . . . What?"

Andy had a gift for writing them. His theories were clever, elegantly expressed, connecting details that most of us had overlooked. *Endlessly insightful,* Mom had written on the top of one about the then-unsolved East Area Rapist's crimes, and she hung it on the fridge, where it stayed for years.

Andy's killer could have walked through the kitchen, looking for a pen with which to write the note. Then he could have seen Andy's name on that handwritten report and had all he needed to fool us.

I tell Elijah this, in a breathless rush. His gaze lingers on me in a way I don't understand.

"What we really need," he says, "is the note itself. Do you know where it is now?"

"No."

"Hmm," he muses. "Neither does your mother. Or your siblings."

I shrug. "I don't know where it ended up."

After I read it, I never wanted to see it again.

Elijah cocks his head. "The last words you thought you'd ever hear from Andy and no one knows what happened to them."

"I didn't think they were the last words. I was sure he'd come back. Or that I'd find him."

"Mmm," he acknowledges, scribbling again. "Well, it would be very helpful to the investigation if you could locate that note." His eyes, dark as leeches, latch onto my face. "Let's talk about the party."

"What party?"

"The birthday party for you and Andy. The night he went missing."

I wouldn't call it a party. We didn't get presents or decorate the house. There was dinner, and a sticky too-sweet cake from the market, and then we capped off the night by honoring our namesakes, Andrew Borden and Elizabeth Short, aka the Black Dahlia. We lit candles for them, chanted the words, blew out the flames — just like how, on Charlie's birthday, we honored the Lindbergh baby, and on Tate's, we honored Sharon. And then we'd do it all again on the anniversaries of their murders.

Add to that the Honorings for the Blackburn Killer's victims, and people like Kitty Genovese and the Boy in the Box, and it's a wonder there was ever a single day in which our lips didn't part for our prayer. The squares in our Honoring calendars have always been crowded with ink.

"Can you tell me again," Elijah says, "what it was like that night? Any tension between family members?"

Not *between* family members. The tension was all in Andy, just as it had been for days. By the time we sat down for dinner, he couldn't hold his fork without his knuckles turning white.

But Elijah isn't looking at me, or even his notebook, as he waits for me to answer. Instead, he scans the room, lingering on a portrait of Linda Cook, her permed hair and small mouth, before moving on to Peggy Lynn Johnson, her oval face and prominent gums. Tate was sure to paint both women so they were smiling, and I see Elijah register that, eyes hungry and curious, his hand prepared to jot down assumptions about the room, our family, this house.

"Are you like your father?" I ask him.

He snaps his head toward me. "What?"

"Edmond Kraft was obsessed with us. He was so fixated on exposing whatever dark secrets he'd convinced himself we had that he was willing to break laws to spy on us."

"Break laws?" He arches a skeptical brow.

"He'd trespass on our property. We'd see him out there, creeping around."

My mind returns to the women outside. I wonder if they've given up and left, or if they've only multiplied, swarming like flies on something dead. I think of Ruby, too. Her massive eyes. But at least Ruby stayed in the woods when she watched. At least those women were only on the driveway. Edmond helped himself to our entire lawn, inspecting the grass as if searching for drops

98

of blood, running his hands along the stones of our house as if one would pop out to reveal a hidden tomb. It always agitated Andy. He'd see Edmond's patrol car return and his fist would instantly tighten. Later, he'd head out back, pick up his ax, and take his frustration out on the trees. Dad had the opposite reaction, watching with amusement as Chief Kraft poked through our hedges, wrote down notes about nothing. *Let him,* Dad would say.

"Are you like your father?" I ask Elijah again.

Whatever mask he's been wearing drops in an instant. It's jarring, really — how quickly he goes from detective to defensive.

"No," he says. "But this isn't —"

"But you've followed in his footsteps," I push. "You're a police officer. You're here, aren't you? Investigating crimes on Blackburn Island. Investigating us."

"I'm questioning your family because your brother was —"

"I see how you're looking at this room. It's the same way your father used to look at us."

Elijah's mouth hangs open, a fish caught on a line. He shakes his head.

"My relationship with my father is complicated," he says, and there's not a note of authority left in his voice. Instead, he sounds sad.

"To be honest," he continues, "I resented him for most of my life. I hated that he paid such little attention to me so he could basically stalk you all instead."

The word *stalk* surprises me. I wouldn't have expected Edmond's son to see it that way.

"But my father's in a nursing home now," he adds. "Early onset dementia. He began to need more from me than I could handle, and I . . ." He raises a helpless hand. "Most of the time, when I visit, he doesn't know me. So I've had to let a lot of things go. It's hard to hold grudges against someone who can't remember what they did to earn them."

"But you agree," I say, "that the way he treated my family wasn't right."

Elijah tilts his head, thoughtful. "He used to keep these Lighthouse notebooks," he says after a moment. "Black journals where he'd tape in photos he took, record every detail he could discover about your family. There was this filing cabinet in our house, and you'd open it and see dozens of these things, organized according to year."

Elijah scowls at his knee, then flicks something off his meticulously ironed slacks. "He didn't hang on to a single photo of me, but" — he chuckles bitterly — "he had those notebooks."

He says this while holding a notebook of his own.

"So yes. I know what my father did with your family was inappropriate. And I hated it. Though, admittedly, as a kid, I hated it for my sake instead of yours."

He chuckles again, a mirthless sound. "I saw you once, you know. You and Andy. My father had taken me with him, for one of his drop-ins. I stayed in the car, and I saw the two of you, playing around with John Fritz in the yard. You were running from him, and he couldn't keep up — his leg, you know — and Andy pulled you behind some bushes to hide.

"Mr. Fritz was baffled at first, and then alarmed. He called your names, frantically searching for the two of you. And I saw Andy peer out from behind the bush, and he was laughing.

"It wasn't until Mr. Fritz was a foot away that Andy jumped out at him. And he was so startled he fell back onto the ground, wincing and grabbing his leg as soon as he went down. And your brother's laughter . . . Even from the car, I could tell there wasn't any playfulness in it. Only cruelty."

Silence pools around us. I remember that day, the shock of seeing someone I cared about lying on the ground, someone who — despite his limp — seemed so solid and strong. But it wasn't cruelty that kept Andy from noticing what he'd done to Fritz; it was this unnameable energy, this fierce rebelliousness, that would well up inside him. And before it came out as whacks against a tree, it would come out like that: tricks on Fritz or Mom; frenetic laughter that, I'll admit, seemed inappropriate, at times.

"I told my dad about it," Elijah says, "when he returned to the car. I thought he'd be proud of me. He was always looking for reasons to mistrust your family, and here was this . . . really mean thing I'd seen." He taps his pen against his notebook, a slow and steady rhythm. "Only . . . you know what my dad said? 'Don't waste my time, kid. I'm not looking for mean. I'm looking for evil.' "

He strikes the paper harder with his pen. Once. Twice. I blink both times. "So no," he says, "I'm not like my father. Because I'm not looking for evil. I'm looking for answers."

His gaze slinks away, taking in the stacks of newspapers on the shelves, as if the answers he seeks are filed with the stories of all those victims. Then he studies another of Tate's paintings and makes a note.

"But you're suspicious of my family," I say — because it's clear to me now: it's not just Fritz he suspects; it's all of us. *Any tension between family members?* he asked.

"I'm not ruling anyone out," Elijah confirms.

The temperature in the victim room drops. Cold snakes beneath my clothes.

"Getting back to it," he says. "I wanted to ask you about your sister's Instagram." He glances at his notebook as if he needs the reminder. "Die-underscore-orama, I believe it's called? Die_orama?"

Dread punches at me. I'd almost forgotten. Right now, Tate is in town, buying supplies for a diorama in which our brother will be glued, for eternity, to an ax and a grave.

"What about it?" I snap.

Elijah's eyebrows shoot up. "A few of the crime scenes she depicted of the Blackburn Killer's victims — the positions the bodies were found in, where on the shore they washed up — they're . . . oddly accurate."

I cross my arms, let out a huff. "That doesn't surprise me."

"No?"

"She's obsessed with accuracy. She researches each case until she can't see straight anymore. And then there are her 'studies.' "

Elijah flips back through his notebook, hunting for something. Then he taps a page. "Her hashtag BehindTheCrimeScenes posts?" He says *hashtag* like it's a made-up word. "I found those particularly interesting. Sketches of every angle of the crime scene."

I nod. "So she can perfect the details before she commits them to the diorama. Like I said: obsessed with accuracy."

I bet she's out there right now, collecting handfuls of dirt to make the hole in which Andy was found appear more authentic.

"And where does she get her information?" Elijah asks. "When she researches the cases."

"I don't know. Newspapers? Internet? You'll have to ask her."

He scribbles once again. "It seems there's a lot you don't know."

"They're not my dioramas."

"I don't just mean this. Where the note went, for example."

"I told you —" I start, but then I'm stopped by a noise at the door, someone on the other side trying to push it open.

"For fuck's sake," I hear Charlie say. His grunts are muffled through the wood, the knob turning uselessly. Elijah glances at me, puzzled, but I just shrug. This house is old and the doors tend to stick. Some keep you in. Others keep you out.

The door gives way, and Charlie barrels through. His hair is tousled, face red, and he has a streak of dirt on his sweater.

"Detective Good Boy!" he says. "Sorry, I didn't know Dolls had company."

"He's not company," I say.

Charlie smirks as he heads for the shelves. Running his hands over the newspaper folds, he plucks some out, letting them fall to his feet. Soon, the floor looks carpeted in black and white.

"What are you doing?" I ask, and I can't help the shrillness in my voice. I see flashes of victim names — *JonBenét Ramsey, Christopher Byers* — as he plucks and drops, plucks and drops. This isn't how Mom taught us to handle the papers; she always warned us to be careful with the pages, make sure our hands were clean and the corners never bent. Then again, Charlie often flouted Mom's wishes when it came to respecting victims — goofing off during Honorings, wagging his candle in the air instead of holding it solemn and straight.

Andy and I giggled at it then, but now, seeing those murdered people tossed so casually to the floor, my chest feels tight.

"I'm pulling out options for the LMM," Charlie replies.

"The LMM?" Elijah inquires.

Charlie stops, head turned over his shoulder to strike me with a mock scowl. "You didn't tell him, Dahlia?" He spins around, rubbing his hands together. "The Lighthouse Memorial Museum. In honor of our brother and father. Tate will debut a new diorama, we'll be —"

"A diorama of what?" Elijah interrupts.

Impatience creases Charlie's forehead. "Andy, of course."

Elijah gives me a curious look before returning to his notes.

"For one day only," Charlie continues, "we'll be showcasing family artifacts. Exposing our history, our traditions. Basically, we'll be giving the people of this island exactly what they've always wanted: our lives splayed open. All you can ogle!"

Elijah scrawls until his fist falls off the page. "Why?" he asks.

Charlie smiles, slick and taunting. He's slouching a little toward the left, his usual posture. When he was a teenager, I always thought it looked like one side of him was

106

heavier than the rest, like his skinny body that seemed to be all limbs was always off-balance. Now, it only makes him look casual, like he's leaning against an invisible doorframe, like the museum he's planning isn't strange at all.

"Why not?" he answers. "We've got nothing to hide. You'll have to come, Detective."

Elijah bites the inside of his cheek — exactly the same way his father did, whenever he was sniffing around, certain of something. He meets Charlie's eyes, and I watch as they stare at each other, gazes hard and unyielding.

"You can count on it," Elijah promises.

SIX

The doorbell won't stop ringing. I try to block it out, burrowing deeper into my beanbag chair, but it shrieks through the air, cutting through my walls. I curl up tighter, fetal and aching.

It's been a day since those women stood in our driveway, but now, from the sound of it, people have gotten bolder. Charlie's voice booms up the stairs — "Well, hello!" — every time he opens the door, and it makes my head, already pounding from a second night of too many tears, feel like it's splitting wide open.

Another chime rings out, quieter than the bell downstairs, and it takes me a moment to recognize it as the sound of a text. I fumble for my phone, lost in a fold of the beanbag chair, and when I finally find it, I stare at a message from Greta.

Just checking in. Here whenever you need me. Police are saying there's no apparent connection between the Blackburn killings and Andy's death, but it's hard not to go there, right? Let me know if you want my help, or a blueberry muffin, and I'll be on the next ferry.

I know what she means by help. I can imagine her, ravenously reading the news, typing notes into her "Thoughts & Theories" document, which has grown a hundred pages since I met her. I don't doubt she wants to be here for me, that she's genuine in her offer of support. But I know a part of her must be tingling at the knowledge of another murder on Blackburn Island. It's the same part of her that showed me, one Halloween, a picture she'd found in which someone had dressed as a Blackburn Killer victim. They were wearing a light blue — not ice-blue — dress, and they were grinning like a jack-o'-lantern, pointing to the cursive *B* they'd drawn on their ankle. *People are sick,* Greta said, but her eyes, bright and gleaming, lingered on the photo.

I don't want that for Andy. For him to be a thought or theory in someone's obsession with a killer — even if Greta's right: it is hard not to go there.

I shove the phone into my pocket. Later. I'll find words for Greta later. Right now, I need something for my headache — ibuprofen, or a sleeping pill even, something to

109

knock me into a state of blank unconsciousness.

The doorbell rings again before I make it down the stairs. I hover on the landing as Charlie, unaware of my presence, arranges his face into a look of cheerfulness and thrusts open the door. "Well, hello!"

From here, I can't see who's on the other side, but I watch as Charlie receives a casserole dish covered in aluminum foil.

"Thank you so much," he says, cradling it like a baby. "That's incredibly kind of you. My mother's all but banned us from the kitchen while she auditions for America's Next Top Cookie Chef, so this is much appreciated."

There's a murmur I can't make out as the casserole bringer replies.

"No, no, it wasn't like that," Charlie says, "but have you heard about the memorial we're holding? I think you'll find that all your questions will be answered then."

He runs through the details of his grotesque museum, words I'm already tired of hearing — *artifacts, exhibits* — before thanking the visitor again, smiling and unhurried. When he closes the door, his smile slips off his face and he puts the casserole on top of the credenza, where, I see now, others have already been placed.

He looks up as I walk down the stairs. "It's like a food bank in here," he says.

"Why are you even answering?" I ask. "You know they just want to gawk."

Charlie studies my face as I reach the first floor. "Your eyes are puffy," he says, lip curled in distaste. "I have a cream for that, you know. Remind me later to give it to you."

He heads toward the living room, but he's stopped midstep by the bell once again. He tries to nudge me aside as he lurches for the knob.

"Hey." I slap a palm against the door. "You don't have to answer it."

Charlie pinches his lips together, looking at my hand as if it's a spider splayed on the wood. Then he plucks it off.

"Of course I do," he says. "Don't you get it? The PR team is coming to *us.* They'll spread the word to the rest of the island and we won't have to lift a finger. Well, except to . . ." He nods toward the casserole dishes on the credenza. "Why don't you go deal with those? And maybe check on Mom? I think I smell burning again."

I smell burning, too. Last night, Mom thrust a pan of too-dark cookies at us. "Snickerdoodles!" she proclaimed proudly. But Tate was the only person to take one,

111

nibbling politely at its crispy edges.

Again, the bell, piercing and insistent, and when Charlie opens the door, it's to a trio of girls, each one ponytailed and smiling.

"Well, hello!" he says, and then, turning to wink at me, "No casserole?"

"What?" One of them laughs. "No, we're, uh . . . Is Tate Lighthouse here?"

Charlie crosses his arms over his chest. "Tate Lighthouse," he repeats, as if the name is unfamiliar. "You don't look like islanders."

And they're not. I know it before the one in front responds. They're tourists, lured by Tate's Instagram toward an island with nothing to offer them. No cutesy shops. No soft, sandy beaches that, even in November, might provide a relaxing place to stroll. All that's here — all they care about being here — are the dark, jagged rocks on which the Blackburn Killer's victims were found.

"We go to University of Rhode Island," the girl chirps. "We read online that . . . Sorry, is Tate here? We figured she'd be back."

Charlie chuckles, clearly entertained. "You know my sister?"

"Your *sister*. Wow." She turns to her two friends and the three of them laugh, nervous but giddy. "No, sorry — not personally, but —"

"Tate!" Charlie yells up the stairs. I jump at his sudden interruption. "You have visitors!"

A few seconds of silence, then footsteps from above, followed by the creak of a door. When Tate descends the stairs, I'm surprised to see her looking disheveled. Well — her version of disheveled, anyway: a smudge of mascara beneath one eye, hair more limp than wavy. Even her lavender sweater looks rumpled.

"Friends of yours," Charlie says, opening the door wider to reveal the three suddenly bashful girls.

"No, no," the girl in front says. "God, we wish, but" — she blurts out a giggle — "No. We're just really big fans, and we . . . we heard about your brother." She sobers, mouth flattening. "We're really sorry."

The girls' eyes are stapled to Tate, their sympathy directed only at her. And I don't need strangers and gawkers to tell me they're sorry, but it would be nice, maybe, to get some acknowledgment — that the person here with the biggest hole in them is me.

"Thank you," Tate says, her lashes lowered, appearing more demure than I know her to be. "That's really kind of you."

"Oh, you're welcome!" the girl says. "And we were wondering" — she looks back at her friends, who reply with the tiniest nods — "could we get a selfie with you?"

"Oh," Tate says. She edges toward Charlie, who quickly steps in.

"Sorry, no," he says. "She's not really dressed to impress right now, as you can see. *Yuck,* right? She hardly slept last night. She's been working 'round the clock on a new diorama."

The girls, who'd slumped a little at Charlie's refusal, perk back up.

"Really?" two of them say in unison.

"Can we . . . can we see it?" the other one asks — and though I've never interacted with Blackburn's tourists before, it's clear these girls feel they have as much a right to our lives as the residents do. My skin crawls with their audacity, their fervor.

"Absolutely!" Charlie says, closing the door just a little, concealing Tate as she tiptoes back up the stairs. "My sister will be debuting it in four days, at three o'clock, at an event we're calling the Lighthouse Memorial Museum. LMM, for those acronym lovers among us." He points to one of the girls' sweatshirts, where URI is stitched across the chest. The tourists giggle again.

114

"We'll see you there?" Charlie asks.

They nod, seemingly starstruck at the thought.

"Great," Charlie says. "See you soon. Tell your friends!"

The second he shuts the door, his grin goes slack. Without his theatrical brightness, he's visibly tired. His sweater hangs off his shoulders, too big on his lanky frame.

"Well," he says, looking with heavy eyelids toward the boxes he's piled in the living room, "back to work."

"Charlie, why are you doing this?"

"I told you," he says, weary and annoyed. "We're setting the record straight, proving to the islanders that we're not the monsters they think we are. We're just . . ." — the last word comes out on a sigh — "people."

"But those weren't islanders. They were tourists."

He pinches the bridge of his nose like he, too, is battling a headache. "Things have changed since we lived here, Dolls. The tourists basically *are* the islanders. They come for the stories of the Blackburn Killer, and by the time they leave, they've heard all those rumors about us; they're tweeting about Murder Mansion before the ferry's even docked." He looks at me, the whites of his eyes zigzagged with red. "That's not the

115

legacy Andy would have wanted for us." He clears his throat, gaze sinking toward his feet. "Neither would Dad."

I stand up straighter, surprised to hear him mention Dad. I know he's why we came here to begin with, but when there's a hole blown open inside you, bubbling with acid at the edges, burning through you more and more each moment, it's hard to notice the pain of a paper cut. And honestly, I have no idea what Dad would have wanted for us. By his own admission, he didn't *know what to do with girls;* Tate and I weren't invited to be part of his legacy.

"Sorry," I say, "I know you —"

I'm cut off by a noise at the door — a knock this time instead of the bell — and it's as if someone's pulled a string at Charlie's back; he lights up and breaks into motion.

"Well, hello!" he says, tearing open the door.

"Hi," a voice says, husky and unsure.

"Can I help you?" Charlie prompts.

I crane my neck over his shoulder to find Ruby Decker standing on the porch. The moment she sees me, a wrinkle in her forehead relaxes. "Hi," she says again.

Charlie looks back and forth between the two of us. "This a friend of yours, Dolls?"

He doesn't recognize her. Which makes sense. She would have been only seven when he left at eighteen, and I don't remember her being the Watcher until Andy and I were ten.

"This is Ruby," I tell him, "Lyle Decker's granddaughter."

"Hello, Lyle Decker's granddaughter. How can we help you?"

Ruby ignores Charlie, gaze pointed at me. "I remembered something."

"You remembered something," Charlie repeats. "How satisfyingly specific. Would you care to —"

"Come in," I say, and Ruby slips through the door, not even glancing at Charlie.

"Sure, yeah, come inside," he says. "Oh, and you've tracked some dirt in on the floor, that's good. I wanted the house to be clean for the LMM, but this is better."

He crosses his arms, leering at Ruby, who peers up at him with wide, unblinking eyes. "What?" she asks.

"Nothing," I say. "We can talk upstairs."

"What's the LMM?" she asks, following behind me, but when I turn to answer her, I see she's already forgotten the question. She's studying the photographs along the staircase, mouth ajar.

"Andy told me about these," she says, so

117

reverentially, like she's finally seeing a masterpiece in person she'd previously only read about in a textbook. She leans toward one in particular, where Mom's parents smile in front of a wall of mounted guns, arms stretched wide as if in awe of their company's success: *all of this is ours.*

It's a photo I've often wondered about, given that Mom hates to even think of her parents' work. After she told us the most chilling detail of their murder — that the gun that killed them had been one they'd manufactured — she never let us ask about it again. *I don't want anyone to think,* she said firmly whenever we tried, *that because they created something that killed so many people, it was karma that they were killed by that thing in return.*

But wasn't this picture just a reminder of that, with the guns lurking behind them, almost taunting their proud, carefree smiles? Sometimes I think Mom overcompensates, that maybe she's the one who believes their deaths were karma, and the guilt about that is what keeps her insisting that victims of murder must be honored.

At the bottom of the stairs, Charlie watches us, interest and irritation battling on his face. A few moments pass before he plods off toward the living room. "Well,

118

hello there!" he says to one of the boxes.

"Come on," I tell Ruby, and she trails me reluctantly to the second floor.

"Which one is Andy's room?" she asks, following me down the hall.

I nod toward a closed door near mine. Ever since I arrived, I've tried not to look at it, and now, even just gesturing to it sends a jolt of pain ricocheting through me. What ghosts are trapped inside that room? What dust of Andy and me? I stop abruptly, causing Ruby to crash into me from behind.

"Whoa," she says. "Are you okay?"

My lungs are hot and tight. "Sorry," I manage, and I lead her toward my room, turning my face from Andy's.

After we enter, I close the door behind us and make my way to the bed. The old mattress groans as I sit, and if Ruby's notices the tissues littered across my blankets, she doesn't mention them. Instead, she walks toward the window near the corner of the room, hunches down, and rubs her hand along the wall.

"What are you doing?" I ask.

Without answering, she approaches the window closest to me, mere feet from the bed, and repeats the hunching and rubbing until her fingers find the grooves Andy carved into the wall.

"Here it is," she says, smiling at me. "I've always wanted to see it."

And for a moment, it feels like I'm breathing through a straw, like I'm only allowed a sip of air.

"He told you he carved his name here?" I ask.

She nods, tracing the letters of his name, letters I stared at for years while I waited for him to come home.

"Why?" I say.

She looks at me, lifts one shoulder and drops it. "He told me lots of stories about you."

It's not the answer I was expecting. My eyes sting with a warning, and I reach for one of the tissues on my bed.

Ruby stands from her crouching position, scanning the rest of the room. There isn't much here. My bed. An old dresser. A desk with a drawer that's always jammed. The beanbag chair that's identical to Andy's. He'd often drag his into my room, and we'd flop onto the chairs in sync, waving our arms and legs to make "bean angels." With Andy right next door, spending as much time in my room as he did in his, I never felt the need to adorn my walls with pictures or to pretty the hardwood floor with a rug. For years, Andy and I filled the room with

120

laughter, with stories, with silence we sometimes wrapped ourselves in like a blanket — and afterward, when he was gone, the emptiness felt like a promise: he'd come back for me; he'd never leave me so unfinished.

"You and I could be friends, you know," Ruby says. "Like Andy and I were. I'd really like that. It gets so lonely here, up on this island."

She stares at me so intensely I have to look away.

"I don't live here anymore," I say toward the wall. "I'm leaving as soon as I know what happened to Andy. You said you remembered something. What was it?"

"I could visit you," she pushes. "Wherever you live. Grandpa will be dead soon anyway."

My eyes slingshot back toward her face. "Whoa. That's —"

"It's just the truth. He's been sick for so long — basically as long as Andy's been gone — and that's felt like forever to me. Haven't the last ten years felt like forever to you?"

When I don't respond, she takes a step forward.

"So I've been thinking: when Grandpa does die, it's time for me to move on. Leave the island like I always wanted. I'll sell the house, and . . . maybe I could stay with you for a while."

She moves even closer, her thigh touching the edge of the bed.

"My place is tiny," I tell her, scooting back an inch.

"That's okay. I don't take up much space."

"No, it's . . . barely bigger than this room."

"Well, we could always get a new place. Something we pick out together. We could go to . . ." She trails off, examining my face. "Oh," she says. "I'm freaking you out." She slumps onto the bed, plunks her elbows on her knees, her forehead on the heels of her hands. "Andy always told me I come on a little strong. And I don't mean to, I never . . ." She lifts her head to look at me. "I'm just nervous I won't have anyone, once Grandpa goes. It would be nice to have a friend to live with. After."

Tears shine in the corners of her eyes, threatening to spill.

"You don't even know me," I say.

"But I knew your brother."

As if knowing Andy is the same as knowing me. Which, maybe it is, but still: how bold of her to assume she knew him that well in the first place. So they hung out sometimes. So they talked and wrote down

122

silly phrases. What bean angels did the two of them ever make? Where in her room did he sign his name?

Shaking my head, I stand from the bed and take a step back, putting some distance between us. "What did you remember, Ruby?"

She looks at her hands, knotted together in her lap, and nods as she sighs. It's as if she was expecting my impatience, but is still disappointed to hear it.

"It was a week before Andy . . . died," she begins. "We were supposed to meet up the next night; that's what we'd planned, anyway — but I was too excited to see him." She shrugs. "So I decided to watch your house."

She stands up and leans against the wall and peers through the sheer curtain hanging over the window.

"Andy's room didn't have any curtains like this," she says, skimming her fingers along the fabric. "And since it faced the backyard, I could see in a bit, whenever the light was on."

I swallow as she caresses the curtain. It isn't lost on me that she asked which room was Andy's, but she seems to have already known.

"But his window was dark that night," she

says, shooting a glance my way. "And it seemed strange to me. I'd started watching around eleven thirty, and I stayed there, hoping I'd catch a glimpse of him when he got ready for bed. But the room just kept being dark."

She pulls one end of the curtain aside, staring out the glass. "I waited for so long. And it was hours — the middle of the night, really — before I saw anything at all."

My heart thrusts against my ribs. "What did you see?"

"Your groundskeeper," she says.

"Fritz? In the middle of the night? That can't be right."

My entire childhood, Fritz always left at six p.m. on the dot. He'd take the last ferry back to the mainland, head off to a home I still find difficult to picture. I glimpsed him often, over the last seven years, as I watched the ferry from my window, and it took seeing him in that context, off Blackburn Island, to realize I knew nothing of his life beyond our house.

"He was heading toward the shed," Ruby says, ignoring my disbelief, "and he was carrying something — something large and . . . and heavy, it seemed. Something in a big, black bag. And then I —"

"What makes you think it was Fritz? It

124

would've been dark, right? Difficult to see clearly?"

She gives a dismissive wave, annoyed to be interrupted. "His height," she says. "His build. The way he was kind of" — she lurches across the floor a few feet, mimicking Fritz's walk — "staggering. His limp is easy to recognize. Even at night."

"Okay, but —"

"And then," she says sharply, eyes latched to mine as she walks backward, returning to the window, "I saw Andy." She leans against the wall. "He was creeping behind your groundskeeper — behind Fritz — like he was secretly following him. He was walking so slowly, so carefully, his feet didn't make a sound."

She angles her body to face the window again. "Fritz went into his shed. And a minute or so later — so quiet, so careful — Andy did, too."

Andy in Fritz's shed? I can't imagine that. The shed has always been off-limits. *There's too much that's too sharp in there,* Fritz told us. *It's a dangerous place for kids like you —* even though he was fine with Andy leaning his own too-sharp ax against the exterior. I was always so curious about that shed, curious about the part of Fritz that was closed off to us when the rest of him was wide

125

open — but Andy never cared. When I asked what he thought was inside it, he said, *Something unnatural, I'm sure.*

"Could you see what they were doing in there — through the windows or anything?"

"Oh no," Ruby says, shaking her head. "I didn't get close enough for that. Grandpa always told me to stay away from the shed."

"From . . . from *our* shed?" I frown at the echo of Fritz's warnings.

"Yeah, it was one of his rules. He caught me near it one time when I was, like, five. I'd wandered off into the woods, I guess. And when he found me there, he got so mad. And it just became this thing after that: *Don't go anywhere near the Lighthouses' shed.*"

"But why?" I ask. Besides the obvious reason — people shouldn't trespass — I can't imagine why Lyle Decker would care about our shed.

Ruby shrugs. "I don't know. Just Grandpa being Grandpa. He was always telling me where I could and couldn't go."

"Okay, well — What happened after," I press, "when Andy and Fritz came *out* of the shed?"

"I never saw them come out. They were in there for so long, and it had already been so late to begin with, that I went back home. I

126

was worried Grandpa might wake up and check on me, which he used to do a lot. But I asked Andy, the next day, what he'd been doing in the shed, and he denied it even happened."

She lifts her hand, touches the space right over her heart, and begins to pick at her shirt. Squeezing and plucking — the same thing she was doing yesterday: a nervous tic, perhaps.

But why is she nervous?

"He got pretty mean about it," she says, "insisting I was seeing things. So I dropped it. He was in such a mood after that — for *days*. I didn't want to upset him even more."

"So . . . wait. This happened a week before Andy . . . ?"

She nods.

Cold coils through me. Is this why he was so wound up, the week before our birthday? I remember how taut he seemed, his back rigid at the dinner table, his eyes squinting and skittish. Did something happen in the shed to set him off? And why didn't he tell me he went inside?

Without warning, Ruby whips her head my way. "But it was probably nothing, right?" she says, suddenly dismissive of this story she crossed the woods to tell me. "It

127

wasn't like your groundskeeper was breaking in somewhere he shouldn't have been. I mean, the shed, it's . . . it's *his* shed. He has all sorts of reasons to go in there. No matter the hour, right? So maybe something was broken and needed to be fixed really fast. And maybe . . . maybe Andy wasn't following Fritz or sneaking up on him, like it seemed; maybe he was just helping him with something. Or maybe . . ."

I stop hearing her. I see her mouth moving, releasing reasons into the air, but I'm snagged on the fact that pricked me the moment she mentioned *the middle of the night.*

Even two days ago, during the most extraordinary of circumstances, when Fritz dug up bones in our woods, he asked the police if they could finish questioning him by his "usual departure time," so he wouldn't get stuck on the island. Because Fritz has always left — always, always, *always* left — promptly at six p.m.

So why would he have still been here in the middle of the night?

Or if he left our house at six as usual, why didn't he get on the ferry? Why did he return after dark?

SEVEN

I follow Ruby out. Part of me wants to make sure she actually leaves, that she doesn't crouch between trees, waiting for us to walk by the windows and perform our misery for her. The rest of me is on a mission: find Fritz.

From the side yard, I watch Ruby amble through the woods in the back — slow-going, but going nonetheless. Then I scan the landscaping out front, the evergreen hedges, the dormant rhododendrons, the hydrangeas whose petals are dead. I don't see Fritz, or any of his tools, anywhere. I'm about to turn toward the backyard when a voice calls out to me.

"Hey."

I don't recognize the boy who's climbing over the crest in our driveway. He looks about eleven or twelve, so he would have been a toddler when I lived here, if he's even an islander at all.

129

"Hi . . . ?" I say.

He juts a chin toward the house. "My mom says they found a body in your backyard." I hear snickering behind him, and he glances down the driveway toward a part hidden from me by the pavement's curve. "Can I see?"

"Yeah, can we see?" another voice, bodiless as a ghost, pipes up.

More snickering. A whisper of *Murder Mansion* carried on the wind.

"My brother is dead," I tell him, and I wish my voice didn't quiver.

The boy checks over his shoulder again before taking a step forward, a mean little smile warping his face. "Isn't that, like, a party for you guys?"

I hesitate only a moment before running toward him, a growl rising up from somewhere in my body, an animal part of me I didn't know I had. I make it just a few yards before the boy's eyes widen. "Go! Go!" he yells to his friends, his sneakers already slapping against the pavement.

In the quiet that follows, I pant out the energy that surged through me like electricity. Boys like that, their gossiping parents — those are the people Charlie would have us open our house to. And if he wants to play docent to our dad's death, our brother's

130

murder, the parts of our childhood that are none of their business, then fine — but I don't want to be here to see it.

I have to find out what happened to Andy. Then I have to leave this place for good.

But first, I need to talk to Fritz. I need to know what happened in the shed a week before our birthday, because there's a rotten, slithering thing in my gut telling me it's somehow connected to that ax in Andy's skull. And I need to disprove that theory. Because wouldn't it mean that Fritz is connected too?

The backyard is empty when I round the corner of the house. Once again, no Fritz, no tools. Just a handful of leaves tumbling across the grass. As I step into the woods, I see the police tape, a yellow smudge bouncing in the breeze, and I force myself to focus on other things. The trees with scars from Andy's ax. The nearly naked branches.

Fritz's shed.

Its brick walls are as dirty as I remember. Ivy hugs the corners, threatening to fill in all four sides, transform this shed into a living thing. I asked Fritz once why he didn't scrape the ivy off — or do whatever it is that keeps climbing plants at bay. *Who am I to take away its home?* he had answered, and he'd stroked the side of the shed like it was a pet in need of soothing.

"Fritz?" I call from just outside. Only the wind answers back. As I open the door, its hinges creak, and within the sound, I hear an old warning: *You're not supposed to be here.*

Inside, shadows splay against the walls, dowsing the equipment in darkness. I blink a few times, letting my eyes adjust, and when I see that Fritz isn't here, I almost turn to leave.

But something about Ruby's story keeps my feet on the floor. She said Andy seemed to be following Fritz in secret, trying to remain unseen. But this shed is only so big; I can stand in its center and see every corner, every scrap of unused space. Fritz's equipment is lined up neat and tidy along the perimeter of the room, leaving the middle of the floor, a large square covered in gray outdoor carpeting, wide open. So if Andy really was sneaking behind Fritz that night, how would he have remained undetected once he entered the shed?

Feeling like a trespasser, I study the unfamiliar space. I run my palm along the handle of the push mower, touch a leaf still stuck in the tines of a rake. From the wooden counter along the back wall, I pick up bottles of chemicals and packets of

132

seeds. I have no idea what I'm looking for, but my fingers itch to search.

Crouching beneath the counter, I pull out a bucket, rummage through the gardening gloves inside it, then push it back in place. When I reach for another one, I tug too hard and tip the bucket over. Hundreds of nails spill out.

"Shit," I breathe.

I sweep up the nails with my hands. Some have scattered, as far as the middle of the carpet, and as I crawl toward them, something jabs into my knee. I lift up my leg, expecting to find a nail on the floor beneath it, but all that's there is a patch of bare carpet. Except — there's a bulge in it, a few inches long, unnoticeable unless you're down this close. I run my hand along it and feel something hard beneath the rug.

It could be anything. A skinny rock. A pencil nub. More than likely, it's nothing worth discovering. But that itch in my fingers — it has me reaching for the corner of the carpet, and now I'm pulling at the edge, which resists my grip. I yank harder until it slowly peels away, making a ripping sound as it goes.

There's some kind of tape on the bottom, keeping it from coming free. But now I stand and jerk my arms backward and a bigger section of the carpet pulls up. I examine the uncovered floor, part of me expecting that skinny rock, or that pencil nub. But what I find instead is a hinge.

A trapdoor.

My fingers latch around its handle, a metal ring in a recessed hole. I lift the ring so it swings outward, and I give it a good pull.

The door doesn't budge.

Above the handle, there's a keyhole, the kind for an old skeleton key. It glares at me defiantly, a dark unblinking eye.

I yank on the handle again, with more force this time, as if the problem is my strength and not the fact that the door is locked.

What could be down there? What could Fritz need to lock away, then cover over with a carpet? I think of his warnings about this shed: *There's too much that's too sharp in there. It's a dangerous place for kids like you.* Only, looking around again, I see that everything dangerous — pruning shears, pointed trowels, an ax that isn't Andy's — hangs from hooks on the wall, too high for a child to reach.

I return my attention to the handle. Was this door the real reason Fritz told us to keep out?

And when Ruby saw him carrying something through the woods that night — *something in a big, black bag* — is this where he brought it, to the space beneath the floor?

And did Andy, creeping behind him, see something he shouldn't have? Something that rattled him, darkened his mood, turned him sleepless and fidgety until the night he was killed?

As I stare at the door, the lock stares back, daring me to find its key.

"Do you know there's a trapdoor in the shed?"

Mom spins around at the sound of my voice. She's at the kitchen sink, wiping flour off her face, and the room smells like vanilla and char — a meager improvement from just the char. Cooling on the stove is a pan of peanut butter cookies, but I only identify them as such from the jar of Jif on the counter.

"Dahlia!" Mom says. "Here, have one!"

She picks up a cookie with a spatula and holds it toward my mouth.

"No, I'm —" She pushes it closer. "I'm fine, just —"

"No one's eating my cookies," she pouts, and she looks so dejected, so unlike the woman who staged crime scenes in the

135

victim room, stretching out on the floor with her feet together, hand on her stomach — the exact position in which Elva Zona Heaster was found.

"I know they're a little . . . dark," she continues. "But I'm getting better, I swear."

"Why don't you take a break?" I suggest. "You've been baking nonstop."

"I don't need a *break*," Mom snaps, and the cookie drops to the floor. We look at it there, split into three chunks. Mom closes her eyes and takes a slow breath.

"I don't need a break," she repeats, calmer now. "I want to do this for you. You're all going through so much. You've lost your father, your —" She thrusts out her hand to cup my face. Instinctively, I back away, but she catches my cheek in time. "Andy!" she continues. "Oh, Dahlia, you've lost Andy."

The stroke of her thumb feels like a scrape.

"So have you," I say.

She nods, face pinched, as if she's concentrating on holding something in. Tears, maybe. Or words.

"Yes," she says after a moment, hand slipping from my face. "Yes, I lost him, too."

She inhales shakily and points her gaze away from me. "I just want to do something to comfort my children. I've never made

136

you cookies before. What kind of life is that? Going without cookies from your mother. My mother made me cookies all the time, and I . . ."

Her lower lip trembles, but she sinks her teeth into it, biting hard.

"Hey," I say, "we did all right. And anyway, Andy and I were more into pie."

I mean to make her smile, but instead, she lifts her eyes to mine, horrified.

"I don't know how to make pie," she says. "I can barely make these goddamn cookies!"

I flinch in surprise. I've never heard her curse.

Andy was the one to teach me swear words, which he learned while hunting with Dad. *He said "fuck" when the deer got away,* Andy relayed one day. *And he warned me not to repeat it. Especially around Mom.*

Fuck, I said quietly, cross-legged on my bed.

Fuck, Andy parroted. He shifted his body so it mirrored my own.

Fuck, we said together, clapping hands over our mouths, catching the laughter that frothed from our lips.

Now I blink. I do it again and again — until I don't see him in front of me anymore, until there's only Mom, and the kitchen,

137

and this gutting absence that will never be gone.

"I was kidding," I say. "Cookies are great. I'm just not hungry right now."

Mom pushes strands of brown hair back toward her floppy ponytail. "Oh," she says. "Well, I've been putting them in Tupperware when they're done. You can have your pick, once you're ready."

"Thanks." I attempt a smile. "But — Did you hear my question when I came in? About the trapdoor?"

Mom turns back to the stove, using the spatula to transfer the cookies to a cooling rack. "A trapdoor? Where?"

"In Fritz's shed. Under the carpet."

"Oh," she says. "That." She lifts another cookie and slides it into place with the rest.

"What's it lead to?" I ask.

"Just a little basement area. My family used to use it for storage. But the shed's been Fritz's domain for decades now, basically since I was a teenager. I imagine it's still just storage. Old tools and such."

"Do you have a key for it?" I ask. Because her answer doesn't satisfy me. If Andy had seen Fritz with *old tools and such,* it wouldn't have left him so unsettled.

She tilts her head, considering. "I don't know," she says again. "It's possible your

138

father made a copy of Fritz's — but I doubt it. It's Fritz's space. We've always trusted him to use it right."

"Where *is* Fritz? I didn't see him outside."

"Oh." Mom waves a hand through the air, casually dismissing his absence. "He needed some time off after —" Her hand jerks to a stop. "After the other day," she finishes a moment later. "He's understandably shaken."

"When will he be back?"

"I'm not sure. I told him to take all the time he needs. But you know Fritz. He never stays away for long."

I nod. Even on days he designated for time off, we'd see him sometimes, lumbering around our lawn. *All this sun,* he explained once, pointing toward a hot August sky. *I was worried about the peonies.*

"Why are you so curious about the trapdoor?" Mom asks. She's set her spatula down, and now she's regarding me with a tilt of her head.

I respond to her question with another. "Are you sure you don't have the key?"

She shakes her head. "I'm sorry, I don't know."

It seems there's a lot you don't know. I hear Elijah's words, gently accusing me of something, when he last brought up the note.

139

"What about Andy's note?" I try, and Mom startles a little, her lips parting. After a moment, she closes her mouth, then turns away to grab a binder from the counter behind her. She opens it to a seemingly random page, running her finger down a handwritten recipe.

"I found my mother's baking book," she says quietly. "So now I can make those raspberry cookies."

"Mom," I say. She doesn't turn back to face me, but her finger goes still. "Andy's note. Do you know where it went? Elijah Kraft thinks it might be evidence. That whoever did this to Andy" — even from behind, I see Mom wince — "might have written it to make us think he ran away."

"I don't have it," she mumbles. "I already told him that."

"Well, somebody must. Do you think maybe Dad —"

"I don't know!" she cries, spinning around. "Don't you think I wish I knew? I never saw it after that day. It just — The note just disappeared!"

Tears overwhelm her eyes, and she clears them away with furious blinks. Then she smiles, a ghastly slash of teeth across her face.

"Now, please," she says. "Let me make

140

these cookies for you. Please, Dahlia. I have to."

Mom's unraveling. And she's wrong, too. The note has to be somewhere. It didn't just disappear into thin air, unwriting Andy's — or the killer's — words. That terrible morning, we passed it around, hand to hand to hand, and someone had to be the last to hold it. And then what did they do — just toss it in the trash?

Maybe, actually. It fits with the rest of my family's carelessness, the way they treated Andy's absence like it wasn't worthy of concern. But I can't bring myself to imagine it: this solid piece of evidence, gone, destroyed. Long since decomposed.

I try Charlie next. I find him in the living room, kneeling in front of the coffee table, writing with black Sharpie on a small piece of white cardboard. He's got another Sharpie gripped between his teeth, and he squints in concentration.

The room is a mess. Empty boxes are tossed into one corner, heaped into crooked towers, and there are piles of stuff — candles, DVDs, papers, portraits I recognize as ones taken from the victim room — spread throughout the space. I step over a heap of murder documentaries and find myself inches away from a collection of guns — five or six, at least, stacked together like logs in a fire. I read the card that Charlie has placed beside it: *Daniel Lighthouse's Hunting Rifles.*

"What is this?" I ask.

Charlie cranes his neck to see past the piles and down at my feet. Speaking around the Sharpie in his mouth, he says, "An exhibit."

"You're displaying Dad's guns?"

He pulls the marker from between his teeth. "That's usually what an exhibit means, yes."

Mom will hate that. She always turned away from Dad's rifles, stung by the sharp reminder of her parents' deaths.

"But why?" I ask. "I thought the whole point was to have the islanders see us as humans instead of . . . violent and dangerous."

"That's right," Charlie says. "And what's more human than killing animals for sport? Or, in our case, for dinner?" He smiles at me, but when I don't return his grin, he leans back against the couch and huffs. "Don't tell me you're some kind of vegetarian or something." I cross my arms and don't respond. "Oh god. Vegan?"

"No. Stop. I'm not anything. I just think

you could be doing something a lot more useful with your time."

"Like what? Baking cookies?"

"Like helping me figure out who murdered my brother."

Charlie's smile disintegrates. "He was my brother, too," he says, voice cold. "And that's the police's job."

"Then help *them* figure it out. They're looking for Andy's note, you know."

Charlie twirls his Sharpie between his fingers. "I'm aware."

"So? Do you know where it is?"

"I do not."

"How is that possible? How can no one know?"

Charlie shrugs, hunching over the coffee table again. He squints at a piece of cardboard, holding it down at one edge as he drags the marker across it.

Portrait of Catherine Susan "Kitty" Genovese, he writes, *painted by Tate Lighthouse, age fourteen.*

And now, beneath those words, he's drawing a line, about three inches long, and leaving an inch-wide space before adding a dot. It looks like a sideways lowercase *i.* Dropping my eyes toward the card for Dad's guns, I see the same mark.

"What is that?" I ask.

143

"What's what?"

"That." I point toward the card beneath his fingers. "That weird *i* thing you're doing."

He stares at the card, brow furrowed, as if seeing the mark for the first time. "It's not an *i*."

"Then what is it?"

"It's . . . I don't know, you've never seen it before? Tate calls it my trademark flair. It's just what I do when I write things. Rent checks, grocery lists, whatever." He shrugs. "Everything's boring without it."

At another moment, it might have struck me as sad — how I know Charlie so little that I don't even recognize something he considers to be his "trademark flair." But this is a moment too close to that other one: *He was my brother, too.* And that moment has only underscored how quickly Charlie left, so soon after we discovered that Andy was gone. *I've got an audition,* he said to me, *a once-in-a-lifetime opportunity: Brutus in* Julius Caesar. *Andy will turn up, Dolls. Or else he won't, and that's the way he wanted it. But I've got to go for now.*

Only it wasn't *for now;* it was forever.

I remember thinking how appropriate the role was: Brutus — the man who stabbed in the back someone so close to him that his

144

name became synonymous with betrayal. (I only knew the play in the first place because of the gruesomeness of Caesar's murder; even the literature Mom taught us always ended with somebody lying in their own blood.) And though I know, now, that there's nothing Charlie could have done, it still boils me up inside to recall how quickly he left.

He looks up at me, brows raised. "Is there something else I can help you with?"

"Maybe," I say, tamping down my bitterness. "You know Fritz's shed?"

"The thing that's been on our property our entire lives?" Charlie asks, picking up another piece of cardboard and holding his Sharpie above it. "Nope, never seen it. What's it like?"

"There's a trapdoor inside it," I say, ignoring his sarcasm. "Under the carpet. Do you know anything about that?"

He straightens.

"A trapdoor? No. But I've never been inside the shed. Don't you remember it wasn't allowed?" He rolls his eyes before continuing. "Why do you care about a trapdoor?"

"Ruby Decker said she saw Fritz and Andy go inside the shed in the middle of the night, about a week before Andy was murdered."

"The middle of the night?" Charlie glares at his cardboard. "That can't be right; Fritz—"

"Always leaves at six, I know. And when I went to ask him about it, he wasn't in the shed, and I ended up finding the trapdoor. Which is locked, of course. And Mom isn't sure what's down there, but she said it's like a basement or something."

Charlie leans against the couch again, shrugging as he crosses his arms. "So? What are you thinking?"

"I don't *know* what I'm thinking, that's the problem. But maybe Fritz is keeping something down there, something . . . illegal? Maybe he's growing drugs! And maybe Andy found out by following him one night, and Fritz . . . Fritz . . ."

". . . killed our brother?" he finishes for me. "To protect his *drugs*? Are we talking about the same Fritz here? The guy who worships at the altar of spiderwebs? The guy who sings to grass to make it grow?" He chuckles. "Actually, maybe Fritz *has* been on drugs this whole time. It would explain a lot."

"This isn't funny."

"I'm sure that Fritz would agree! You're all but accusing him of having a grow room

146

under the shed and murdering a kid so . . . what? Dad never found out? You're grasping at straws, Dolls. But, hey, if you're so worked up about this door, why don't you go ask Fritz to unlock it for you?"

"He isn't here right now. And Mom doesn't know where the key is."

"Well, see? There you go."

"There I go, what?"

"Dahlia, I need to concentrate. The LMM is only four days away, and I can't have you buzzing around me like this with theories about how the mildest, meekest man in the world might have axed our br—"

He stops the second he looks at me. And I guess I'm grateful — that he has enough kindness in him to leave that image incomplete.

"Sorry," he says, shifting his eyes back toward the cardboard. "Just let it go, Dolls, okay? You're going to make yourself sick."

He lifts his hand to continue writing. And he's right, about one thing at least. It doesn't make sense, the idea of Fritz — gentle, sweet, easygoing Fritz — killing someone he'd only ever been kind to before.

But still —

"I'm going to find that key," I announce.

147

EIGHT

Every morning, there's a moment when I don't remember Andy is dead. For that tiny sliver of time, he's still out there somewhere, sitting on a park bench maybe, draped in the shade of an abundant oak. Or he's seated at a table in a restaurant, contemplating the chair across from him I do not fill. Or he's standing on a boardwalk, scowling at an ocean that's deep and indigo and will not take him home.

It hurts, of course — imagining him, in all those places, living a life without me — but it's nothing compared to the pain I feel when the moment ends. When I open my eyes. When I blink to find that my lashes are stiff from last night's tears. When reality trudges inside me, crushing my lungs.

And on this, the third morning in which I'm yanked upon waking into a world where Andy is dead, I roll over to find that my bedroom door has been removed while I slept.

At first, I'm certain I'm seeing things. But my door is gone, its hinges empty and useless, gripping nothing but air.

I spring out of bed, march to the gaping hole, and I see down the hall that other doors are missing too — all of them, it seems, except for the one to the bathroom. I grip the doorjamb as I shiver. It's unnerving — not just the mystery of where the doors have gone, or how I managed to sleep through their removal — but the effect of the doorlessness itself. The hallway is flooded with sunlight when normally it's dim during the day, our rooms shut tight whether we're in them or not.

I make it only two steps down the hall before I have to stop: Andy's door is missing too. I try to snap my gaze away, but it's too late; I've seen inside. His room is still so similar to mine — same bed, same dresser, same beanbag chair — and somehow, that guts me harder than if every trace of him had been erased.

I can't linger here when his room is open, festering like an unbandaged wound. Spreading my hand against the wall, I steady myself and keep going. When I reach Tate's room, I find her walls unchanged from years ago, displaying the different phases of her childhood art: melancholy watercolors of our gray mansion; monochromatic sketches of the living room, victim room, kitchen; oil portraits of her namesake, the corn silk of Sharon Tate's hair and the bronzer on her cheekbones the only color on Tate's walls at all.

Hunched at her desk, back facing the doorway, Tate is cast in a glow from the lamp beside her. Her hands work at something on top of the desk.

"Where are the doors?" I ask.

She jumps at the sound of my voice but doesn't turn around. "Charlie took them," she says.

"Why?"

"Something to do with his museum."

Anger ripples through me, sending me stomping into her room.

"He's going to display our *rooms*? That's — This whole thing is ridiculous, but that's taking it way too far. You have to talk to him, Tate. He'll listen to you."

She waves a hand, swatting away my words, and it's such a Charlie gesture.

"I don't think he's displaying them," she says. "But even so, let him grieve how he wants to, okay?"

Her voice is flat, inflectionless. Gone is

150

the warmth with which she greeted me my first day here. Gone are the jarring hugs, the doe-eyed *how are you doings.* Now, here she is, the Tate I'm most familiar with: working Tate, distracted Tate, *give me a minute* Tate. When Andy and I were kids — just five to Tate's fourteen — we'd try to climb all over her before she'd nudge us away, deeply embedded in one art project or another. Sometimes she glued together household items — spoons, peppermills, thimbles — making sculptures that only Charlie could identify: *Oh, cool, a grandfather clock.* Other times, her fingertips were smudged with paint as she eyed a photo of Bessie Darling or Lynn Eusan and committed them to canvas. Either way, Andy and I got used to the distant, detached tone with which Tate spoke (a tone that, years later, she would mask with exclamation points in her emails), and now as she sits with her back to me, her hands still tinkering with something on the desk, I don't have to peer over her shoulder to know what she's doing.

I do it anyway, though. I stand on my tiptoes, look at what she's making. She holds a hot glue gun in one hand, and with the other, she moves dirt, real dirt, back and forth across a square of painted Styrofoam, her fingers raking it into place.

And now I see: she's already dug a hole, already made an ax. It's whittled from a pencil, attached to a blade that shines with aluminum foil.

The floor tilts. The room spins. I have to grab her shoulder to keep from spinning too.

She whips her head to the side, narrowing her eyes at my hand. "What?" she spits out.

"How can you do that?" I ask, and I'm so dizzy with despair that the words sound like a plea, not the sharp accusation I intend them to be.

Tate sighs, turning back to the dirt at her fingertips. "I have to," she says.

"No, you don't."

"I do, Dahlia. And I'm sorry if it hurts you, or if it makes things harder. But you've seen my Instagram. This is what I do."

What she does. What she does is pin those women to their damp, sandy graves. In her diorama of the Blackburn Killer's second victim, Stephanie Kepler lies on the shore almost as if she were sunbathing, one arm flung above her head, the other at her side. Her blond hair is blown across her face, and the dark, glassy water is stalled midlick at her branded ankle. Tate crafted the dress so it always looked wet, the bodice of the gown

152

so sheer it gave a glimpse of Stephanie's nipples beneath. *Pornographic,* one commenter said. *Authentic,* wrote most of the rest.

"It's how I process and cope," Tate adds.

"That's bullshit. Your whole Instagram is bullshit. All those dead women? We processed and coped with their murders every time we had one of their Honorings. So no, your Instagram isn't about that at all. It's about attention. It's about *you.*"

"You're damn right it's about me!" she fires back, her blue eyes like the center of a flame. "It's what I have to do, Dahlia, just to . . . just to be okay."

Tears gather in her lashes but they do not fall. She's breathing heavily, nostrils flaring in and out, lips stitched so tightly together they make a perfect seam.

"What does that mean?" I ask.

She shakes her head, silent for too many moments. Finally, she gestures toward the base of the diorama, exposing the dirt beneath her nails. "This is the only thing I'm good at," she says quietly. "My Instagram, it's . . . the only thing that connects me to other people. I don't know how to make *friends,* Dahlia. Do you?"

The question startles me. Of course I think of Greta, the way she shoves her hair behind her ears when she takes an order at the café, the way she blurts out murder facts to unsuspecting customers.

"I have a friend," I say.

"*A* friend," she echoes, as if I've proven her right. "Well, who can blame us, right? Making friends wasn't exactly a lesson in Mom's curriculum. Me, I have Charlie, and there's an old lady in our building who brings us soup sometimes, and . . ." She trails off, helplessly lifting her hands. "Now our brother is dead, and the only people in the world who care about that are the people in this house. But a diorama will change that. My followers *care* about the people I post about. The one I just did of Jessie Stanton? It got a thousand Likes in three minutes."

Jessie Stanton — the last woman to be murdered on the island, the same month we found Andy's note. Blackburn swarmed with police when she died, like it always did after a woman washed up, but within a week or two, they'd already moved the investigation from their tiny satellite base on the island back to the mainland. They promised to comb through interviews, sift through photos. They promised to find the clue that would lead them to a killer who had eluded them for years.

154

I remember now that that's why Dad refused to report Andy's runaway to the police. *They've got their hands full with that poor Stanton woman. We're not going to distract from their investigation by having them chase after someone who chose to leave.* I didn't think of that when I saw Tate's diorama of Jessie, posted only a few weeks ago. I was too busy focusing on the details that Tate had meticulously re-created: the emerald nail polish on Jessie's toes; the *B* on her ankle; the rip in the blue gown, like an intentional slit up the dress, which newspapers said was likely from her body crashing against the rocks.

"So I can only imagine how many my own brother will get," Tate continues.

"How many what?"

"Likes."

My lips part, my breath hitching between them. "You're doing this for *Likes*?"

She frowns. "You're not listening. I'm doing this to . . . to . . ."

She stops, shakes her head, as if it's too much to explain.

"This is the *only* thing I'm good at," she says again, tears finally brimming over. "So what else would you have me do?"

I survey the grave she dug in the Styrofoam, that tiny blade that glints in the light.

It's only a matter of time before she builds Andy's body, too, before she places it in that dirt, sticks it beneath that blade.

"I would have you do a lot of other things," I blurt. "You could be helping me figure out who did this. You could be stopping Mom from baking herself into a psychotic break. You could be —"

"I don't see you doing any of those things," she says, tongue whipsharp, tears so quickly dissolved. "How exactly are you helping Mom? How are *you* figuring out who did this? Last I heard from Charlie, you went to your room after talking to him yesterday and haven't come out until now."

I open my mouth to lash out a response, but nothing comes. She's right. As much conviction as I had yesterday, promising Charlie I'd locate the key to Fritz's trapdoor, I found myself suddenly and overwhelmingly exhausted, unable to do much more than head upstairs to my bed and hide beneath the blankets. There, in the darkness I created for myself, I drifted to sleep, and when I finally woke up, Andy was dead again, and my door was gone.

"Fine," I say. "Maybe I haven't done enough. But at least I'm not planning to exhibit the worst thing that's ever happened to our family."

156

Tate looks at the dirt on her desk. Then she picks up the tiny ax, twirling it between her fingers. "It's not the worst thing," she says.

"Excuse me?"

She meets my gaze, pain swimming in her eyes. "Worse has happened to our family."

Air sputters out of me.

"Like what? Dad? Dad's death? We barely knew him, Tate. He acted like you and I were Mom's kids alone and all he had to do was tolerate us. So how could you possibly say that losing him is worse than —"

"I don't care that Dad's dead," she says. Then she jolts, as if startling herself with her own admission. "I mean — That didn't come out right. I just mean . . ." She sighs. "Never mind, Dahlia, okay? I need to get back to work."

I'm about to argue, but I'm stopped by a sound in the hallway: footsteps, followed by something banging against the wall.

"Shit," Charlie mutters.

I march into the hall to find him holding up a door with one hand and rubbing at a new mark in the wall with the other.

"What are you doing with the doors?" I demand.

"Dolls!" he exclaims, like he's happy to see me, like he didn't sneak into my room

157

to unscrew my door while I slept. "I'm so glad you asked!"

Even feet away, I can smell him; bourbon seeps through his pores.

"No doors until after the LMM is over," he explains. "You all need to get used to feeling exposed. I had a director once, Lorenzo Fichera" — he pauses, as if waiting for me to recognize the name — "who made me stand in Times Square in my underwear as an exercise in vulnerability. So just be grateful I'm not sending you half naked into town."

Seconds pass. "Are you serious?"

"Hey, I don't make the rules. And anyway, this'll be good for us. There's too much *hiding* going on in this house, you know? Too much squirreling away. Mom in the kitchen, you in your bed —"

"Mom's not hiding," I cut him off. "She's . . . manically baking."

"Well. Either way. Nobody's immune." He uses both hands to lift the door. "This is Mom and Dad's. But you're right, she probably won't even notice — since it's a door, not a cookie tray. This is the last of 'em up here, though, so I'll do the kitchen next."

He sweeps past me, carrying the door with ease, despite how lean he is, arms still twig-thin even in his thirties. Mouth ajar, feet

158

frozen to the floor, I watch him go. When he disappears down the stairs, I take in the hallway around me. Bursts of sun, from the windows of open rooms, pour onto the carpet — an old runner that's been here forever but only now reveals its stains. Dark splotches mar its red like blood clots in a vein.

I avert my gaze from the space where Andy's door should be. Down the hall that branches off to the right, I see light splashing out from Mom and Dad's room.

Curiosity pulls me toward it, a place I haven't seen inside in decades, not since I was five or six. I'd had a bad dream — the Black Dahlia, split in half on the grass, was still alive, reaching out to me, her new smile bleeding all over her teeth — and I pounded on Mom and Dad's closed door. When Dad opened it, I told him I had a nightmare, looking past him for Mom, who, a notoriously deep sleeper, didn't seem to have stirred. *Go back to bed,* is all he told me, and he shut the door in my face. After that, whenever a nightmare troubled me, I went to Andy's room, crawled beneath the blankets he was already holding up to let me in.

Now, I linger in the doorway, absorbing details of a room that still feels off-limits. Not that it was, really. Not officially, like

Fritz's shed. *It's important that everyone has their own space,* Dad once said. As if space was our problem in this massive, echoing house. Still, he proclaimed, *You can't go in someone else's space unless you're invited in* — which I later learned, from one of Greta's favorite TV shows, is how vampires have to live.

My eyes sweep across the room. The big bed. The reading chair beside a full-length mirror. The dresser made of dark, shiny wood. And on top of the dresser, a set of keys.

My heart kicks when I see it — this reminder of the trapdoor, the dark unyielding lock, the key I swore to Charlie I'd find. Mom said Dad might have it, and the ones on the dresser are definitely his. I recognize them from his key chain, a piece of antler whittled down to a few inches long. As I hurry toward them, I quickly find that all of them are regular, no skeleton key among them that would fit the lock in the shed's trapdoor. But my pulse beats faster, spurring me on.

I open the dresser drawers, rummage through my parents' socks, underwear, pants. I look through each of their nightstands. I even crouch on the floor, lift up the bed skirt, and search beneath it for boxes that may be keeping keys. When I find nothing unusual, I turn toward my parents' walk-in closet — the door of which Charlie has kept intact. Once inside, I feel past the hanging clothes for hooks on the walls. Then I search the clothes themselves, palming the pockets of Dad's shirts and jackets, waiting to register something hard and metallic.

The smell of him wafts off the hangers, gamy and musty, and it strikes me suddenly, as I run my hands along his hunting jackets, that even this doesn't make me miss him. Whatever weight I felt from his death when I headed back to the mansion — it's gone now, crushed beneath the boulder of mourning Andy. And honestly, it's freeing in a way, Dad being dead. For ten years, my body has housed a vibrating bitterness toward him, and now, it's a relief, knowing I have no reason to try to forgive him anymore.

I wrench apart the final cluster of coats, ready to pull each pocket inside out if I have to — but my hands go still when I see the back of the closet. Instead of a blank, uninterrupted wall, I'm met with another door.

Tentatively, I reach toward it, hair pricking up along my arms. When I turn its knob, I expect resistance, but it opens easily, without so much as a creak.

I stare into the dark void I've revealed. Then I activate the flashlight on my phone.

It's a passageway, no wider than four feet across, and as I point my light straight ahead, I can't even see where it ends. The walls are unfinished; exposed studs and cracked beams reek of mildew. I creep in farther, my empty hand spread out toward the side, until it brushes against something.

I swing my phone toward the planks of wood beside me. Taped to them — all over it, it seems — are sheets of paper. They overlap, colliding with each other, and when I step closer and shine my light on one in particular, my knees almost buckle.

It's a drawing of Andy. His eyes closed. Blood streaming from his head.

Hand covering my mouth, I look at another. Andy, again, clearly dead, face slack, cheek pressed to the ground.

The edge of each drawing touches another, forming a horrifying mosaic, a grotesque collage. I follow the trail of sketches — dozens of them; dozens! — looking ahead as much as I can, avoiding these apparitions of Andy, and when they finally stop, there's a few yards of space before I reach a new door. I open it, struggling for air, and find myself in another dark room. My flashlight bounces around, and when it highlights something I recognize — magenta jeans, crumpled on the floor — I rest against the doorframe so my mind can catch up.

I'm in Tate's closet, which apparently connects with Mom and Dad's. And those drawings, I understand now, are Tate's studies for the Andy diorama, completed in the same style as the ones in her #BehindTheCrimeScenes posts: pencil on paper, innumerable attempts at getting the victims' poses exactly right. I can picture the ones she did for the Blackburn Killer's victims as clearly as if I've pulled them up on my phone. For Amy Ragan, the fifth murdered woman, Tate drew her legs alone at least a hundred times, posting her sketches over a number of days, garnering more comments that way, more Likes.

The man who stumbled across Amy during his morning walk told the papers that her leg had been bent at such a strange angle that at first he thought it was broken, that *that* was why she was lying there motionless — a broken leg, a horrible but commonplace injury. But as soon as he started running toward her, he registered the ice-blue gown, and his feet froze on the sand. Turns out, Amy's leg had been mangled by the force of the waves tossing her back onto shore. Tate wrote in the caption of one round of studies that she needed to get the leg just right, because to do so would capture the true violence of the murder: not just the strangulation that killed her, not just the *B* mutilating her ankle, but the reminder that she had been thrown into the ocean. *Like a cigarette butt,* she wrote. *Like a rock skipped across water, purely for entertainment.*

Now, my heart throbs: just like she did for the dioramas of the Blackburn Killer's victims, Tate has sketched Andy over and over, practicing for the position of his body, the anatomy of his wounds, so she can glue and paint him permanently into place. Dead. Always dead.

I stand up, step back into the passageway, and close the door quietly behind me. I can't risk her hearing me, investigating the sound. I can't risk a conversation with her right now when all I have in me is the capacity to claw at her, to shout.

Stumbling back along this gruesome hall, led by the light on my phone, I almost make it out. But I'm stopped by the drawings again, even as I try so desperately not to see them. My gaze shifts there anyway, without warning, and now I'm inches from a sketch I didn't linger on my first time through.

In this one, Andy's eyes are open, and they're so *him,* so *his,* the crinkling of them so agonizingly exact. They stare out at me like they did a million times before — and I can see him, free of this paper, real and alive, squinting at nothing but air, just before he stomps outside to grip the handle of his ax.

Or another time, the blazing annoyance in those eyes, the night of our sixteenth birthday, Tate and Charlie whispering at each other behind a closed door while Andy itched to talk to them, ask them about life away from this house. He'd had his questions lined up for weeks, and he was so furious they'd locked us out, I thought he might yell those questions through the wall, louder and louder until they thrust open the door, let him inside just to shut him up. *We don't need them,* I reminded him — and the implication was: *because we have each other.* But the next morning, I didn't have him anymore. So I had nobody left at all.

Tate has rendered him perfectly — except for the wound at his temple, which leaks graphite blood all over the page. The ax itself is missing, as if the killer, off paper, has lifted it above his head to take another swing. And no matter how many times I blink, Andy's eyes never close; they still

165

stare out at me.

Or out at the person with the ax.

I'm going to scream. I feel it bubbling up like bile in my throat, ready to spew out. But when I open my mouth, I hear a different sound, the chime of my phone announcing a text.

You want that muffin yet?

Greta. I call her without thinking, my legs shaking as I step out of the passageway and back into Mom's closet.

"I guess you do!" she says in greeting, and I slump against the wall, sink to the floor, Dad's hunting jackets brushing my shoulders.

"My sister is sick!" I tell her. "She's doing a diorama of Andy, and she's done all these studies of his death, and she's taped them up in this weird passageway behind her closet. And I mean" — I glance at the shadowy hole leading back to that hall — "why would she put them in there, where she can't even see them, if the point is to use them as references for the diorama?"

As Greta hesitates, I barrel forward to answer my own question. "I guess she wanted to hide them — from me, probably, because she knew I'd react this way if I saw them. But you know what? Putting them in there like that — that just means she *knows*

166

what she's doing is messed up. And yet, she's still over there, spreading dirt on Styrofoam, making an *ax,* building his *body.* It's disgusting! All of it! And then there's Charlie. And my mom! They've all gone completely crazy!"

I huff into the phone, catching my breath.

"What's happening with Charlie and your mom?" Greta asks.

So I tell her about the museum, and the cookies, and our doorless rooms. Then I tell her the rest of it, too. About Ruby Decker, and what she saw the week before Andy died. About the door in the shed, and Mom's explanation that doesn't sit right. I tell her about the missing note, about Elijah Kraft, about the people on this island who still won't leave us alone. I tell her everything you're supposed to tell your closest friend, and when I'm done, I feel like my skin's scraped off, like someone's wedged apart my ribs, like my heart is beating in open air.

I wait for her to respond.

"I'm so sorry," she says finally. "And yeah, your family's being really weird."

I close my eyes, comforted by the acknowledgment.

"That trapdoor, though," she continues. "That's intriguing. The carpet, the lock.

167

Why go to such lengths to hide some extra equipment?"

"I don't think it *is* extra equipment."

"No, I don't either," Greta agrees. "But if Andy saw it, like you think he did, why wouldn't he have told you about it? Especially if it shook him up so much."

I've been trying not to think about that, how there might be something else he kept from me — first Ruby, now this — when, all along, I thought we shared everything.

"I don't know," I say. "It doesn't make sense. But I just have this feeling that the shed is connected somehow. To what happened to Andy."

"Then you have to break in."

I scoff at how simply she says it.

"I'm serious," she insists. "You have to go with your gut. You know my friend Alan, from my message boards? He was camping with his grandmother once, same spot they went every summer, when all of a sudden Nana gets this weird feeling and makes everyone pack up and leave. A couple days later? A dead body was found right near their campsite."

Goose bumps swell on my skin, even as I shake my head. "I don't think there are dead bodies under the shed."

"I know, but . . . gut feelings exist for a

168

reason. Now, do you want me to walk you through how to pick a lock? I'm not saying I once broke into an abandoned building because I thought it was the scene of a cold-case murder when actually it was just an old doctor's office, but . . . let's just say: I know how to get in places."

I picture the lock again, that small black hole in the wood. I see the possibility of Fritz, returning to work, finding me tampering with a door I'm not supposed to know about. Then I see Andy, the week after he followed Fritz to the shed, when his eyes wouldn't stop darting, when he rushed through meals, hardly even tasting his food.

And now, standing up from the closet floor, I answer Greta.

"I'll pick the lock. Just tell me what to do."

NINE

The door to the shed is cracked open.

"Fritz?" I call.

He wasn't shearing the hedges out front, or raking leaves onto a tarp in the yard. There weren't any tools left out that would indicate he's back. Still, I peek into the shed, expecting to find him there. When I don't, I slink inside.

Dropping to my knees, I peel back one corner of the carpet, but it's as resistant as the first time I tried to yank it up. Tugging back enough to look at the bottom, my heart hammers at what I see: fresh tape applied to each edge.

But if Fritz isn't here, then who would have done that? And why?

As I throw the carpet back, the dark lock reveals itself. I've brought two bobby pins, which Greta said I would need. I open one and remove the rubber tip, then bend the other at the closed end to create a lever. I follow Greta's directions, inserting both pins into the hole, pushing the first in deeper, twisting upward as I use the lever for tension, but all I hear are futile scrapes against the wood. Greta admitted she'd never picked a lock for a skeleton key.

I look around for something else to try and am just about to grab a screwdriver when a throat clears behind me. I stiffen, spinning toward the open door.

"Ruby," I say. "What the hell?"

"Maybe this will help," she says, and at first I'm not sure what *this* is; she's got her fingers on her sweater again, picking at the fabric along her sternum, just like she did the other times I saw her. But now she hooks a finger under her collar and pulls out a thin silver necklace. She grasps its pendant. Only — I squint through the space between us; she's hard to see, backlit from the sun outside — it's not a pendant at all. It's a key.

A small skeleton key.

"Where did you get that?" I demand.

She unclasps the necklace, slides the key off the chain, and holds it out to me. "Try it."

I eye her for another moment, her face giving nothing away, and then I grab it from her. Kneeling in front of the door, I put the

171

key to the lock — and it slides in so easily, offering a satisfying *click* the moment my wrist turns.

For now, I keep the door closed, snapping my head back toward Ruby. "Where did you get this?" I ask again.

"It was Andy's," she says.

The answer pushes me back, my weight thrust onto my heels. "What?"

"He was playing with it the last time I saw him. On his birthday. We met up, and —"

"Wait, you saw him on our birthday?"

"Of course. Not till late at night, but yeah."

A sickening feeling slithers through my stomach. *Late at night* means she saw him after I did, when I thought we'd both gone to bed. *Late at night* means she might have been the last person — besides his killer — to see him alive.

"We were arguing that night," Ruby says. "And I hate that. I've always hated it — that the last conversation we had was a fight." She gestures toward the key, still slotted into the lock. "But he kept *fiddling* with it. And it was driving me crazy. I was already upset — we were having an important conversation — but it was clear he was distracted, just playing with the stupid key. So I grabbed it from him."

172

I look at it again: dark brass, a circle at its end. I don't remember ever seeing it before.

"He let you have it?" I ask.

"Well . . . he was mad at first. He, like, lunged at me."

"He *lunged* at you?"

I can't picture that. Despite the handle of his ax that fit into his palm like it had been made for him alone, despite the growls that thundered through him each time he whacked at another tree, I never saw a whisper of violence in Andy. Not toward a person anyway.

"He didn't hurt me," Ruby's quick to reply. "He didn't even touch me. And when he saw how startled I was, he backed down immediately. He was like 'Sorry, sorry, sorry,' and then he put his head in his hands and just . . . grunted. This really primal grunt. It scared me a little because I'd never seen him like that. Not even when I watched him with his ax. So I ran off, ran back home. And I still had the key."

She bites her lip, combing one hand through her hair, examining her split ends. "He didn't come after me. I thought he would. I thought, at the very least, if he didn't want to apologize about our fight, then he'd want to get the key back. But he just let me go. And I never saw him again."

I blink and I'm there, inside that night, standing beside Andy as he watches Ruby run away. I see him squint into the darkness, and maybe that distraction — eyes pulled toward the diminishing girl in the woods — was enough to keep him from noticing someone behind him, raising an ax over their head, ready to swing it down onto —

But the key. Why did he have it?

"Honestly, I thought it was his house key," Ruby says. She sinks to her knees beside me, running her hand over the bottom of the door. "I even tried it in your front door a couple weeks later, but —"

"You tried to break into our house?"

"No, not break in. I thought I had a key. But it didn't work. So I put it on a chain and I've been wearing it since then. To remember Andy, I guess. The last thing I had of him."

She reaches for the key in the lock. Tracing the round end of it with her finger, she loops around the dark metal circle over and over. Then she pulls the recessed handle. The door creaks as it starts to open.

I shove it back down. "What are you doing?"

"We should see what's inside," she says. "Maybe this is where Andy ended up that

174

night I saw him enter the shed. You're thinking that, too, right? That's why you were trying to pick the lock."

"There's no *we* in this, Ruby. This doesn't concern you."

"But," she protests, lower lip protruding like a child's, "I gave you the key."

"I know, thank you for that. But now . . ." I gesture for her to go.

"But you clearly want to get in there, and you wouldn't even be able to if it weren't for me. I could have kept it, you know. It's been mine for years. It's special to me."

"Sounds like you stole it," I say. I hear the unkindness in my voice, but I don't know how else to speak right now. I have no idea what's beneath the trapdoor, or why Andy had the key that night; all I know is I need to get in there. And I need to do it alone.

Ruby's eyes seem to shrink, squinty with hurt. "Andy was right about you," she says. My shoulders rear back. "I told him he should bring you sometime, when we met up at night. I was interested in getting to know you. But he said you wouldn't go for it. That you were too closed off."

"Closed off?" The words are high-pitched, indignant, and I'm unable to meet Ruby's stare.

"He said you had problems trusting people. That you only really trusted him. I remember thinking that sounded sad. And lonely."

My eyes sting at the corners. My throat burns. She's wrong. My childhood — sitting on my beanbag chair with Andy, crouching beside him in the credenza, making forts from leaves and twigs — was happy. I was never lonely until the morning after our sixteenth birthday. Never sad until he didn't come back.

"I trust people fine," I reply.

But really, who was there to trust in our house? Tate and Charlie, who cocooned themselves together, cooing over each other's art and ambitions? Dad, who treated me more like a chore than a child? There was Mom, I guess — but she was consumed by her curriculum, obsessed with acquiring new papers, new films. And when she wasn't teaching us, she was stuck on the stairs, gazing at her parents on the wall, promising herself she would protect us from their fate, would ensure we knew that the worst could come for anyone. And yet I didn't know — for a decade I had no idea — that it had already come for my twin.

"Then let's open it," Ruby says. "Together."

I don't like her insistence, the way she's

176

needling her way into spaces she doesn't belong. It's consistent with how she's always been — our Watcher — but it's still unnerving, like there's something in this for her.

"Ruby. Please just leave."

Her gaze combs my face. She chuckles a little: *you can't be serious.* But when I only watch her in return, she shakes her head, dusting off her knees as she stands.

"Fine," she says. "Hope you find what you're looking for."

I don't know what I'm looking for, I want to hiss. *I can't fathom what Andy might have seen down there, what unsettled him so much, left him fidgeting with the key on his last night alive.*

"Go," I insist as Ruby lingers in the doorway.

With a final huff, she turns away and closes the door behind her, plunging the shed into shadow. I wait for my eyes to adjust, listening to the softening crunch of her footsteps outside. When the only thing I hear is the steady pulse of the ocean, its waves a whisper even in this closed room, I take a deep breath and take hold of the handle.

As the door yawns open, a dark pit gapes at me from beneath the shed floor. I turn on my phone's flashlight, shine it into the

177

hole, but all I see is a set of stairs that lead to more darkness. I don't allow myself to wait or second-guess. I don't indulge the chill that's inching up my spine. I sink my foot onto the first step and begin to descend.

The air gets colder the deeper I go beneath the shed, and soon I'm standing on a concrete floor. My phone illuminates an overhead bulb in the center of the low ceiling, but when I pull its dangling string, it doesn't turn on.

There's nothing in the room — no furniture, no equipment — except for a wooden chest against the farthest wall.

I go to examine it, my light catching on its sealed combination lock before I see that its lid has been split open, the wood caved in. The chill lingering in my spine explodes into a shiver.

Andy.

I recognize the anger, the frustration, the desperation in the broken box, the same I saw whenever I'd rub my fingers along the cuts he inflicted in our trees.

Andy was here. With his ax — which he used to hack into the chest. That means he must have been down here before Ruby took the key from him. And maybe that's why he was so on edge with her. Maybe he'd found something he wished he hadn't.

I reach into the jagged hole that Andy created, but my hand gropes at nothing. The wall behind the chest is blank and gray, offering no answers. Slowly arcing my phone across the room, I investigate the rest of the space, inching along the perimeter, sticking my nails into every crack I see. So far, it's only a concrete room, icy and empty — but that doesn't make sense. Why would Fritz put nothing down here but a chest, then go to such lengths to keep the room sealed up?

It's not until I reach the last wall that I know. My throat goes painfully dry.

There are photographs, taped all over the wall, edges overlapping. They're snapshots of a woman — of several women, I think: here, there's a lock of red hair, limp across a shoulder; and here, a blond ponytail, curled at the end; here, a pale ear, jutting out from beneath a black bob.

Then I notice an arm in a sheer blue sleeve, an ankle burnt with a B. I notice wide-open, glassy, unseeing eyes.

My lungs burn and my joints lock.

I've seen that same shade of blue, that same shape of a *B* — in studies, in dioramas, I've seen it a hundred times. But instead of Tate's renderings, which could only sketch them in pencil onto pages, or craft them out of porcelain and cloth, these photos are of real bodies.

Real women.

All of them dead.

I clamp a hand over my mouth. As I breathe through my fingers, cold air rushing into my lungs, my mind slows. Then it catalogs each photo, separating them from the horror of the whole.

There's the nape of a neck, pink from the grip of a rope. A pair of lips, parted and purple.

There's a hand, its fingers curling inward. A foot, its toenails emerald green.

The foot belongs to Jessie Stanton then. Part of me is lucid enough to link that detail to Tate's diorama. What Tate didn't capture, though, was the way the nail polish chipped in the right-hand corner of Jessie's big toe.

There's a leg, stretching from the hem of the ice-blue skirt that, on this woman, cuts off at the calf. This would be Erica Shipp. The third victim. The papers said she was too tall for the dress.

There's a round breast, nipple hard and dark beneath the sheer fabric.

There's a birthmark on a wrist — the way they identified Alexis Shea, the sixth woman. Her husband didn't need them to lower the sheet from her face in the morgue; he saw her wrist poking out and knew.

There's a tattoo on a collarbone: *the world is wide and I am small* — Stephanie Kepler, the second victim.

There's red hair on a shoulder: Claudia Adams, the fourth.

There's an ear with a diamond stud. A crooked nose, the crest of a cheekbone, a freckle that's —

When did Andy see this?

My mind veers without warning, steering away from the neatness of facts, and now I'm in it again, the constricting terror, the vise around my ribs. The photos grow blurry the longer I look, but really, *when did he see this?*

It couldn't have been the night he followed Fritz. Maybe he snuck after him into the shed, glimpsed the top of his head as he descended into the hole, but didn't see this room himself until our birthday. And then, returning aboveground, stunned and undone, the key still in his hand, Ruby intercepted him.

That's the only excuse I can think of for why he wouldn't have told me himself, wouldn't have dragged me down into this room, held a light to this wall so we could absorb the shock of it together, our mouths gaping and dark.

He would have wanted me to know. I'm

181

certain of that. He wouldn't have wanted to be alone in the discovery of what Fritz kept locked in this room.

But the ax got to him first.

No, not just the ax. The hands gripping it. The arm muscles tight and flexed. The shoulders that must have strained back. The face that —

The face that would have been the last the Blackburn Killer's victims ever saw.

I suck in a breath. Elijah Kraft said the M.O. wasn't the same, that there was no evidence to suggest Andy was a victim of our island's serial killer. But that's because Andy wasn't killed for sport, or ritual, or whatever motivates an evil man like that.

Andy was killed to keep a secret.

I stretch my arm toward the photos, touching a slack lip, a pulseless wrist. But at the sound of something above me, my hand snaps back. Heart pounding, I fumble with my phone to turn off my light.

Seconds accumulate as I listen. And then: the ceiling groans; tentative footsteps creep.

"No," I hear.

And even though it's just a syllable, more moan than word, it's a voice I know so well. The same voice that always warned us to keep out of the shed. The voice that said, *It's a dangerous place for kids like you.*

182

TEN

"No," Fritz says again. "No, no." I crouch on the concrete, covering my head with my hands.

The quiet that follows is heavy with Fritz's presence. He isn't speaking anymore, but I can feel him, looking down through the trapdoor — which I've stupidly left open. I've never been scared of him before, but as my mind pieces together the wall behind me, this hidden room, Fritz's insistence that we never enter the shed, terror vibrates through me. I picture him, feet above me, reaching for a tool he can use as a weapon.

But here, the image falters. Fritz with a weapon?

Even now, even with the photos I'll never stop seeing, I can't imagine him intending to do harm. Not to these women. Not to Andy. Not when he's a man who let us hitch a ride on his tarp of leaves, dragging us around the lawn on what he called his "magic carpet."

But don't we all have darkness? Pitch-black parts of ourselves that even those who love us can't see? Andy had the trees, his ax, the stormy thing that bubbled up inside him, desperate for release. And not just that. He followed Fritz to the shed one night. So he must have known, somehow; he must have had a feeling that something wasn't right, that something *unnatural* was afoot. But he kept that hidden from me. And if Andy could carry things inside him I never would have guessed at, then surely Fritz could, too.

My head jerks at another sound from above. The footsteps stutter across the shed, and then — one second of nothing, two seconds, three — it seems they're gone.

I wait another minute to be sure before I approach the stairs. Legs shaking, I climb my way up.

The shed above is instantly warmer, even in the chill of November. Out of the hole, I turn to leave — and then I go still. Fritz stands, arms crossed, at the threshold, his body like another door, sealing me in this space.

"Why were you down there?" he asks.

His voice is steely. Colder than I've ever heard it. His eyes seem distant, as if detached from the moment, and he shuffles toward the center of the shed. I edge backward — "Fritz, wait" — until the wooden counter stops me.

Fritz stops, too. Then he slams the trapdoor shut.

The sound reverberates, throbbing in my ears. He bends down to grab the key, but I'm younger and faster, plucking it from the lock, curling my fingers around it.

He looks at my closed fist, his expression flat and blank as an empty plate. And it's that — his stoicism amid such horror — that sharpens my fear into rage.

"What was that?" I demand. "In that room. On the wall."

It's a stupid question. But there's a wild, desperate part of me that hopes I've got it all wrong, and until I hear him say it, until he defines what was down there, that part of me will wonder if my rage is meant for someone else.

"Trophies," Fritz says.

My fingers loosen and the key slips against my palm.

"Tro-trophies?" I stammer. "That's what you call them?"

It's a common enough term. Robert Hansen, the "Butcher Baker," kept his victims' jewelry. Ivan Milat, the "Backpacker Mur-

185

derer," collected the camping equipment of the people he killed. But hearing the word now, about the photographs I just saw — faces with swollen lips, necks reddened by rope — I feel dizzy.

Fritz lumbers forward, arm outstretched, fingers bent into hooks. I recoil, pressed against the counter with nowhere to go. Turning my head, I squeeze my eyes shut.

He doesn't touch me. Instead, there's a squealing, sliding sound, and when I open my eyes again, he's holding a roll of double-sided tape, removed from the drawer left open beside me. He crouches down on the floor, careful with his bad leg, and rubs pieces along the edges of the carpet. He works quickly, methodically. He's done this many times before.

Words lurch into my throat. "Is that what Andy was? A trophy?"

Fritz stiffens, tape hanging from one finger like a strip of molting skin. For several moments, he's doesn't move — a blinkless, frozen figurine. Then, without warning, his palms strike the floor as he slumps onto his knees.

"Andy," he groans. He's hunched like someone about to retch. "That poor boy." He lifts his head, nearly in tears. "I didn't know he . . . I would have never . . .."

186

But he doesn't tell me what he would have never. The sentence dissolves as I watch his cheeks grow wet with silent crying.

Who is this man? Whose legs did I hold on to as a kid, laughing as I used him as a barrier during tag with Andy? Surely this isn't the same man who lifted his arms like branches, pretending to be an impenetrable tree that Andy couldn't find me behind. Surely he's not the man who let Andy pretend to chop at him, my twin's hands gripped around the handle of an invisible ax, Fritz slanting, then stooping, then staggering to the ground, at which point Andy erupted into cheers.

"Andy," the man on the floor now murmurs. He slams his fist against the wood, a spurt of anger that makes me jump.

"Andy," he repeats.

Each time he says his name, the shed seems to shrink around me.

I need to get out of here, get away. I need to call the police.

But as soon as I take one step, Fritz jerks out an arm and seizes my ankle. I cry out, try to shake him off, but his hand tightens like a tourniquet.

"Wait," he says. "We don't have to seal it up. Help me get rid of it all instead."

His eyes flick to the trapdoor, half covered

187

by the carpet. Anguish has slipped from his face, replaced instead by desperation. And finally, I can picture it: Fritz wearing that same expression when he discovered Andy knew what was beneath the shed. Some cool, stunned part of me can even understand it — almost: the fear of getting caught, the instinct toward self-preservation.

I look down at my foot, his hand circling it like a cuff, and somehow, I find the strength to crouch down beside him, to bring my lips right next to his ear.

"You're disgusting," I murmur.

He sucks in a breath. His grip loosens. Wrenching my ankle free, I take off running.

Right away, tears blur my vision, springing up with every step. I'm not sure if it's sorrow or fear that keeps them coming — part of me is still too numb to know — but it doesn't matter. My body is ahead of my mind, erupting with sobs as if trying to shed the shock of what I've witnessed.

Ripping open the back door, I burst into the house. Then I race down the hall until I collide with Charlie, who's rounding a corner.

"Jesus, Dolls," he says.

"Don't let Fritz in here!"

Charlie recoils, startled by my shout.

188

"Why not?"

I shake my head, reaching into my pocket for my phone. My fingers tremble as I punch in the passcode, failing two times before I get it right.

"What are you doing?" Charlie asks.

I dial 911.

"What's in your hand?"

Phone to my ear, I open my other fist, surprised to find the key still inside it. Charlie reaches for it, right as the dispatcher picks up, and I snap my fingers closed.

"The Blackburn Killer," I blurt. "I know who it is. Please. Get here now."

Silence oozes for a moment, until the dispatcher asks for my name and address. But I'm staring at Charlie, who's rigid and astonished, working to put it together. Finally, he looks at the back door. His brow furrows; his lip curls back. "Fritz?" he says.

"Ma'am? Can I have your name please?" the dispatcher asks.

"Sorry," I say. "Dahlia Lighthouse. I'm at 16 —"

Charlie snatches the phone from my hand. Then he ends the call with a stab of his finger.

I gape at him. A flurry of emotions — panic, confusion, disappointment — sweep across his face.

"Dahlia," he says, and his voice is coarse. "What the hell have you done?"

The police march in and out of the shed, a trail of ants with cameras and clipboards. From here, at the kitchen window, their white gloves make their hands look porcelain; their bright blue shoe covers could be mistaken for slippers. I watch the scene with drowsy detachment, standing between Mom and Tate as my mind moves at a sluggish pace.

You're in shock, Elijah told me when I mumbled apologies, slow to comprehend his questions. *Take your time.* But time has only dragged me further from the shed, making me wonder if I dreamed those photographs, if Fritz's hand on my ankle was only a hallucination.

Behind us, Charlie keeps grumbling. He grips a bottle of Glenlivet, storming back and forth across the tile. Every so often, he pauses, shoots an angry glance out the window, and scoffs.

"Unbelievable," he mutters now, the first coherent word he's said since Elijah and his team arrived.

"I've been working relentlessly," he says, "to show people we're nothing to be afraid of, and now we've got police traipsing

190

around our yard like we're a gang of criminals. Thanks a lot, Dolls."

"Knock it off," Tate says. "It isn't her fault."

Charlie scoffs again, rolling his eyes until they land on the bowl Mom deserted when I ran into the kitchen, crying about what I'd found. With his free hand, he stirs furiously at the wet ingredients, slugging his whisky with the other.

His resentment rouses me enough to respond.

"Are you really saying I shouldn't have called the police? I was supposed to just — let it go, the fact that, under our shed, there's a . . . a . . . ." — I fumble for the words — "serial killer's headquarters?"

"We don't know that's what it is," Charlie says.

"You didn't see what I saw! The photographs. Fritz's trophies. That was *his* word. What *he* called them."

Charlie frowns at that. "Trophies," he repeats, finally sounding disturbed.

Beside me, Mom lets out a tiny whimper as Tate shakes her head.

"I still don't understand," Tate says. "Fritz *confessed*? He said he was the Blackburn Killer?"

"Not in those exact words. But he asked

191

me to help him get rid of the evidence."

Tate turns to Charlie. They exchange a dumbfounded look.

"And there was a chest," I continue. "In that room, a locked chest. Only it had been broken into. By an *ax*."

I wait for their gasps of comprehension, the catch in their throats as they register that Andy has entered this story. They all stare at me, though — Tate and Mom wide-eyed, Charlie squinting.

"An ax!" I say again. "And the chest was empty, but . . . but Andy was there. The night of our birthday!"

Tate scrunches her brow. "How do you know it was that night?" she asks, and I realize I've left so much unsaid. I fill them in on what Ruby saw: Andy fidgeting with the key, and the week before that, Andy sneaking behind Fritz as he carried a —

I freeze in my retelling, stopped by a realization, a timeline snapping together.

"Oh god," I moan.

"What?" Tate asks.

I knead my forehead with my knuckles. "Ruby said Fritz was carrying a big bag into the shed, a week before our birthday. That would have been right around the time Jessie Stanton was found. Which means — He was probably carrying Jessie."

Another moan drains from my lips.

That dark energy that had been fizzing off Andy the days before he died. Now I know its source — even if parts of it remain a mystery: how much he witnessed in the shadows of that night; if he knew exactly what Fritz had done, and to whom. But he saw enough, it seems, to wreck him for the rest of the week. So why, then, did he swallow down his discovery, never telling anyone — not even me?

I see the chest again, its splintered wood conveying desperation. Maybe he'd been waiting for evidence, for proof — the kind he gained access to only on the night he was murdered.

I take in a shaky breath, numb again, unable to feel the tears I know I must be crying.

"I think Fritz killed Andy," I say, and my voice is so flat, so distant, it sounds like it's coming from somebody else. "I think he killed him for what he saw. When I asked Fritz about that, he kind of crumpled, said if he'd known, he would have never. I don't know what that means, but . . . he didn't deny it."

Charlie and Tate stare at each other, silent. Mom's hand flutters up to cover her mouth.

"I can't believe it." She lets out another

whimper, though her eyes, shifting to the scene outside, remain dry. "I've known Fritz for decades. We trusted him. My parents. Daniel and I. How could he have —"

Her question cuts off as Charlie nudges her aside to look out the window. An officer is walking from the shed, out toward the side yard, a clear plastic bag in his hand. Even from here, I can tell what's inside it: a photograph.

Charlie groans. "Everyone's going to know."

"Maybe not," I say. "Elijah told me not to speak to reporters. He said they don't want this public yet."

"Yet," Charlie echoes with contempt. "And where is Detective Good Boy, hmm?"

"He took Fritz away for questioning."

But before that, he disappeared into the shed while two other officers stood outside, guarding our groundskeeper. Fritz leaned against a tree, gaze far off, defeated, as if waiting for the moment they'd haul him away. When Elijah finally emerged from inside the shed, he nodded to the officers to follow him, and they each wrapped a hand around Fritz's arms, guiding him as he limped dutifully after the detective.

Now, officers continue to enter the shed as their colleagues exit. Whenever someone

194

comes out, there's a heaviness to their gait, like they're trudging through mud that sucks at their shoes.

"I can't watch this anymore," Mom says. She turns to the kitchen island and digs a measuring cup into the canister of flour. She doesn't scrape off the excess, like Greta always does when she makes the café's muffins. Instead, she dumps the heaping cup into the bowl of wet ingredients before shoving it back into the flour.

"It's too much," she murmurs. "This is all too much." She plops more powder into the batter. "First Daniel. Then Andy. Now you say Fritz . . . And the shed!" The measuring cup clatters onto the marble as her hands, shaking, hang in the air like she doesn't know what to do with them.

Tate rushes toward her. She tries to embrace her, but Mom shrugs her off. "No, no, this is all my fault."

"*Your* fault," Charlie says. He gulps from the bottle still clenched in his fist. "Do tell, Mother." He smiles, wolfishly, as whisky glosses his lips.

Guilt fills Mom's eyes as clearly as tears.

"I built our lives around victims of murder," she says. "I taught you about them, held Honorings for them. And now, here they are, all over our backyard. Andy" —

pain tightens her expression — "Andy was killed here. And god only knows what happened in that shed. So maybe . . . maybe it was karma, for the way I chose for us to live."

There's a beat of silence, all of us absorbing this strange theory. I've never heard her speak of karma without the context of her parents — the guns they made and were unmade by in return.

Charlie belts out a guffaw. "I'm sorry, but that's insane." He laughs some more until, abruptly, his smile evaporates. "If you're going to blame yourself for anything, how about you start with what you missed."

Mom's eyes grow wide. "What I missed?"

"Dahlia says Fritz has a murder den under our shed. Shouldn't you have known that something was going on? Shouldn't you have seen *something*?"

"Hey," Tate says. "We never saw anything either. We . . . we were here for years, as close to it as anyone" — tears clump like mascara in her lashes — "and we had no idea." She shakes her head, continues in a whisper. "We had no idea, Charlie."

"That's . . . that's not the same," Charlie says, but for a moment, he seems flustered. He rubs the back of his neck, then reaches for Tate's hand, squeezing it once before

196

letting go. "No, it's . . . it's not the same, Tate."

He slams his gaze onto Mom. Drinking his whisky, he glares at her over the bottle. "We were *kids,*" he adds when he swallows. "Mom was the adult. If anyone should have known . . ."

He trails off, his implication heavy in the air.

Mom gapes at him in horror. Then she spins toward her bowl on the counter, stabbing at the clumps of flour with a spoon.

"Ah, great plan," Charlie says. "Cookies will solve everything. What do you think — should I offer the officers some of your previous concoctions? Nothing works up an appetite quite like photos of dead women."

"Charlie," Tate says sharply, swiping away her tears. "You're being cruel."

"Oh, come on."

"You are. And I know you're scared, but —"

"I'm not scared," he says, voice rigid.

Charlie and Tate stare at each other — wide, wordless moments — and I see something pass between them, a message relayed in the silent shorthand they have with each other. It always annoyed me, their invisible words I never learned to read, but right now I'm grateful for it, grateful for Tate, especially, the only one who can crack through Charlie's meanness like it's nothing more than the thinnest layer of ice.

"Well, I'm fucking terrified," she tells him softly. "So could you please ease off everyone? What's happening out there is no one's fault. No one's in this room, anyway."

Charlie looks at the bottle in his hand. Then he raises it to his lips, gulping it down like he's dying of thirst. As he turns to face the window, Tate glides into place beside him, the tension between them instantly dissolved. Now, sharing the same view, the two of them lean together. It's almost imperceptible, how they're propping each other up, but I know that if one of them were to move, the other would stumble.

I ache for that. For someone to keep me standing. Which means I ache for Andy.

Without thinking, I take a step toward them, bend toward Tate as if to lean on her other shoulder. But then I see a freckle of brown paint on her jaw, and immediately, I recoil.

How could I forget? While I was descending into the room beneath the shed, she was dipping a brush into paint. While I was tracing Andy's footsteps, crouching over the same chest he once split apart, she was building our woods, tree by tree. And when

I illuminated those women, shining a light on their branded ankles, their strangled necks, she was staring at death, too, preparing our brother's miniature grave.

They're oddly accurate, Elijah said of her dioramas — and it's a sickness really, how committed she is to getting them right. I think of her studies in the passageway, the sketches manic, obsessive, edges overlapping like —

Like the photos beneath the shed.

My body jolts at the comparison, one I haven't registered until now.

I look at Tate again, watching as she nestles closer to Charlie, resting her chin on his shoulder. Together, they stare at the woods outside, at the police scattered between the trees.

I see it again — photos taped to a wall; sketches taped to studs — and a chill winds up my spine. But it's too much right now, trying to make sense of that similarity, so I shake the thought from my mind.

ELEVEN

Elijah returns after dark.

When I open the door to his insistent knock, it's like opening it to the past. For a moment, it's his father I see on our porch, with a smile he's biting back, certain he's finally got us. *I always knew,* I hear him saying, *there was something evil here.*

But then I blink, and it's Elijah there, glowing gold in the porchlight. He was unexpectedly kind to me, earlier today, his voice gentle as he asked the questions, as he encouraged me to take my time. Standing with him in the backyard, his team already gathering, I regarded the shed like if I turned away, it might start creeping toward me. Elijah shifted then, blocking that terrible, ivied place from my line of sight, and I managed a grateful flick of my lips before seeing the view his moving had exposed: the yellow tape of Andy's grave. The other crime scene in our woods.

Now, I expect Elijah to tell me that Fritz has made a full confession. Already, I feel the burden of the looming challenge: reconciling the man I thought Fritz was with the monster he turned out to be; modifying every memory where I saw him be good to Andy. But then I notice the officers behind Elijah. There are five of them, out on the walkway, looking off to the sides as if scanning our yard for danger, for shadows that move with a human shape. They each rest a hand on the gun holstered to their belts, while Elijah, dressed in his usual slacks and coat, forces a tight, toothless smile.

"We have a warrant to search your house."

He holds up some papers, and I stumble back in surprise, a movement he takes as an invitation to enter.

"I'll be the judge of that," a voice growls behind me.

I smell Charlie before I see him. His cloud of whisky precedes him.

"Actually," Elijah says, passing him the papers. "Judge Matthews was the judge of that, as you'll see from the signature."

Charlie skims a finger down the first page, elbowing me aside as I try to read it, too. "You're looking for . . . evidence and instrumentalities of a crime," he says. "Well. I believe my sister already gave you free rein

201

of an entire shed full of evidence."

"You can keep reading," Elijah says.

Behind him, one of the officers wipes their feet on the front mat, an oddly polite gesture for someone invading a home.

Charlie's head snaps up. "You're looking for the brand."

"The Blackburn Killer's brand?" I blurt. "Why would it be here? Shouldn't you be searching Fritz's house?"

Elijah opens his mouth to reply, but Charlie, still reading, steamrolls over him. "This says the warrant can only be executed in the daytime, six a.m. to ten p.m. And it's" — he pulls his phone from his pocket, clicking it to check the time — "9:47 right now. I hardly think you can do a competent search in thirteen minutes. I suppose we'll see you in the morning then?"

He steps forward, as if to usher the officers out, but Elijah stands firm.

"As long as we begin before ten p.m.," he says, "we can be here as long as we need to. So, yes. Maybe we will see each other in the morning." Something almost mirthful glints in his eyes as he glances beyond us toward the back hall. "Who else is on the premises right now?"

"Premises!" Charlie echoes. "Such an official word for someone who's going to be

202

rummaging through our underwear drawers."

Elijah ignores him, looking at me to answer.

"M-my mom and Tate," I say, and I hope he doesn't mistake my stutter for nervousness. Mostly, I'm bewildered, watching his gaze slink across the foyer, sharp and suspicious.

"We'll need to detain you all for the duration of the search," he says.

"Detain us?" I picture handcuffs, cold against our wrists. "Are we under arrest?"

"No," Elijah says. "Not at this time."

Fear ripples through my confusion in slow, icy waves. "I don't understand. What about Fritz?"

"We've let him go for now."

"You've *what*?"

"Amateurs," Charlie grumbles.

Elijah's gaze is cool as it shifts from Charlie to me. "He remains a person of interest," he says, "but without direct evidence connecting him to the room beneath your shed, we have no reason to hold him."

"It's *Fritz*'s shed," I remind him.

"On your family's property."

Elijah nods to the officers, prompting a couple to head upstairs while two others breeze past us toward the back hall. The fifth, stocky and bald, remains in front of the door, a statue with crossed arms.

"While my colleagues conduct the search," Elijah says, "I need to question you all individually."

Question us. In the past, he's said *interview.*

"I'm happy to do it here, if you'd like. Or I can take you down to the station."

I gape at him, unable to form a response. Even Charlie is silent, fingers creasing the warrant.

"Here then?" Elijah says after a moment. He gestures to the man behind him. "Officer Bailey will sit with you while you're waiting."

He takes in the living room to his right, squinting at the towers of empty boxes, the artifacts of our childhood that Charlie's organized into piles. Then Elijah smiles, a flash of his father in his teeth.

"How does the dining room sound?"

"You're doing a great job, Officer Babysitter."

Charlie's at the head of the table, the place where Dad always sat. Mounted on the wall behind him is a deer head, the lashes around its dark eyes thick and feminine. Andy used to stare at that head when we ate the animals he and Dad had hunted, his jaw working at meat he'd eventually spit out when no one but me was watching.

Now, the deer looks like a headpiece Charlie's wearing. He grins at Officer Bailey, who stands by the doorway, expertly ignoring his taunts. He's been guarding us for almost an hour, ever since Elijah took Mom to the victim room for questioning.

Across from me, Tate is slumped over, cheek resting on her arm. Her hair spills onto the table in a messy pile, which Charlie — between quips — braids with restless fingers.

From upstairs, there's a thump, followed by a sound like furniture sliding across the floor. Charlie glances at the ceiling.

"Are you sure you're safe in here?" he asks Officer Bailey. "If we're as murderous as you think, who knows what we might do? Maybe you should call one of your friends for backup."

Finally, the officer acknowledges him. "Is that a threat?"

"No, Officer," Tate says. Sitting up, she throws a glance at Charlie that slaps the smile off his face. He looks away like a chastised child before his eyes bolt back to hers.

As their gaze lingers, I see it morph,

deepening into something anxious and fear-ful. When Tate slides her hand across the table, Charlie grabs it, his fingers squeezing hers until his knuckles turn white. I study their shared look, their clasped hands, and a thought blazes through my mind.

They know something.

Tate winces as footsteps creak across the floor above us. She glances at Officer Bailey, finds him momentarily distracted by the deer head, and mouths to Charlie, *They're in your room.* Charlie nods, slightly, then loosens his grip on her hand just to tighten it again.

For the past hour, I've remained baffled about the warrant — why are the officers stomping through *our* house instead of Fritz's? — but at the sounds from upstairs, from Charlie's room, my siblings seem like they're bracing for the ceiling to crash onto their heads.

The thought pulses again: *They know something.*

As if hearing the accusation, they let each other go, and it's then that Mom returns. She shuffles to the table in her slippers before sinking into the seat next to Tate. As Mom releases a heavy sigh, Tate's quick to rub her arm, to put her head on her shoul-der, but I'm still staring at the space between her and Charlie, trying to find the secrets they passed through the air.

"Your father should be here for this," Mom says, and the comment shoves a laugh out of Charlie.

"Oh yes," he says, "he's missing quite the party."

"I just mean," Mom clarifies, "that he always knew how to handle things like this."

"Murder investigations?"

"Of course not." Mom sets her elbows on the table, massaging her forehead. "He knew how to talk to the police. Every time Chief Kraft came by, Daniel was able to allay his concerns."

Charlie laughs again, loud and booming, and even Tate suppresses a smile.

"What?" Mom says.

"Dad never *allayed* anything. He was an asshole to Kraft."

Mom's hands fall into her lap, her back straightening. "No, he wasn't."

"Yes, he was," Tate agrees. "Where do you think Charlie gets it?" She nods toward Officer Bailey. "He didn't say much to him, which was part of it, of course — it drove Kraft crazy — but when he did respond, he always had some slick, sarcastic remark. He loved to toy with him."

Look around, Dad said to him once. *Any*

bodies you find are up for grabs.

"*Toy* with him," Mom repeats. "No. I don't think so. Daniel handled the police, the same way he handled everything in this house. Clogged pipe — who called the plumber? Smoke detector chirping — who changed the batteries? He may have been . . . gruff, sometimes, and he certainly wasn't chatty. But he took care of us. He kept us safe. And" — she sighs again — "there's not another man in the world who would have put up with me."

"Hey," Tate says, scooting closer. "No one had to *put up with* you. Why would you say that?"

Mom waves off Tate's sympathy. "You know what I mean. I wasn't a typical mother. Nothing like my own. I didn't read you bedtime stories. I hardly ever cooked. I taught you about the Alphabet Murders before the alphabet itself. And Daniel . . ." Tears pool in her eyes, turning them as glassy as the mounted deer's. "He was fine with all that. He was *not*" — she grimaces before using Charlie's phrase — "an asshole."

"Dahlia?"

Our attention jolts toward the doorway, where Elijah stands, notebook in hand. He squints at Dad's deer, studying the animal

208

like he thinks he knows it personally. Then he turns to me, expression dark.

"You ready?" he asks.

We resume our positions from the other day — him on the couch, me in the armchair. The victim room, lit by a single lamp on the couch's end table, is painted with shadows. Even Elijah's face has an inky sheen.

He starts by repeating his questions from this afternoon — how I discovered the trapdoor, where I got the key, what made me so intent on going down there — and again, I slog through the answers, which, I'm surprised to hear myself articulate, all lead back to Ruby.

"Tell me about your father," he says next.

"My father?"

I try to conjure his face, but for a second, all I see are his clothes: heavy tan jackets, boots with inch-thick soles. I can't bring to mind the man that Mom just spoke about, the one she swore took care of us — sons, daughters, and wife alike. All I see is how he looked each time he went out the door, and I realize that whenever I imagined us burying him, I pictured him lying in his coffin, still dressed for hunting.

"What about him?" I ask.

Elijah shrugs, affecting a casual air. "What was he like? What did he do all day? It doesn't appear he had a job, so I'm curious."

He touches his pen to his notepad, eager to write.

"You mean you're suspicious," I say.

Because suddenly I get it. The warrant. The thumps from upstairs. Even Mom's unprompted praise, the second she returned from speaking to Elijah. If I wasn't so horrified, I might laugh at how long it took me to understand.

They think Dad was the Blackburn Killer.

My body responds first: head shaking, pulse racing, cheeks heating with furious disbelief. Then I spit out the words that disprove their theory.

"Whoever killed those women is the same person who killed Andy," I say. "Andy saw the room under the shed, and the Blackburn Killer murdered him for that. And my father would never have killed my brother. His *son*. So he wasn't the Blackburn Killer."

"That's interesting," Elijah says, jotting something down. "Your defense of your father is predicated on the idea that he never would have killed your brother. Not that he never would have killed seven women."

My mouth drops open, ready to whip out

210

a reply. But it hangs slack as his words sink in. "No," I finally mutter. "I didn't say that. Of course he didn't kill those women."

He stood at Honorings, he chanted the prayers for Melinda, for Stephanie, for all the Blackburn victims. And beyond that, he was a simple man who greeted each morning by stepping outside, inhaling the crisp, salty air of this island. He was a quiet man who loved to hunt.

Hunt animals, I remind myself, after a single queasy second. *Not women.* Contrary to what the islanders think, we did not live in Murder Mansion.

"Is this about your father?" I ask Elijah. His hand, sprinting across his notepad, stops.

"No," he says, meeting my gaze. "It's about yours."

"Edmond never found the evil he was looking for in my family," I press on, "so you must be trying to do it for him. To carry on his legacy or whatever, because —"

"I don't want my father's legacy."

"Because, otherwise," I continue, "none of this makes sense. It's Fritz's shed. He called the photographs *trophies.* He asked me to help him get rid of the evidence. So I don't know what story he told you, but to me, it was pretty clear who the Blackburn

211

Killer was. Who my *brother*'s killer was."

"You know, it's funny," Elijah muses. "You've done a complete one-eighty on your groundskeeper."

"I — What?"

"When I spoke to you about him the other night, you were adamant that he wasn't a killer."

My skin flushes hot again, blood surging to the surface. "Haven't you been listening? Didn't you *see* the shed? Everything's changed since the other night. Everything but your family's suspicion of mine."

Elijah watches me, chewing the inside of his cheek.

"In a way, I get it," I say to his silence, "if that's what this is about. I understand, better than most, the pull of family."

The pull of Andy, anyway. How, for every moment we lived together, I could always feel him in relation to me, like a cord connecting us, wrapped around both our waists. If one of us moved, we felt the tug of the other, even from different rooms. And when he was gone, I thought I still felt him out there, pulling on his end sometimes, trying to show me where he was.

Elijah sets his pen on top of his notepad, which he balances on his thigh with one palm. "Dahlia. I assure you that my ques-

212

tions have nothing to do with my father. The fact is: photographs that we believe belong to the Blackburn Killer are in the room beneath your family's shed."

"Fritz's —" I start to say, but he puts a hand in the air.

"There were also blue fibers found in the hinges of the chest in that room. Fibers that appear consistent with the gowns the killer dressed his victims in. We'll know for sure if they're a match once we hear from the lab."

I stare at him, absorbing this new information. All these years, I never saw the actual dresses. The only way I knew how to picture them was from the miniature replicas that Tate stitched for her dioramas. Now, I shiver, realizing how close to me they always were.

Is that what Andy found in the chest that night? Maybe his ax grazed the fabric as it bit into the wood. Or maybe, by then, the gowns were gone — Jessie Stanton being the last to ever wear one.

"If you think it was my father," I say, "then why would the murders have stopped? He's lived here all this time, but there hasn't been another murder on the island since Jessie Stanton. Doesn't it make more sense, then, that the killer would be someone who . . . who died, or maybe left the island, or . . ."

213

I trail off, hearing in my own words an argument for Fritz's innocence, too.

But he knew what was under the shed. At the very least, he knew.

"Fritz called them trophies," I reiterate limply. "So why else . . . How could . . ."

My questions wither as I shake my head.

Leaning forward on the couch, Elijah sets his notebook on the cushion beside him. I watch him fold his hands together, and I'm surprised by how thin his fingers are, how clean his nails. Without his pad and pen, he looks almost vulnerable. A detective without a weapon.

"I promise you," he says, and for a moment, I hear kindness, patience, tucked back into his voice. "I interviewed John Fritz extensively. And his answers, coupled with our findings in the shed, did not warrant his arrest at this time. We've let him go for the time being, but as I told you when I first arrived, he remains a person of interest in the case."

I let out a breath, my shoulders relaxing. "Okay," I say.

Elijah flicks his attention to the left. There's a space there, on the wall, prominent as a missing tooth. Two days ago, Elijah pointed to the portrait of Kitty Genovese that hung in its place. Charlie must have

214

removed the painting, planning to include it in his museum, but now, Elijah watches the empty wall like the space itself is a kind of clue.

Tension squeezes back into my muscles as he slides his eyes, narrower than before, back onto mine.

"Person of interest," I say, echoing the phrase he used for Fritz. "But not suspect. I've seen enough documentaries to know there's a difference."

"We'll be thoroughly investigating every possibility," Elijah says, and it's like he's reciting from those films, parroting the lines of detectives who, so often, never caught the killer at all.

He reaches for his notebook again.

"Now," he adds, smacking the pad onto his lap, "let's get back to your father."

TWELVE

All throughout the mansion, the rooms look like a tornado swept through, leaving nothing untouched. Furniture is askew, drawers ajar. Clothes are strewn; books are splayed. It's been twelve hours since the police left, ducking back into the darkness, empty-handed but for the warrant they came with. Still, the house retains the feeling of strangers inside it.

Charlie's in the living room, working on his museum like yesterday never happened. He's already fixed what Elijah's search undid: the piles of DVDs, the towers of newspapers, the pyramids of Honoring candles. Bent toward the coffee table, Charlie slams his fingers against the keys of an old typewriter, focusing on it with the intensity of a surgeon.

Beside him is a glass of brown liquid, and as he retrieves a white card from the typewriter, he takes a sip. I should be relieved, I guess, that he's not slugging straight from the bottle anymore.

"Would you like a monologue?" Charlie asks, and it's only now I realize that I've been hovering in the doorway, drowsily observing him.

"What?"

"Usually people don't watch me like that unless I'm performing." Half a smile slithers up his cheek. "I could give you a little Stanley from *Streetcar,* if you'd like."

"I'm good," I say, weaving through empty boxes toward the couch. "What are you doing?"

"Remaking the artifact cards." He gestures toward a messy pile of his handwritten labels, right beside a tidy stack of typewritten ones.

"Why?" I touch one he'd written on, tracing that sideways lowercase *i* he scrawled beneath them all. *Murder Report: The Black Dahlia,* this one says.

He slaps my hand away. "The first ones looked amateur."

"Even with your trademark flair?" I ask, pointing to that mark beneath the words. There's mockery in my voice, implied air quotes, but he takes the question seriously.

"It looked too busy. These are cleaner. More precise. But here, if you're going to

217

miss it so much . . ." He grabs a Sharpie, grabs my arm, and before I understand what he's doing, he's scrawled the sideways *i* onto my hand. Then he smiles up at me, eyes bright with mischief.

I yank my hand away, rubbing at the ink that's already seeping into my skin.

"Is this really appropriate? Carrying on with your museum after" — I pause — "yesterday?"

"It's more appropriate than ever! You handed Fritz over on a silver platter, and what did the police do? They came for *us*. And they found nothing, of course, but that won't keep people from talking. From painting *us* as the murderers. Is that what you want?"

"I don't . . ." I shake my head, struggling to process his response, which seems so far from the point. "I don't really care what people think. I just want to know who killed Andy."

He picks up his drink and throws his head back to down the rest of it. "Well," he says. "You have your priorities, I have mine."

My breath catches. I go so still it feels like my heart stops beating.

"I mean . . ." Charlie tries to backtrack. "That's not what I meant. Andy's important to me, too, obviously, I just — I don't know

218

what you want from me, Dolls. I'm not a detective. But this" — he opens his arms to encompass the room — "this is something I can do for Andy."

"For Andy? You've got to be kidding. You're calling this the Lighthouse *Memorial* Museum, but where's the memorial part of it? All I see are films and paintings and a bunch of old homework."

And Dad's guns shoved into the corner. I wonder what Elijah thought of that, if one of the times he pulled Mom from the dining room last night — "Just another quick question, Mrs. Lighthouse" — was to ask her about them.

"I can't keep explaining the LMM to you," Charlie says, staring into his empty glass. "But it's as much about setting the record straight about Andy as anything else. Showing people that he was . . . Fuck, he was human, okay? He was a kid! He didn't have it coming to him because he lived in Murder Mansion."

Charlie tips his head back again, lips on the mouth of his glass, trying to extract a final drop.

"And what do you think's going to happen when they hear about the shed?" he continues. "Or serial killer headquarters, as you called it. They'll lump Andy in with the

219

Blackburn Killer's victims, and that's what he'll be forever — part of *that* story. It makes me sick just to think of it."

It makes me sick, too. That's why I haven't returned the texts from Greta that I woke to today. Any luck with the door?? the first one said, and I couldn't bring myself to tell her, to confirm that she'd been right the other day, when she suggested a connection between the Blackburn Killer and Andy. She's been my friend for years, but for longer than that, she's been a self-proclaimed "true-crime junkie," a "citizen detective," a person who's "literally obsessed with the Blackburn Killer." I want, for a little longer at least, for Andy to be mine. Not an eager, all-caps post on a message board. Not an update on a serial killer's Wikipedia page.

Also, Greta wrote next, I'm sure you're working with the police about your brother, but do you want my help looking into anything?

I don't know exactly what she does each day, when she's at her computer. I know she makes requests for public documents, consults with retired detectives. I know she pores over police records, discusses theories with people like her. But beyond that, it's a mystery to me. Even when we sit side by side, working our separate searches, I've never felt tempted to glance at her screen, a place I didn't think I'd find Andy. So what would it mean, for her to help me? How long would it take her to follow the police's footsteps and start asking me about Dad?

"They think Dad might be the Blackburn Killer," I say, and Charlie's forehead wrinkles.

"I'm aware," he says. "I imagine I was badgered with the same questions as you."

We didn't talk about it last night. Sitting around the table, one of us gone at a time, we mostly kept quiet. Even Charlie, returning from his own interview, stopped trying to taunt Officer Bailey. Instead, he sat, arms crossed, beneath Dad's deer, face scrunched in an indignant scowl.

"What do you think," I ask, "about that theory?"

Charlie's eyes blaze with pain. It's so quick, gone as soon as he blinks, but for a moment, I see Andy in him — the burst of emotion that would surge across his face, right before he stomped toward his ax — and it opens something up in me, an instinct to reach out, to offer my palms to Charlie as a place to put that pain.

"I think it's ridiculous," he says, voice hard, vulnerability tucked away. "I think

221

they're desperate, they're —" He stops to squint at me. "Why? What do you think?"

I shrug. "The same, I guess."

"You *guess*."

After the police left, I lay in bed for a long time, gaze scratching the ceiling as I tried to see things as Elijah did. I remembered that, when I asked how Ruby knew it was Fritz that Andy snuck after in the woods, she said it was the man's height, his build, which, for Fritz and Dad, is about the same. But Ruby also said she saw Fritz's limp, and Dad was always solid and sturdy, his walk more akin to a heavy-footed march.

No matter how long I tried last night, the sky blushing with light when I finally fell asleep, I couldn't see Dad as the man in the shed, the Blackburn Killer, the person with such horrible secrets to protect. More important, I couldn't see him murdering Andy, the son he partnered with on hunting trips, the son he looked at with a cool sort of pride whenever he served us venison stew.

To be fair, though, when I tried to picture Fritz with the ax, it was difficult to imagine, too.

"It's just, he and I were never close," I tell Charlie. "So when Elijah asked me questions about him, there wasn't a lot I could say beyond the basics. But you actually spent time with him, so . . . what was he like? What'd you even talk about, all those times you went hunting?"

"We talked about nothing."

"Nothing? You didn't say anything to each other?"

"Not really." Charlie scans my face, reading my skepticism. Then he snorts with impatience. "I don't know, Dolls. He mostly talked about nature. The beauty of nature. Appreciating nature."

I think of the deer head on the dining room wall, the dinners we ate chaperoned by its crown of antlers, its watchful yet unseeing eyes.

"How is killing animals appreciating nature?" I ask. "Seems like a contradiction."

Charlie straightens his cards. "Not to him. He had this philosophy: nature is a continuum, with these discrete, sublime moments that most people miss because life moves so fast."

Now he leans back on the couch, brows pushed together, as if remembering Dad is like pressing a fresh bruise. And I know that pain, of course I do. Except my memories of Andy aren't bruises; they're seeping, open wounds.

"I don't understand," I say, and Charlie grunts.

223

"For Dad," he explains, "there were two options: we leave the deer to age and die and rot — by which its beauty lessens — or we freeze it in the prime of its beauty; we mount its head on our wall." He gestures out the doorway, in the direction of the dining room. "We eat and appreciate its meat *while it's still delicious.* His words, not mine. I, for one, hate the taste of venison."

He grimaces dramatically, then hunches forward again, attention back on his typewriter. As he pecks at the keys, I shift closer to read: *Daniel Lighthouse's Hunting Rifles.* I look at the guns in the corner of the room. To me, they're still just weapons, not tools with which to preserve beauty.

"What else was he into?" I ask. "I know he liked to cook — or at least he *did* cook, but —"

"Dahlia, what is this?" Charlie cuts in. "You're starting to sound like Kraft with all these questions. Next thing I know you'll be pulling out a warrant."

He glares at me, a challenge in his eyes, but the mention of the warrant jerks me back to last night, his hand clasped with Tate's, their gaze tight and anxious as footsteps thudded upstairs.

"Why were you so worried when they were searching your room?" I ask.

224

The twitch beneath his eye is immediate. The thin skin spasms.

"I wasn't worried," he says. He yanks the card from the typewriter and drops it on top of the others, upsetting the tidy pile.

"I saw Tate mouth to you that they were in your room, and you were staring at each other like you were scared they'd find something."

He shakes his head. "You must've been seeing things." He sets another card into the typewriter, twisting the knob to get it perfectly in place. He rests his fingers on the keys, but he doesn't type. "Makes sense, after the day you had."

The day I had. As if my discovery in the shed was devastating to me alone.

"Is there something you're not telling me?" I push.

He exhales slowly, scrutinizing the blank white card.

"This is exactly what Kraft wants," he says. "For us to turn on each other." Behind Charlie, the living room windows rattle in their frames, jostled by the wind. "Better for us to stick together, don't you think?"

Right now, the skin around his eyes is crinkled exactly like Andy's. The resemblance is so remarkable that, for a moment, I struggle to breathe. But then I blink and

225

he's Charlie again — skinny, smirky Charlie, the corners of his lips quirked in private amusement.

"We have to trust each other," he says. "You have to trust us. Me, Tate, Mom — we're all you have left."

In a way, he's right. Without Andy — without the possibility of Andy — I'm painfully untethered, no cord around my waist to tug me through my days. It would be nice, maybe, to feel like I'm still a part of something, an essential piece of a greater whole. For so long, I've pushed my family away, angry that they never looked for Andy, that they left me alone in my bleary pursuit of him. But now I know: from the moment I started searching, he was already gone. Their help wouldn't have mattered. We still would have ended up here.

Now, I wince against a rush of images: the police tape, the grave, the photographs in a concrete room. It seems impossible that I could ever stand in this house, on Lighthouse land, without feeling utterly haunted. Even harder to imagine: sharing a life with my remaining family, unshadowed by the darkness that, for years, crept unnoticed in our own backyard.

As Charlie types, the bones in his hands flick beneath his skin, same as they did when he squeezed Tate's fingers last night. No matter what he says, I'm sure of what I saw: they stared at each other, their mouths set in grim, identical lines.

"You do trust us," he says, shifting his eyes from the typewriter to me, "don't you?"

I watch him for a while, waiting for a flash of Andy in his features again. Finding none, I turn to go, unable to answer him yet.

There's a shattered eggshell on the kitchen floor. Its yolk, glossy as sunlight, oozes between the tiles. A rack of unburnt cookies cools near the oven, edges perfectly golden.

Mom's slumped over the counter, silent and motionless, arm on the marble, forehead on her arm. I watch for the rise and fall of breath, listen for a moan or cry. When she remains as still as a grave, I step over the egg to approach her, stretching out a tentative hand.

As soon as I touch her, she jolts. "Dahlia! Oh!"

I jump back, palm pressed to my chest.

"Here!" she says.

She pirouettes toward the cookies, scoops one up with a spatula, and places it on a napkin that she pushes into my hand. I look at the chocolate chips studding the top of it, and the scent that wafts toward me is

227

sweet and familiar, whiffs of Greta's café. For the first time since returning home, my mouth waters; my stomach churns with hunger.

"Thanks," I say, and I take a bite. The cookie is soft and buttery and warm. I give an appreciative groan as I lick the chocolate off my teeth. "Wow. It's good."

Mom beams, hands tucked toward her chin, clasped as if in prayer. Her smile reaches her eyes, lighting them up, and it completely transforms her, the slumped woman from just moments ago now bouncing on her toes.

"How are you doing?" I ask. "After yesterday."

Her smile dims, flickering once before disappearing completely. She looks at the egg on the floor but doesn't bend to clean it up. "I'm . . . managing," she says carefully. "How are you?"

She glances at the sink, the cookies, the gaping hole where the kitchen door once was, and it's strange, watching her try this hard to avoid my gaze. Even when she told us how Dorothy Stratten, once a Playboy playmate, was found naked on the carpet, her brains blown out of her head in chunks so big that "one resembled a whole roast chicken," she stared at me and Andy as if

228

daring us to look away.

"Managing," I agree.

Mom reaches into a cabinet for a plastic container and begins placing the cookies inside, three neat little rows.

"Fritz called," she says, matter-of-factly, and right away, my skin feels shivery, my forehead moist. "He said that, given the circumstances, he's going to take some more time off."

"Time off?" I practically yell. "I hope you told him he's fired! At the very *least,* he's fired."

Mom freezes for a second, a vein jumping at her temple. But then she shakes her head, stacking more cookies on top of one another. "Detective Kraft said they let him go. They don't think he's the . . . the Blackburn Killer." Her movements slow, the spatula gliding to a midair stop. "Or Andy's. And I know what you said yesterday, but the more I think about it, the more impossible it seems, that Fritz could have —"

A timer bleats, startling us both.

"My shortbread!" Mom cries. She opens the oven door, shoves her hand into a mitt, and pulls out another tray of cookies. These are pale and square and glistening with heat. She sets them on the stove and shakes off her mitt.

"Here!" she says, grabbing one with bare fingers, then dropping it instantly. "Ow!"

"Mom! They just came out!"

The cookie she tried to give me is now a broken lump. Beneath it, the delicate crust of another shortbread is crushed.

"Oh," Mom moans, as if the loss of two cookies is too much to bear. Then her "oh" morphs back into "ow" as she looks at her fingers, shiny with grease.

I guide her to the sink and hold her hand beneath the water. She's stiff at first, but then she leans against me.

"Thank you," she whispers, head tipped toward mine. When I shut off the faucet, she exhales a chuckle. "Decades of lighting Honoring candles and I never once burned myself. But now . . ." She holds up her hands, twisting them to show each side. "I'm marked all over."

"What did you say to Fritz?" I ask.

She pushes some flour off the counter and into the sink.

"I told him that makes sense. Taking time off."

"You . . ." I gape in disbelief, watching as she walks to the pantry and runs her fingers over ingredients like words in a book. "You realize, don't you, that the reason the police don't think Fritz did it is because they think

Dad did."

"Yes," she says, pulling out a bag of walnuts and scouring its label. "And I told Detective Kraft that that was impossible. For one thing, if my husband were going out in the middle of the night to . . . to kill women, and do whatever in that shed, wouldn't I know? Wouldn't I wake up each time he left or returned?"

I don't remind her that she sleeps like the dead. *Like the murdered,* Charlie always joked.

"Besides," she continues, putting the walnuts back on the shelf, "Daniel has an alibi for the night Andy —" Even with her back to me, I see her stiffen. "The night of Andy."

"What alibi?"

"You remember," she says confidently, turning to face me again. "He was sick that night, on your birthday. He made it through dinner and the Honorings, but then he was up all night because he was sick as a dog. He kept running back and forth to the bathroom."

As she speaks, something lightens in me — because I do remember his queasiness, the way he grimaced each time he swallowed. I even remember that, the next morning, when I screamed upon finding the

231

note, when everyone but Andy came running, Dad looked unusually exhausted, his skin tinged with gray. And though I already told myself Elijah must be wrong, I still feel buoyant with relief at the memory.

Until I think of Fritz.

"So if you're sure it wasn't Dad, then that means it was Fritz. And you're just chatting with him on the phone!"

"We weren't *chatting*," she insists. "It was a very quick exchange."

"With a murderer!"

"Stop it!" she says. "We don't know that! Fritz has always been a . . . a very gentle man."

For a second, I feel the flare of pain in my ankle, the bruises Fritz left when he grabbed me yesterday. I found the marks last night as I peeled back my socks for bed, head still ringing with Elijah's questions.

"And if he's guilty, then why would he call?" Mom continues, throwing up her hands. "It must be a misunderstanding —"

"A misunderstanding! What exactly was misunderstood?"

"I don't know, Dahlia! Okay? I —" She shakes her head. "I hate to even think of it."

She puts her palms on the counter, looking at the marble so she won't have to look at me.

232

I don't know this woman, the one averting her eyes. Where is the Lorraine Lighthouse who raised us? The one who used cooking twine on her own body to demonstrate how the Glamour Girl Slayer bound his victims. The one who planted herself, almost daily, on the staircase, face sad and stony as she stared at her parents.

Mom has always been single-minded in her devotion to people who were murdered. Now, a day after learning that a serial killer kept his trophies beneath our shed, she's choosing not to think of it, not to demand an explanation when a suspect calls our home.

"But Mom —"

"I can't discuss this anymore!" she cries. "Not right now. Please, I'm . . . I'm exhausted."

She takes in the mess around her: the dirty dishes, the egg still shining on the floor, the cookies she only half packed up. Then she sighs so deeply it sounds like the crash of an ocean wave.

"I'll take care of this later," she says. "I need to lie down for a bit."

She looks so tired that I feel a pull toward sleep myself. As she shuffles away, I ache to lie down, too. But Andy — always sleeping, never sleeping, from now until forever —

233

needs me to keep pushing. For answers, for evidence, for something that will connect Fritz, without a doubt, to the room beneath the shed.

I turn to the window, homing in on that building, its white brick choked by coils of ivy. A perimeter is marked by fresh yellow tape, tauter than the one that flaps around the family plot. And it's there, near those little headstones, that something seizes my attention: a figure in dark clothes, hunched in the woods not twenty yards past those graves.

A chill scampers up my spine. The figure is too small to be Elijah Kraft — or even his father, a knee-jerk option I consider. I try to see the person more clearly, but they remain just a blur of black among the trees.

I rush to the hall closet, push past coats to the shelf in the back, and I grab the binoculars that look as if they haven't been moved since the last time Andy and I used them. Grief gushes up, quick and acidic, but I swallow it down, hurrying back to the kitchen.

I aim the lenses into the woods until I catch a hazy glimpse of the person's dark clothes. Inching the binoculars into the right spot, I twist the knob until the world clicks into perfect focus — and then I gasp.

For a moment, I'm hurtled back in time. It's Ruby, crouching on our property, just like she did when we were kids.

But that's not what startled me.

Yards from the place where Andy's body was discovered, Ruby Decker, clutching a shovel, is digging a hole for something.

Or she's digging something up.

THIRTEEN

I've barely shrugged my coat on before I'm out the door, calling Ruby's name. The wind snatches my voice, blowing it back toward the house, and in the distance, Ruby stabs her shovel into the ground, so focused on digging that she doesn't even hear me.

I'm jogging toward her, closing the space between us, but when I reach the crime scene tape, it stops me like a finish line.

Now I'm rooted here, close enough to really see it — the spot where Andy was buried — and my throat is burning, my lungs are heaving; the air is thin and not enough.

Ruby's shovel whispers against the dirt, jerking me back to her intrusion. I hear the ocean breathe, its endless in and out, and even though Andy hated all the water locking us in, I soothe myself with its sound.

Steady again, I veer around the grave and march the remaining yards to Ruby, who won't stop digging, still oblivious to my approach. When she pulls back her arms to pierce the ground again, I grab the end of the shovel and yank it toward me, forcing her off-balance.

"Hey!" she protests.

"What are you doing?" I demand. "Why are you here?"

But she keeps going, frantically tossing soil to the side. Moments later, when her shovel clangs against something, Ruby drops to the ground. She flings the shovel away and claws at the dirt until a patch of silver appears. Slowly, carefully, like she's excavating a fossil, she reaches into the earth and extracts a tin box. She rests it on her lap, skimming her fingers across it but leaving it unopened.

"What is that?" I ask. "How did you know it was here?"

"I put it here," she says softly.

"Why? What's in it?"

The wind circles us as I wait for her to speak. Dead leaves whirl.

"Andy's birthday present," she says, and I pull in a surprised breath.

She shakes the box and something slides inside it. "I gave it to him that night," she continues, before adding an indignant huff. "I probably shouldn't have bothered. I knew, before he even opened it, that he was distracted. Holding that key. Fidgeting with it."

She whips her gaze up at me. "What was down there? Under the shed."

I shift my feet, struggling not to see it: painted toenails, collarbone tattoo, a bolt of red hair. Ruby waits for me to answer, eyes wide and alert, but I can't bring myself to tell her. More than that, there's something in the way she watches me, so eager so soon after crying, that makes me think I shouldn't. Elijah said he wasn't going public yet, and no matter how good of friends she was with Andy, Ruby wasn't one of us. It isn't her right to know.

"It's just a basement," I lie.

Ruby's brows pinch together. She cranes her neck to look toward the shed, its perimeter of police tape bright and unavoidable.

"The cops were here," she says.

"Yeah," I admit. "They were searching the shed." My heart drums as I deepen the lie. "Seeing if there were clues about Andy. Since it's so close to where he was found."

She squints at me, skeptical, but I nudge my chin toward her box. "What was the present?"

She lingers on me for another moment. Then she drops her attention toward her lap, smoothing her hand over the box's lid before sliding it off. "I made it for him," she says.

She sinks her hand into a froth of tissue paper to pull out something familiar, an embroidery in a wooden hoop. I recognize the pattern of flowers from the one hanging in her living room: *Ruby loves Grandpa,* it said. This one is almost identical — same perimeter of yellow and purple hollyhocks, same white fabric, same navy thread for the letters. In fact, if not for one altered word, I'd think this was the one from Ruby's wall.

But that altered word: it's a name, actually.

Ruby loves Andy.

"It was supposed to be a kind of confession," she says.

I sink down beside her, feeling punched, lungless, just looking at the letters of Andy's name. They're so smooth, so graceful, so unlike the ones he carved into my wall, or the inside of the credenza, or the handle of his ax. Those were skinny and sharp, quick cuts in the wood that surprised me a little when they didn't bleed. But these — Ruby took her time with these. And I don't know why it's knocked the wind out of me, seeing his name like that, painstakingly stitched.

"I was in love with him," she says, pushing her hair out of her face as the wind tousles it. "That's probably not a surprise. But it was a risk, giving him this, even though I was pretty sure he felt the same."

"Did he?" I hear myself ask. Because there are things I knew about Andy without him having to say a word: when his stomach hurt; when something simmered in his veins, ready to send him straight for his ax. And there are things he ran out of time to tell me: what he knew about the Blackburn Killer, what he saw beneath the shed. But him loving Ruby — that doesn't fall into either category.

"What made you think he loved you?" I say. I try to sound neutral, but I understand there's cruelty in asking.

She narrows her eyes at me. "You know we were together, right? You know we weren't just friends?"

I'm still for a moment. But then I straighten my spine, wanting to look as tall as a kneeling person can. "Andy never had a girlfriend."

She laughs at me, dryly. "He might not have used that word," she says. "But we were each other's first kiss. First . . . everything, really."

I shake my head, dizzy with the revelation, this piece of his life he never let me

240

know. Did he keep it a secret because he didn't believe I could take it? Because he knew I didn't understand how to love, how to trust someone, outside the two of us? My eyes burn, remembering how he told Ruby I was too closed off to hang out with them. Closed off. Like an empty room. Like a dead-end road.

"It was supposed to be cute," Ruby says, "telling him I love him like this." She traces the embroidery with her finger. "He liked the one in my living room, so I just thought . . ." She trails off, seconds passing before she continues. "But he got weird as soon as he opened it. He said that I didn't love him, that I couldn't. That I didn't even really know him."

I feel a spike of satisfaction: *See? This closeness was all in her mind.* But when I notice her crumpled expression, like Andy's rejection is happening now, I swallow my meanness down.

"I told him that wasn't true," she continues. "That I *did* love him, I wanted a *life* with him, off this island, just like we'd talked about." She stares off into the trees in a vacant way that reminds me of Dad's dead deer. "I even told him I wanted us to get married someday. Start a family together. I wanted to have loads of kids — I still do — so I'd never, *never* be lonely."

For a moment, I want to laugh. The notion is so absurd: fifteen-year-old Ruby planning a permanent future with Andy, picking out kids' names, writing them down like ingredients for a recipe. But the moment passes quickly, and the next one wallops me — thinking of children with Andy's crinkly eyes, his cowlick he could never keep down. Would his kids have crouched in credenzas, making mischief in the dark? Would they have felt, just a little bit, like mine? The possibilities are a dull blade, taking too long to slice me open.

"That's when he really freaked out," Ruby says. She sets the embroidery back onto the tissue paper. "He was like, 'Family? You think *I* can start a family?' He said it proved how much I didn't know about him. Or where he came from. How *unnatural* your family is —"

I tense at that: Andy's word in her mouth.

"— how any kid of his was bound to be unnatural, too. He went on and on like that: 'Who knows what I'd do to a kid? Who knows what's in my blood?' Which was so stupid. So insulting. Like I'm supposed to believe he's, like, a vampire or something."

"Vampire?" I repeat.

Ruby shrugs. "That's what he was acting

242

like. Like he was some evil creature destined to do bad things. I mean, what kind of thing is that to say? 'Who knows what's in my blood?' "

She's right. It's an odd, almost eerie concern, one I never heard him express.

"He'd talk all the time about us leaving this place, and then the second I tell him I love him, he's not sure he can build a life with me? What else had we been doing all those months, if not planning for a future together?"

She hangs her head, her voice so quiet, so fragile, I have to lean in to hear her.

"Anyway, I ran off after that, taking his stupid present back home. But I grabbed the key first, like I told you — because that was the infuriating thing. He was yelling at me, refusing to let me love him, and the whole time, he was only half there. The other half was thinking about that damn key. Or what it opened."

Her earlier question idles in her eyes. *What was down there? Under the shed.* I have to work harder this time to pretend like the answer is nothing.

"So why is the embroidery *here*?" I ask. "Why did you bury it? In our woods."

"I had to hide it from my grandfather," she says. Then she sighs. "Andy broke my

243

heart that night. So when I got home, I was a mess. And when Grandpa came to my room to check on me, I couldn't stop sobbing. I was lying on my floor, in a pile of Andy's notes — you know, the ones we'd write together, the funny little phrases? I'd kept them all." She wipes her nose before rubbing her fingers on her jeans. "And Grandpa was like, 'What's all this? What's got you so upset?' And I was so sick of hiding that I loved someone. I knew that was Grandpa's biggest fear: that I would fall in love and leave him. Just like my mother. Just like his wife. But I couldn't fake it anymore. That love is who I *was* right then. Do you know what I mean?"

Her question reaches into me, tugging at my starkest truth. Because yes. I do know what she means. My love for Andy is who I've always been.

I can't say that, though. My throat is a closed fist. So I nod, encouraging her to go on.

"I showed him the notes. They didn't make sense to him; they were all like *your hair is made of wishes and salad forks.* Silly phrases that no one had ever thought of but us. But I told Grandpa what they meant: we'd had a relationship, we'd loved each other. Or so I thought."

244

She pulls the embroidery out of the box and scrapes at the thread with dirty nails. It's as if she's trying to unstitch the letters, unwrite her love for Andy after all these years.

"So I thought," she repeats, the words even wryer this time.

My voice is pinched when I speak. "I think you just . . . you caught Andy at a bad time."

She glares at me. "What does that mean?"

"Nothing, just —" I force a shrug. "You know how he was, right? With the trees? Sometimes, some . . . bad feelings came over him, and he had to hurt something to get them out. I just think that, that night, that something was you."

She bites her lip, considering. "But it was his birthday. Your siblings had come back to celebrate. What bad feelings could he possibly have had?"

I see the photographs again: the dark *B* on an ankle, someone's skin singed from the brand.

Where *did* the brand end up? I wonder if it was part of what Andy found when he hacked open the chest, if it was with him that final night, in his pocket maybe; if when his clothes decomposed in that awful grave, the soil swallowed it down, deeper than the police would later dig.

Instead, they dug for it in our house.

I focus on Ruby. "Families are complicated," I say. "It was the first time we'd all been together in eight years. It could have easily stirred up frustration. Resentment."

She doesn't seem convinced. "When I asked him if he really didn't want me to love him, he said, 'I don't want you to love me.' No hesitation. He made his feelings perfectly clear."

She picks at the embroidery again, scraping a tight thread. "So I told Grandpa what happened: I loved Andy, we'd talked about leaving, I thought we'd make a life together, but he'd rejected me. And then Grandpa — he got so mad. He grabbed some of the notes and, like, shook them in his fist, mumbling that he was going to *get that Lighthouse boy.*"

I recoil at the phrase. "*Get* him," I repeat. My skin tingles with unease.

"I'd never seen him so enraged," Ruby continues. "But more than that, he seemed hurt. Reading those notes, he could see we'd been close. And I tried to tell him: I wasn't my mom, or my grandma; loving Andy didn't mean I loved *him* any less — but the next thing I know, he's storming out of my room, slamming the front door, and I didn't see him for the rest of the night."

All at once, the ocean and wind crescendo, and in them, I hear the snarl of her grandfather's voice, hissing at me how Andy *deserved what he got.* When he said it, I was shocked by how heartless, how hateful, he sounded.

But what if he was even worse than that?

I comb through my memories, trying to gather what I know of Lyle. Turns out, it isn't much, only what I've learned from Ruby the past few days: he's extremely protective of his granddaughter, he didn't like Andy, and he's been sick for almost a decade.

But now, my mouth falls open, the word *decade* resonating inside me like a struck bell. The same length of time since Andy was killed.

Since Jessie Stanton, too.

In an instant, my mind whips toward something else, something I completely forgot in yesterday's tangle of horrors: Lyle used to warn Ruby to stay away from our property. But not only that. *Don't go anywhere near the Lighthouses' shed,* he told her.

When she relayed that story, I couldn't make sense of it. How would he have known

247

about it? Why would he care? But now, pushing these pieces into place, I almost groan.

What if Lyle was the Blackburn Killer? What if the victims ended at Jessie Stanton because he grew too sick, too weak, to murder anyone else?

I focus in again on Ruby, who's still talking.

". . . and I realized a couple days later that if Grandpa saw the embroidery, he'd probably get even madder. I kept thinking, *Maybe Andy will change his mind.* So I didn't want to make things worse for us by having Grandpa stumble upon this. I was already thinking of how I could backtrack, tell Grandpa I was being stupid that night, that I'd had a crush and it was over. But this" — she picks up the wooden hoop and immediately drops it back in the box — "*Ruby loves Andy*? Made to look exactly like the one I made Grandpa? He'd see it as a betrayal. That I'd replaced him somehow. That I was still set on leaving him."

She clenches her jaw, and it's a loud, windy moment before she continues. "So I buried it, here, in line of sight of Andy's window, hoping he'd see me and come out. I was sure, at the very least, that we'd meet up again soon, and when we did, we'd talk,

248

and he'd apologize, and he'd want his present back. I never . . . *never* thought it would be ten years before I dug this up."

Her eyes well up. They're probing mine, wanting something from me. But I feel so removed from her, my thoughts still knotted up with Lyle.

"You have to use it," she says, pushing the embroidery into my hands.

"Use it?" I ask dimly.

"In the Lighthouse Memorial Museum. It's all people are talking about in town, and as soon as I heard about it, I knew the embroidery had to be part of it. Please."

She bites her lip, face twisted and tortured. "Everything between us is so unfinished. I never got to say goodbye to him. I never got to give this back. And I just want to feel like . . . like he has it, in some way. Like he knows that, even though I ran from him, I really did love him." Tears spill onto her cheeks. "Please," she says again.

I watch her for a moment, still somewhere else in my mind. Finally, I nod, and she relaxes.

But as we stand to go, I'm not thinking of the embroidery she thrust into my hands. I'm thinking of the call I'll make to Elijah as soon as I'm back inside. He needs to know that, for all the hours they searched

249

our house last night, looking for the Blackburn Killer's brand, there was another
house, just through the woods, they should
have been searching instead.

FOURTEEN

"You think Lyle Decker used someone else's shed as his trophy room."

Elijah's voice on the phone is skeptical. I picture him arching a brow.

"Think about it," I say, shoving Ruby's embroidery into my dresser drawer. "If you're going to keep an entire roomful of evidence, would you want it on your own property, where it would immediately implicate you if somebody found it?"

I expect Elijah to use my words against me, remind me that the roomful of evidence on our property implicates *us*. Instead, he throws a question back at me.

"Haven't you wondered," he starts, "why your brother was buried in your father's plot?"

I freeze, midpace, in the middle of my room. "Of course I've wondered."

"Do you want to hear my theory?"

I wait without answering, eyes fixed on

my beanbag chair. For a second, I see Andy flopping onto it, before the image shifts, and he's flopping into a grave.

"Actually, it's an extension of a theory *you* mentioned," Elijah says. "That the Blackburn Killer is the same man who murdered your brother." He clears his throat in a way that sounds forced. "As you surmised, we're looking into your father as a possible suspect for the Blackburn murders. So say it's true that the crimes were committed by the same person. If your father killed your brother, in the heat of the moment, maybe, upon learning that Andy saw what was under the shed — again, a theory you articulated — there'd be a benefit, wouldn't there, to burying him in his own plot?"

I see where he's going. But I won't say it. I won't admit that, for one delirious moment last night as I tried to push his questions out of my head, I thought of this, too.

"It would ensure," Elijah continues, "as much as he could, at least, that the body wouldn't be discovered until he himself was dead — when his own grave was dug, when it would be too late to hold him accountable for the crime. For any crimes, in fact."

I'm annoyed by his tone — smug, self-satisfied. I can picture him writing in his notepad, hand hurrying across the page to

252

describe my silence.

"Do you normally discuss your theories with the family of your suspects?" I ask.

Elijah pauses so long I check to make sure the call wasn't dropped. Eventually, he says, "Things are a little different, in this case, given that the suspect in question is deceased."

"So you're not going to look into Lyle Decker," I reply. "Even with what I told you Ruby said. That he was weird about our shed. That he found out Andy hurt her the same night Andy was killed. He said he was going to *get that Lighthouse boy.* And when I saw him the other day, he told me my brother deserved what he got."

"That's all very circumstantial," Elijah says. "But if you have reason to believe that Lyle Decker had access to your shed, that might be another story."

I think of the key, dangling from a chain on Ruby's neck for the last ten years. But that came from Andy, she said, not her grandfather.

"I don't," I concede. "Not really."

I know it's not a perfect fit. The revelations about Lyle don't change how Fritz spoke about the room beneath the shed — calling the photographs trophies, begging me to help him get rid of the evidence —

and it doesn't change that Ruby was sure it was Fritz she saw in the middle of the night. It's possible that, in the dark, she could have mistaken another man for Fritz, but would she really not recognize her grandfather?

"Maybe Lyle was in cahoots with Fritz," I offer.

"Cahoots," Elijah repeats, as if it's a word he's never heard before. "Have you known Mr. Decker and your groundskeeper to be close?"

"No," I admit. "But there's clearly a lot I didn't know about Fritz."

"And — going back to motive here — I'm unclear if you think that Mr. Decker killed your brother as revenge for hurting his granddaughter, or because Andy discovered he was the Blackburn Killer."

My nails stab my palm, the mark from Charlie's Sharpie stretched tight over my fist. "I don't know — both, maybe." I force myself to relax my hand. "That's why I called you, so you can figure it out."

"All right," Elijah says. "I appreciate the info. But while I've got you here — have you had any luck finding the runaway note?"

"No." I glance at my floor, its debris of sweaters left scattered by the police. "But if we still had it, wouldn't your officers have found it last night?"

254

"It wasn't the subject of our search. And anyway, a single piece of paper is kind of a needle in a haystack."

"Well, I asked around. No one knows what happened to it."

"Okay," Elijah acknowledges, but I hear that smugness again. Right away, I know what he's thinking: Dad might have thrown it away. It fooled us, the morning we read it, but if Dad had forged it, if Andy's fingerprints were never even on it, maybe it wouldn't have fooled the police, who would have had the resources to analyze it.

"Lyle had access to Andy's handwriting," I blurt. Because now I'm remembering another part of Ruby's story: after Andy rejected her, she was sobbing on her bedroom floor, surrounded by his notes. Lyle found her like that, and when she told him what happened, he grabbed some of the papers before storming out of the house.

I tell this to Elijah, adding threads to my theory as quickly as my mind can spin them: "It's possible Lyle didn't even have to forge it. *The only way out is to never come back?* That might be something Andy wrote himself. It sounds exactly like him. Which is why I never questioned it."

"Uh-huh," Elijah says, distraction fogging his voice.

255

"Uh-huh? That's it?"

"Sorry," he says, and now there's a sound on his end, like chair legs scraping against the floor. "Something just came in. I have to go."

"Something about Andy?"

"I'll talk to you later, Dahlia."

"Wait. Are you going to question Lyle?"

"I assure you," he says coolly, "I'm following every lead."

But I don't believe him. Even after he hangs up, his voice lingers, allowing me to hear the echo of his father. *I assure you,* Elijah said just now, a phrase that Edmond often used.

I assure you, I'm only doing my job, Edmond would say when Andy, answering the door, squared his shoulders, refusing to call down the hall for Dad. *I assure you — just a quick chat.*

I can't leave this to Elijah, someone brainwashed to suspect us. He's told me — *assured* me — that he hasn't been swayed by his father, but still, he keeps coming after mine. And the longer he looks for answers here, the longer they'll go unfound.

I don't know how the families of the Blackburn Killer victims have managed — living for decades without knowing the truth, enduring the public's fascination with our island because of what happened to *their* daughters, *their* sisters, *their* wives. And all this time, no one has been able to give them justice, to punish the man who derailed their lives.

But I know someone who's hunted that man for years, even after the case went cold. While I squinted at pictures of city streets, she pored over newspaper photos, sweeping a magnifying glass across audience members at public meetings. *I bet you anything,* Greta once told me, *that when police held meetings about the Blackburn Killer, that motherfucker showed up to watch.*

Phone still in my hand, I pull up her number, and as soon as she answers, I hear the café — spoons clinking against mugs, laughter overlapping, the burble of conversation like a distant stream.

"Bad time?" I ask.

"*Perfect* time. I've been meaning to take my break."

The background noises soften, and I hear Greta shutting the door to the stairwell that leads to my apartment. We'd sit there sometimes, splitting a muffin while she rested between shifts, and I'd inevitably think of Andy. Even years after I last saw him, it still felt like a tiny betrayal, sharing a meal with anyone else.

257

"I need your help," I say to Greta.

"Anything."

When I tell her about the shed, I ignore her gasp. I speak for minutes at a time — explaining about Fritz, about Ruby, about Lyle — while Greta whispers a refrain of *holy shit.* Only at the end do I mention Elijah, how he tore our house apart, searching for the brand.

By the time I finally stop, Greta's unusually quiet.

"Seems a little on the nose," she says after a while. "Your father being a suspect."

The response is so unexpected I almost laugh. "What?"

"Just with the way you were raised and all. It's too — I don't know — tidy, I guess, to think that someone who told you all these murder stories was out there murdering the whole time."

"It was my mom who told us the stories," I say. And I don't know why I do that, contradict Greta while she's defending Dad.

"Still," she says, "he was part of that. And I mean, take me, for example. I'm as obsessed with murder as they come. You've seen my murder spreadsheets. But that doesn't mean I actually want to kill someone."

"So you think Elijah's just biased?"

"Well, I get why he did the search. Your family owns the shed, and they can't really ignore that. But do I think your father was this vicious serial killer, and you all had no idea? No. I don't."

I release a long breath. Despite my own theories, my dismissing of Elijah's, there's something about hearing Greta say this that feels especially validating.

"Will you look into Lyle Decker for me?" I ask. "See if there's anything . . . off about him? A criminal record maybe? I don't know. You're always able to dredge stuff up."

"I'm on it," Greta says, a tremor of excitement in her voice. I imagine her scribbling notes on her server's pad, itching to add Lyle's story to her folder of files.

"I'll see if I can connect him to any of the Blackburn victims," she adds. "I actually really like him for this. It's creepy, how overprotective he is of Ruby. What if he killed women as, like, a way to rewrite the story of his wife and daughter leaving him? He couldn't get them to stay on the island, but he can make sure other women never leave."

I pull my cardigan tighter. Outside my window, bare branches shudder. "Wow. That's —"

"I'll dig into your groundskeeper, too.

He's definitely involved in this. Actually, I should go. If I close early, I can get a head start. I'm sure the cops are waiting to announce the shed until they have a concrete suspect — which is good; it means they don't have enough on your dad — but as soon as they go public, it'll make things trickier."

I try to ignore the buzzing of her eagerness, the reminder that, for Greta, this isn't just a favor she's doing for a friend; it's an opportunity. I bet she can't believe her luck: the privileged information, the glimpse into suspects no one else has heard of.

"Thanks," I say, throat tightening. "But please, remember that this is . . . That Andy's not just —"

"This is about your brother. Well, the Blackburn women, too. But right now, it's about Andy, and I promise I won't lose sight of that. You can trust me, Dahlia, okay? You can trust me."

I'm heading toward the stairs when Tate calls my name.

I find her at her desk, hair piled into a knot on top of her head, and her room seems back to normal, the police's mess not evident when I first walk in. Then I notice a sweater sleeve stretched out on the floor, looking like an arm reaching for help, and I realize she's stuffed everything under the bed. Its ruffled skirt bulges out, trying to hold it all in.

"Who were you talking to just now?" Tate asks over her shoulder. Even in profile, I can tell her brows are furrowed.

"My friend."

Her skin is unusually pale, and the muscles in one arm keep tensing, like she's squeezing something in her hand.

"You shouldn't be doing that," she says.

"Talking to my friend?"

She snaps her head in my direction. "Talking to your friend about Dad. About the police suspecting him. You can't just . . . We should keep that private, Dahlia."

Tate turns back to her diorama, which now bears trees so lifelike I expect to see the wind shaking their branches. The hole is still there, waiting for a body.

"Like you're planning to keep this private?" I say, gesturing toward her desk.

She exhales impatiently. "We've been over this."

"Well, sorry, but I don't see why it's okay for you to share Andy with thousands of strangers, but I can't tell my one friend what's going on in the investigation."

Her arm tenses again. I try to see what's

261

in her hand, but she pulls it toward her, tucking her fist into the folds of her sweater.

"There's a monumental difference between the two," she says. "The diorama's only part of it. It's the thing that gets people's attention. And when they read the caption, they'll know that Andy was more than just his death. Telling people about Dad, though?" She pauses to shake her head. "Why would you go out of your way to confirm people's suspicions of us?"

I pause at the word *confirm.*

"Wait," I say. "You agree with the police? You think it was Dad?"

Her eyes flash wide for a moment. Then, just as quickly, they crimp with pain. "Of course not!" she says, the phrase a whip she lashes through the air.

"I just meant," she adds, gaze slinking toward her lap, "that you have to be more careful. You can't be giving people more ammunition than they already have. It's a slap in the face to all the work Charlie's been doing."

"The work? He's turning Andy's death into a spectacle. Both of you are."

"You're not *listening,*" she groans, punctuating her last word by slapping her hand onto the desk. The sound it makes is strange, like a teacup rattling onto a saucer,

262

and when I look at the space in front of her, I see why.

She's built a body. That's what she was squeezing in her hand, what she's just smacked onto the desk: the little doll that, once inside the hole, will complete the diorama.

The body is flat on its back. I brace myself for the four-inch doll to resemble Andy, but when I lean closer, I see it's featureless, still missing the details that would make it seem human — an outfit, a hairstyle, a specific tint to its skin. Right now, it's just a cloth torso with porcelain head and limbs, indistinguishable from the ones Tate has showcased in her #BehindTheCrimeScenes stories, usually posted after the diorama itself, taking her followers through her process, from scattered materials to finished product. I always get goose bumps when I watch those posts, where, at the very beginning, the doll is blank and anonymous, but by the end, it's a murder victim.

My hand trembles as I reach for the doll. I feel the sting of tears.

"You say you're trying to show people that Andy was more than just his death. But how are you going to paint Andy's face? With his eyes open? With crinkles around them?"

She looks from me to the doll, biting her

lip. "You know that's not how I —"

"You're obsessed," I cut in, suddenly so weary, "with showing off his death."

"I'm not *obsessed*."

"Yes. You are." My words are slow, sapped of energy, my shoulders sagging like someone's holding them down. "I saw the passageway."

Tate frowns, forehead creased as she tries to catch up. "Between the closets?" she asks — and just like that, anger flickers through my fatigue.

"Don't do that," I say.

"Do what?"

"Act like you don't know what I'm talking about."

"I *don't* know what you're talking about. I haven't been in that passageway in years."

Now, my tears burn as I swipe them away. "You expect me to believe that?"

"I don't know why you wouldn't."

"How many times did you draw him dead? And how could you *bear* it?" I swallow down the sob that's threatening to escape. "He's our *brother*. And it's like . . . like you killed him over and over."

Slowly, she turns her head from side to side. "Dahlia, I have no idea what you're talking about."

I let out a groan before grabbing her wrist.

"What are you —" she starts, but I pull her toward her closet, open the door, and drag her with me to the second one in the back. Then I yank her into the passageway and push her forward, the smell of mildew sudden and sharp.

"Stop!" she says. "I hate it back here! What are you doing?"

I ignore her, reaching for my phone in my pocket. When I turn on the flashlight, I shine it on the wood, walking a few more feet until the light latches onto paper. I look back at Tate, who's stopped moving, and with a grunt, I grab her again, pulling her toward her nightmare of a collage.

Tate gapes at the wall, taking in her drawings like she's awed by her own skill. Mouth ajar, she runs her hand over one and then looks at her fingers, eyes wide, as if she expects the sketch to have transferred onto her skin.

"These are of Andy," she says.

"And how do you think I felt when I stumbled upon them? How do you think it makes me feel when I see" — I glance at one in particular, my heart stopped by all its gray, graphite blood — "my twin brother looking like this?"

Tate stares at the paper, but her head is

shaking back and forth. "You think *I* did these?"

"Oh, stop it — they're your studies for the Andy diorama! Just like the ones you did for the Blackburn women."

She continues down the passageway, squinting at the other sketches, and I follow her with my flashlight, letting my vision glaze over so I don't have to see them too. Still, I make out the shape of them, the way the papers overlap. A shiver whirls through me.

"And the way they're arranged!" I say. "It's exactly like the photos under the shed."

Tate swings toward me. "Are you going to accuse me of doing those, too? Photographing *murdered* women?"

"Why not! You make dioramas of them!" I shout — but then I hear myself, and I shake my head. "No. Sorry. I don't . . . I know you didn't take the photos. You were a teenager back then."

"Oh, *that's* why I didn't do them! But if I'd been — what, in my twenties? *Then* you could see me killing people?"

"That's not what I'm saying! I'm just — It hurts, okay? Seeing these studies! And it's *weird* that —"

"Dahlia! I've had three days to do the diorama. I haven't had time for studies.

266

What do you think —"

"What's going on? It sounds like a bad production of *King Lear* up here."

We turn to find Charlie in the doorway, lifting a hand as my flashlight blinds him. I jerk my phone back toward the wall, and he steps forward with a slouchy swagger, pulling the smell of alcohol into the tiny space. Shadows pool in the hollows of his cheekbones, and for a second, I'm stunned by how gaunt he is, like weight has dropped from his skinny frame in the last few days alone.

He takes in the papers illuminated against the wood. "What the . . ."

"She thinks they're mine," Tate says, "but they're *not.*"

Her words are so pointed, so adamant, that I finally take notice. My hand slips to my side, casting the light on the floor, blackening the blue of Tate's irises as she turns to me.

"Do you think it's been easy for me, doing this diorama? Do you think I *like* doing it? I told you: I *have* to do it. It's the only way I know to —" She stops as Charlie squeezes her shoulder. She closes her eyes, inhaling sharply. "But *this*? These sketches? I didn't do them."

I rub my forehead, pushing deep circles

into the skin. "But — if you didn't do them, then . . ."

Charlie fills my silence as I trail off. "I think you should listen to her, Dolls," he says, words a little slurred.

"But," I try again, "I don't get it, who would —"

And then a different voice cuts in: "Dahlia."

The three of us turn to find Mom in the passageway, a few feet from the door that leads to her own closet. I point my phone toward her, and it spotlights her exhaustion. Her ponytail, loose and rumpled, is pushed toward one side of her head. Her eyes are circled with shadows. Her arms hang limp at her sides.

She walks toward us, gaze brushing against the sketches taped to the wood. I shine the light on them so she can see them better, but it's only a moment before she looks at us again. Her shoulders slump, like a person defeated.

"Tate didn't draw these," she says. "I did."

FIFTEEN

We're stuck in a relay of glances — Tate to Charlie, Charlie to me, me to Tate — as silence stretches out from Mom's strange confession. With four of us here, the passageway feels tighter, but no one moves to give themselves an extra inch. Even the dust seems frozen, suspended in the air, listening to us breathe.

As Mom views the sketches, a medley of emotions plays across her face: horror, guilt, pain. "This hallway," she all but whispers. "It was a fairly common feature, back when the house was built, in homes of this style. The idea was to connect the master bedroom to the nursery, making it easier for parents to reach their children in the night. To soothe them. Feed them. Keep them safe." She tries to smile, but her lips quiver. "My mother called it the Protection Passage."

"Mom," I say, not bothering to hide my

269

impatience. "Why would you draw these pictures?"

She drags her gaze from the wall, settling it on me instead. "When we thought that Andy ran away," she says after a while, "I couldn't stop imagining all the ways he might die."

A chill creeps over me, starting at my shoulder blades, crawling up my neck.

"I'd see him knifed down in some alleyway, or a man with a gun to his temple . . ."

She trails off, and I know she's thinking of her parents, how the bullet smashed through her mother's skull and hit the glass cabinet beside her, shattering their wedding china. It's a story we've been told a million times, how afterward, once the bodies were gone, Mom had to gather the pieces of plates and bowls, their ivory details outlined in blood.

"And I thought," she says, "I thought that if I got them down on paper — these awful images — then I could, I could ward against them somehow."

Charlie snorts. "Ward against them?"

"I couldn't stop drawing. Every day, another way he could die. Another way I saw him when I closed my eyes. And I think now that maybe I . . ." A tear slips down her cheek. Her voice becomes brittle.

"Maybe the images wouldn't stop because part of me knew he was dead."

Shame flares in my cheeks. Part of me — all of me — should have known, too.

"I drew and I drew and he never came back, just like the note said. So I kept on drawing, and I put all the sketches in here. I couldn't bear to have them lying out in the open. But I couldn't bear to get rid of them either. They were wards. They were protection. But, no — they weren't. I couldn't protect him. He was already . . ."

Her shoulders shake with a sob.

"But Mom," I say, "in all these sketches, you drew him as he actually died. With a head wound." I pause, steeling myself against a wave of nausea. "How did you know?"

I expect her to say she *just knew,* that she intuitively felt how Andy had died, just like I should have known he wasn't out in some city; he was stuck beneath bugs and sludge.

But Charlie speaks first. "That's not true," he says. "Look."

He points toward one of the sketches, and as I focus my light on it, I'm surprised to see he's right. In this picture, Andy isn't limp on the ground, bleeding from the head; he's in a hospital bed, cheeks so sunken they look sucked in. And now I notice that in another, he's crumpled in front of a car, and in another, he's slumped against a wall, a knife protruding from his stomach.

My own stomach churns at these images — but I'm realizing that, ever since I first found them, I never fully took them in. My eyes skimmed along the pictures, clinging to only a few, where, yes, the wound appeared to be in Andy's head. But there were so many others I'd skipped past, overwhelmed by the quantity. Even when I showed them to Tate and Charlie, I blurred my vision, keeping myself from seeing my brother dead.

"I did this to him," Mom says, and now she's pointing at the wall, eyes blazing with the guilt I saw just flickers of before. "It's my fault Andy's dead."

The sentence stabs me — a hot, sharp wound in my chest. As Mom turns to us, I hold my phone low enough to keep from blinding her, but high enough to see how her brows squeeze together, how the creases around her mouth seem to deepen.

"It was karma —"

"This again," Charlie grumbles.

"For the lie I told," Mom finishes.

For a moment, there are only our shared glances, volleyed between me and Charlie and Tate before we return our attention to Mom.

"What lie?" Tate asks.

Mom dips her chin, staring at the floor. "My parents weren't murdered," she says, her voice as quiet as a match being struck. "They died of lung cancer."

Everything inside me goes still. Tate's mouth drops open. Charlie blows out a laugh.

"I'm sorry, *what*?" he says. "Is this a joke? Have you been slipping something into your cookies I don't know about?"

I snap my head from him to Mom, waiting for her to make some sense. She's hugging herself, her lips moving without sound. After a few seconds, her breath solidifies into words.

". . . within months of each other," she's saying. "They'd been smokers for decades. For my father, it was just — something everyone did. His father, his grandfather, everyone at the company. It was part of the culture. Cigarettes were passed around like cups of coffee."

I lean closer, unused to hearing her speak of their business. It was irrelevant, she always said. Whatever harm the guns they made might have caused, it didn't mean their murders were karma. But now — there

273

weren't any murders at all? My head swims as I try to catch up.

". . . and my mother picked up the habit, once she started working with them. Our walls were yellow with smoke. My clothes always smelled. And they got sick around the same time, when I was twenty. I remember thinking how unfair that was. *Both* of them? Not one but both?" Her eyes shift back and forth, pacing the floor like feet. "It was a terrible disease. Stage four. Spread to their liver, their bones. Went to my mother's brain."

Tears drip down her cheeks, and there is nothing in me that wants to comfort her, nothing that wants to reach out and wipe her sorrow from her face. All of me — every cell and atom and breath — is fighting to understand.

"She went first," she continues. "And then my father, not far behind."

Tate slumps against the wall, crushing some drawings with her shoulder. "So, wait," she says. "There were no gunmen? No home invasion?"

Mom shakes her head. "Only cancer." She looks at us now, spearing us with her stare. "But that 'only' was the problem. Nobody saw my parents as victims, or their deaths as tragic, because they'd smoked themselves straight into that cancer. People came to their funerals and said, 'Well.' That's all they had to say. 'Well.' And I knew what that meant. It meant 'Well, what did they expect?' Meant 'Well, they did this to themselves.' "

As I watch her scowl at the memory, a realization clicks into place. "Is that what you really meant," I ask, "whenever you said you didn't want anyone to think of their deaths as karma?"

Except she didn't say *deaths*. She said *murders*. She specifically said they were killed by the very guns their company made — a detail so dark I never questioned its veracity, never would have believed that someone could invent it from thin air.

Mom nods, hugging herself tighter. "However they may have . . . contributed to their illness, I still lost them. Both of them. And their loss felt as raw and unfair and — and violent to me as if they'd been killed unexpectedly, as if someone had arbitrarily chosen to murder them because they walked down a dark street too late at night, or they were in the wrong place at the wrong time."

Her last sentence hums in the air, made resonant by its familiarity. How many murder docs did we watch that spouted that same line? *The wrong place at the wrong time.*

"I mourned and I mourned and I mourned," Mom says, her palms open in front of her, as if she's remembering the weight of her grief, trying to hold it in her hands. "And do you want to know the only thing that comforted me?" She closes her eyes, breathes in deeply, then opens them again. "Murder."

Tate grips my arm. I look at her, but she's focused on Mom. Charlie's glaring at the floor.

"Not the committing of it. But the stories. Stories of gruesome, real-life murders. Stories where people are left behind to grieve someone who was torn away from them. Stories where the . . . the terrible cruelty of life was so absolute." Fresh tears dampen her lashes. "Undeniable."

Even in the shadows, I see her gaze drift from us, distant and hazy.

"So I invented a story like that of my own. I sold my parents' house in Connecticut, sold their whole company, and I moved here, to their summer home, the place where I'd spent every July and August of my life. And when people here, who had known my parents, asked what had happened to them, I didn't tell them about the cancer. I couldn't bear to see it again, the doses of sympathy, so uniform and mea-

276

sured, followed too often by that 'Well.' I wanted to see horror on their faces. I wanted them to feel even a sliver of what I felt about what had happened."

She releases a cold, airy chuckle. "They stayed away from me after that. Didn't want the tragedy that had touched my life to creep over into their own. And that was fine. I didn't need them. I had newspapers and books and films and endless, *endless* stories of people like me. People who existed in the interviews. People who said, 'She was so full of life, I don't understand how she's gone.' Or 'I'll never be over it.' " She pauses, her expression now blank. "I think of those lines all the time."

"Mom . . ." Tate says, but either she doesn't hear her, or she can't be stopped.

"Living inside those stories," Mom continues, "gave me something I hadn't had before: validation for my grief."

She takes another deep breath. "And when I met your father" — Charlie's head snaps up — "and he asked me for my story, I told him the one I'd been telling everyone on the island. Then I took him here, to my family's home, and I showed him the papers I'd been collecting. I showed him the true crime books. The films. And he didn't even flinch."

Her face changes, briefly awash with admiration. "He accepted the darkness I wanted to surround myself with. He understood what it meant to me: solace and protection. I wanted my children to be better prepared for the world than I had been. I wanted to warn you all, as early as I could, about how life can just" — she grits her teeth, forcing words between them — "tear you apart."

Teeth bared, shaking her head, she resembles an animal ripping meat off a bone.

"And I wanted you to have those stories to fall back on, if you ever did lose something in a way you couldn't make sense of, even as others tried to explain it away."

Mom shudders, a quick burst of anger before the sorrow, the shame, sweeps over her again, dragging her shoulders down.

"I thought I was giving you tools to survive. But then" — she hesitates, and when I tilt my light toward her face, I see her swallow — "after Andy left, I thought maybe I'd been wrong. Maybe the darkness I exposed him to had actually sent him running, instead of keeping him safe. I thought of him, all alone out there, no money, no access to a bank account, and I couldn't stop seeing everything that might happen to him. And then I couldn't stop drawing what

I saw, trying to . . . to pull those possibilities from the universe. And then . . .”

Her hands shake as she runs them through her hair, disturbing her lopsided ponytail, pulling it from its elastic band without seeming to notice.

“When we learned Andy was murdered,” she continues, “I knew, without a doubt, that I was to blame. I’d made the wrong choice, been the wrong kind of mother.” Her voice narrows to a whisper. “It was karma, Andy’s death. I lied about my parents being murdered, and then my child was murdered in return.”

She sobs once, so loud I jump. Then she buries her head in her hands and cries like nothing I’ve ever heard. The passageway thunders with the sound. The walls could come crashing down.

Tate takes a tiny step forward, the only distance she can move. “Whatever else you did,” she says, trying to be heard above Mom’s noise, “whatever lies, whatever —” Tate turns her head sharply, as if Mom’s confession is only now landing, sudden and stinging, a slap across her face.

“Andy’s death wasn’t karma for anything,” she continues. “That’s just . . . superstition, it’s —”

“Andy was killed with his own ax!” Mom

screams. "Just like his namesake! I called this into the world. I lied about murder and he was murdered." She drags a hand down her face, fingers clawing at her cheek. "And those women. The shed. Murder has been circling us for decades! How can that not mean something?"

"I don't know," Tate says. She looks at me, eyes a little wild, like she's asking me to step in, to speak to our mother, but I have nothing to say.

"I don't know," Tate repeats. "I don't know, I . . ."

She slumps against the wall again, sliding down until she's perched on the floor. I slump back, too, opposite her. But Charlie is pillar-straight. His fists clench, unclench. His nostrils flare.

"I'm so sorry I lied," Mom says between sobs. She presses the heels of her hands against her cheeks, as if to dam up her tears. "I can't undo it, I can't take it back. But I'm so sorry. To all of you. To Andy most of all."

"You're *sorry*?" Charlie shouts. He slaps the wall, making the rest of us jump.

"I am," Mom whispers after a moment. "I'm so sorry."

"Sorry doesn't —" He covers his face, groaning into his hands, and when he speaks again, his slur is gone, each word precise. "What else have you kept a secret? What else did you know and never say?"

I tilt my head, surprised by the rage in his questions. Surprised by the questions themselves.

"N-nothing," Mom stutters. "I don't know what you — Nothing, I swear."

From her place on the floor, Tate touches Charlie's leg. "Hey," she says quietly. "Mom didn't know."

Charlie scoffs.

"Know about what?" I ask.

I point my light toward Charlie's face, watching as his eyes lose the gleam of their anger, as they dim into resentment instead. "The shed," he mutters.

Mom gasps. "No! I didn't! I had no idea."

Charlie shrugs one shoulder, the movement lacking his sharpness from a moment ago. "You lied to us our entire lives."

"Not about that!" Mom cries. "If I had any idea what was down there, I would have . . ."

She continues on, but I'm not listening. I'm focusing, instead, on the sketches again, tugged toward an earlier thought.

"But they're so similar," I say, and silence swells around my interruption. "Mom — why did you tape up your drawings like this?

Exactly like the photographs in the shed."

"Seriously, Dahlia?" Tate stands up with a grunt. "First, you accuse *me* of taking those photographs, and now you're accusing Mom?"

"She accused *you*?" Charlie asks.

"I wasn't . . . I wasn't accusing you," I say. "Or I didn't mean to, anyway. But Mom" — I turn back to her — "did you ever see the wall of photos? Is that why you . . . ?" I gesture to her sketches.

"No! I've never been down in that room, not even when my father used it. It was always just storage, just —" She touches her forehead. "I don't know what else to say. I already told the police."

Charlie stiffens. "Told the police what?"

"They found my drawings last night, during their search. Detective Kraft pulled me aside, and I explained everything as I explained it to you — my lie about my parents, my fears about Andy — but he asked me about the similarity to the photographs, and I told him I don't know! It's just a coincidence."

"What did Elijah say?" I ask. "Did he buy that?"

On the phone today, he was still pushing me toward his theories about Dad. Did he see this wall as further evidence that he

282

might be guilty, that perhaps Dad copied Mom's collage? Or worse, did the connection between the photos and the sketches nudge Elijah toward a different theory? One where Mom was involved with the Blackburn murders, too.

"Did he *buy* that?" Tate seethes. "Why don't you just say it, Dahlia? You think we're all a bunch of killers."

"What? I didn't —"

"You're suspicious of Mom's sketches, suspicious of my dioramas — which, ten minutes ago, you equated to *photographing dead bodies*!"

There's pain in her emphasis, her lips twisted around the words. I open my mouth to protest, to remind her, again, that I didn't mean what I said — but Elijah's theories are whirling through my mind, his questions spinning like yarn into a gruesome knot. At Tate's mention of her dioramas, I feel a strand get snagged.

"Why are your dioramas so accurate?" I ask.

She flinches away. "Excuse me?"

"Elijah Kraft said the crime scenes you depicted get a lot of things right. I didn't think much of it at the time, but — how did you know, exactly, how to position everything?"

Tate looks at Charlie, mouth agape. He returns her gaze with a bewildered shake of his head. When she turns to me again, her expression is furious and wild, her face almost monstrous in the shadows. "What the fuck are you implying?"

"I don't know!" I admit. "I'm not implying anything, I just —" I lean back against the wall, stare at the sketches opposite me: Andy's head bashed in, his eyes forever closed; Andy slumped on the ground, his eyes open but vacant. "I don't know. I don't know."

"We're your family," Charlie says coolly. "You can't be saying things like that."

Now I whirl toward him. "*You're* the one who asked Mom what other secrets she's been keeping!"

"I was in shock. I'm shocked, okay? About her lie. But the way you're talking to us . . . It's like you don't even know us at all."

"I *don't* really know you at all! I've barely spoken to you in the last ten years."

"And that's our fault?" Tate fumes. "How many times have I contacted you? How many emails have you returned? How often did you call to check on Mom?"

"That's not — How is that relevant?"

"It's relevant because you're making such" — her voice cracks — "horrible accusations." Tears pool in her eyes, but I see her trying to maintain her anger. "And if you'd reached out to us even half the times I reached out to you over the last decade, you wouldn't be treating us all like suspects right now."

"Why would I reach out to you? You and Charlie never made time for me and Andy when we were kids. You were always wrapped up in your own cocoon."

"We were *kids*!" Tate says. She swipes at her cheeks. "And you were nine years younger than me. And even if we did 'make time' for you, what would have happened? You think we were in a cocoon? Well, you were like ivy, Dahlia, clinging to Andy all the time."

"I didn't cling to him, we — If anything, we clung to each other."

"I know that's what you tell yourself, but how well did you even know him?"

Charlie reaches for her elbow. "Okay, Tate . . ."

"No," she says, wrenching out of his grasp. "You act like the two of you were so connected —"

"We were!"

"— like you could read his mind, feel everything that happened to him."

"I could, I . . . I thought I could."

"But you didn't even know he was dead!"

For a few seconds, silence expands around us like foam. Then a sound rips out of me — a ragged, helpless sob — as I drop to my knees on the floor.

"I know!" I cry. "I know, okay? I failed him. I know!"

Mom crouches beside me. "Oh, Dahlia, you didn't fail him." She places a hand on my shoulder, but I shrink from her touch.

"You failed him, too!" I yell, and she leaps back. "He hated how you raised us. He said it was unnatural, and he always, always wanted to leave! All because you couldn't face your parents' death. All because you found comfort in *murder.*"

"All right, Dolls," Charlie says.

"And you!" I fling my gaze up at him. "Andy wanted to talk to you that night, to you *and* Tate. He wanted to ask you what it was like to get out of this place. But the two of you were off with each other like always, and maybe if you'd been there, he wouldn't have been alone outside and someone wouldn't . . . wouldn't have . . ."

My head falls into my hands, my tears instantly wetting my palms. My body burns with pain, like fireworks bursting, scorching me from the inside out. I know I'm barely making sense, braiding together a rope of

286

blame that isn't tied to Andy's murder, but I'm heaving and hurting and I'm sick, so sick, of Andy being gone.

When my sobs finally subside, I look at Tate and Charlie and Mom. They're gawking at me, like they have no idea what to do with me. And it's fine. I don't mind. I don't know what to do with them, either.

"Let's go," Tate says after a moment, tugging on Charlie's sleeve.

"But —" Mom starts.

"We'll talk about this later," Tate snaps.

She closes the door behind them, leaving me with Mom in this dim, constricting space.

"What can I —" she tries.

I shoot a hand up to cut her off.

"Not right now," I say, "please," and I glare at the floor until, moments later, I hear her leave.

Alone in the passageway, I put my elbows on my knees, let my head fall back into my palms. Even with my eyes closed, I see the sketches on the wall — Andy bleeding, Andy dead, Andy never coming back. I look at the tears on my fingertips, watching them glisten like glass shards. And all the while, my chest vibrates with a rhythmic, persistent thud I barely even recognize as the thump of my own heart.

287

SIXTEEN

"I have some news."

The phone is pressed between my pillow and ear, and even as Greta speaks, I feel myself tugged toward sleep. Since Mom's confession yesterday, I've been incurably drowsy, as if a sedative swirls in my bloodstream, too potent to resist. And I don't want to resist it, because if I do, I'll have to be awake in this unnerving truth: for all our lives, our mother lied to us as effortlessly as dreaming.

I hear the floorboards creak in Andy's room. It's quick, just a splinter of sound, but as soon as it happens, my stomach sours. It's not the creak itself, achingly familiar, reaching me through the wall we shared; it's that I don't imagine, even for a second, that it might be him. Already I'm growing used to Andy's absence, my heart settling like a house around the empty space he's left.

"Dahlia? Are you there?"

"Mmm," I mumble.

"I found some info on Lyle."

I sit up in bed, blankets pooling around my waist, cool air rushing in to replace their warmth. "What is it?"

"Well," Greta starts, "it's a couple things. First, you know me: I went down some rabbit holes — but I ended up getting my hands on his high school yearbook. Apparently, he grew up here, not on the island."

"Okay?" That isn't particularly newsworthy. Many of the islanders grew up on the mainland before settling here as adults.

"Anyway, there's a picture of him," Greta continues. "With your groundskeeper."

Surprise twangs against my ribs. "With Fritz?"

"Here, I'm texting it to you."

In a moment, the picture comes through. I zoom in with my fingers, first on the caption — *John Fritz and Lyle Decker, co-captains of the boys' lacrosse team* — and then on the image itself: two skinny teenagers, each with an arm slung over the other. At first, I don't see the men I know in those faces; they're too smooth, too slender, too smiling. But as I squint closer, I recognize Fritz's eyes, mirthful but mild.

"They were friends?" I say.

It's difficult to imagine. Back when we were kids, we knew Lyle Decker as the cranky man across the woods, the man who offered us little more than a growl of acknowledgment on the rare occasions we saw him. Fritz, on the other hand, has always been playful and polite.

"I've never seen them together," I add.

"Yeah, well, Fritz was always working when you saw him, right?"

"Still. He was friends with our neighbor, and that never came up? I guess they could have drifted apart . . ."

"But Lyle knew about your family's shed," Greta reminds me. "And he told Ruby to stay away from it. So it seems like he and Fritz kept in touch." She pauses. "I've got theories, of course."

I grip the phone. "Tell me."

She draws in a breath like someone about to sink beneath water. "Okay, theory one: Fritz is the Blackburn Killer, like you originally thought. Lyle knows something is weird about the shed but isn't sure what — just that his old friend gets really squirrelly about it. In this theory, it's just a coincidence that Lyle got sick around the time the murders stopped.

"Theory two: Lyle is the Blackburn Killer, and he got access to the shed from Fritz.

290

Maybe Lyle told him he needed storage space or something, and Fritz is just an innocent party."

"But Fritz knew what was under the shed," I say. "He asked me to help him get rid of it."

"Right. Okay. On to theory three: Fritz and Lyle were working together. Because it's a lot for one person, don't you think? Moving a body, cleaning it, dressing it, branding the ankle, taking the photographs, *then* carrying it down to the shore? That's a lot of work for a limited window of darkness. All this time, the police have been looking for the Blackburn Killer, but what if it's the Blackburn *Killers*?"

A shiver shoots through me, and for a moment, I'm speechless. I pull my blankets toward my chin. "Wow," I mutter. "I never —"

"There's more," Greta says. "In researching Lyle, I found this old newspaper article: *Judge dismisses trespassing complaint filed against chief of police.*"

"Okay . . ." I say. "I don't get it."

"Chief Edmond Kraft — that's the guy who always hung around your house, right?"

I straighten at the name. "Yes."

"According to the article, Lyle saw Kraft 'snooping around' the woods one night, and

291

he filed a trespassing complaint against him. The complaint never went anywhere, but still."

She says that, *but still,* like her next conclusion should be obvious, but I shake my head, confused. "Edmond was always snooping around," I say. "He'd walk around our property, checking everything out. Writing notes. Elijah Kraft says his dad had entire filing cabinets of notebooks, all about us."

"Exactly," Greta says. "So. Theory four: the chief went a little deeper into the woods than usual, Lyle saw him, freaked out that Kraft might discover something about the shed, and then tried to make sure he couldn't go snooping there again."

I hear the smile in her voice, which is higher than usual. It gets this way whenever she's forging a new path through a case, following clues like breadcrumbs, invigorated by the search.

"Of course," she adds, "that just makes theory four an addendum to theory three. Or two. But then there's theory *five.*"

"Five?" I close my eyes against a whirl of dizziness.

"Last one," Greta promises. Then she does it again, that presubmerging breath. "I've been thinking about my message boards, all the theories that have been kicked around over the years about the Blackburn Killer. And one that comes up a lot is that he might have been someone in law enforcement."

My eyes jerk open. "A cop?"

"It's actually not an uncommon theory for cases like this, especially when there's a lack of evidence. Whoever killed those women knew how to make sure it couldn't be traced back to him. And then there's the idea that he could have used his uniform to get the women's guards down before he strangled them. Or he could have approached them under the guise of questioning them: 'Hey, miss, what're you doing out so late?' That kind of thing."

I clench my jaw, picturing that scene: someone abusing the trust stitched into their uniform, using their power to inflict unimaginable pain. Greta's right; it's not uncommon. I know the stories, the names: Gerard Schaefer was fired from his teaching job, rejected from the priesthood, and finally landed as a police officer in Florida, where he murdered Susan Place, Georgia Jessup, and buried them in a park. John Christie, another officer, stowed his victims' bodies under floorboards, in his garden, behind the walls in his kitchen.

And now I'm thinking of Edmond. How he strutted so noticeably around our lawn, never even attempting subtlety. How he sometimes announced his drop-ins with the flashing lights above his cruiser, a reassurance to the islanders that he had an eye on Murder Mansion.

But what if he was never actually investigating us? What if, instead, he was setting us up, laying the groundwork to make us seem suspicious? That way, if the room beneath the shed — his room? — were ever uncovered, people would easily believe that we were to blame. *Well, yeah,* they might say, *I'm not surprised. Police have been looking at the Lighthouses for years.*

The air compresses around me.

"Elijah said Edmond's been in a nursing home," I tell Greta. "Early onset dementia. I don't know how long he's had it, but —"

"That could explain why the murders stopped," she finishes.

"It doesn't explain Fritz, though. Or Lyle,"

"I know," she agrees, and I hear the hunger in her words, the appetite that's been whetted instead of cured. "That's why they're only theories right now. Something's still missing for sure."

We rehash her ideas for a few more minutes. Then Greta ends the call with a promise: "I'm going to try something."

She won't elaborate on what that *something* is, "just in case it doesn't pan out," but as she mentions it, her voice becomes tight, restrained, like she's pinching back the excitement of whatever she has planned.

For an hour after that, I barely even move. The possibilities, the suspects, pin me down — Lyle at my wrists, his breath rasping in his throat; Fritz at my ankles, his long hair scraping my legs; and Edmond at my neck, his fingers squeezing my windpipe like a pen.

They stare at me, eyes dilated, daring me to decide which one is a killer.

"This is ridiculous!"

Charlie's voice booms up from downstairs, disrupting the image of those men. Instantly, my body feels lighter, like I can actually feel them letting me go.

"It's hysterical, how off base you are. Were you one of those color-outside-the-line sort of kids? That doesn't mean you're creative, you know; it means you're wrong."

I lift my head, pointing my ear toward the hall. The doorbell rang a while ago, but until now, I haven't spared a thought for who might have arrived.

"Do you have one of your fancy little *warrants*? If not, I'll have to see you out."

Adrenaline sprints through me. I spring toward the doorway, trying to catch the other end of the conversation, but the person is too quiet. Creeping across the hall, I edge toward the top of the stairs until I'm able to identify the voice.

"It's really just a question," Elijah says.

"Hardly. It's an insinuation."

"It's interesting you'd see it that way."

I descend a few steps until I see them. In the living room, Elijah studies Charlie, whose shirt is rumpled, half untucked, hair sticking up and out, as if he's been grabbing at it. In contrast, Elijah is pressed and put-together, a crisp green folder in one hand, a notebook in the other.

"What's going on?" I ask, and they both look at me.

"Nothing," Charlie says. But his eyes leap like a startled deer's to Elijah's folder.

"I heard something about a warrant," I prompt.

Charlie ignores me, turning back to Elijah. "If you insist on badgering me with your embarrassingly transparent questions, let's do it somewhere else, shall we?"

He takes off toward the back hall, and Elijah follows without another glance my way.

What was in that folder? Charlie's eyes

darted toward it the same way they darted toward Tate when the police were searching his room. He never answered my question about that, never explained the anxiety I saw. *You have to trust us,* is all he said. *Me, Tate, Mom — we're all you have left.*

But Mom's a liar. And Tate cares more about followers than family. And Charlie was nervous about that folder, nervous about the officers traipsing across his floor.

I want to lurk at the victim room door, listen to Elijah's questions, Charlie's answers, but my brother is clearly defensive right now, enough to be wary of an eavesdropper. I'll need to speak to Elijah alone, after he's talked to Charlie. And maybe I should be wary of an eavesdropper, too.

Slipping into my shoes near the door, I'm about to head outside to wait for Elijah when I register how the foyer's been transformed. Small tables with white cloths dot the wide space. A typewritten card announcing the items that will be displayed sits on each table. The items themselves remain in piles in the living room, where more surfaces wait, draped in white.

It looks like a room full of ghosts.

I open the front door and walk into another gray day, clouds low and heavy in the sky. The wind carries the smell of the ocean,

Andy's least favorite scent, and I pull my chunky sweater closed. Elijah's police cruiser sits at the end of our walkway, and as I approach it, voices drift up from the bottom of the driveway.

". . . but that's because it's Murder Mansion. There was some kind of fuss there the other day. Tons of police."

"Well, yeah. They found that boy."

"No, this was after that. Susan said the driveway was packed with cruisers. There was even . . ."

The voices shrink and fade, belonging to walkers on the road. I take a few sips of air, trying to unhear how flippantly one of them spoke of Andy, how, just like Lyle Decker, she referred to him as *that boy.*

"Hey."

Ruby emerges from the trees near the side yard, as if I've conjured her by thinking of her grandfather. Or as if she's been lingering in the woods. Watching.

"Did you talk to the police about me?" Her question is unexpectedly forceful. She squeezes her lips together, waiting.

"I talked to them about your grandfather."

"Why the hell would you do that?"

She flexes her fists at her sides, and as I answer, I watch her hands curl and uncurl.

"There were things you said that I wanted

298

them to look into. Things that didn't add up."

Or added up too well, I keep myself from saying.

"That's none of their business." Ruby steps forward, shoving a finger into the air, so close I can see the dirt beneath her nails. "Grandpa and me — we're just trying to get by. We don't need the police coming over, riling him up, digging into my past with Andy."

So Elijah did question Lyle. I feel a gush of relief, almost gratitude, even as Ruby's finger jabs toward me.

"Your grandfather was riled up?"

"Of course he was! I told you how he gets when it comes to Andy. You saw it yourself the other day. The detective got him so upset, and — You had no right, absolutely no right, to accuse us of anything."

"I didn't accuse *you,*" I say, leaning away, my back against Elijah's car. "Why are you so mad?"

For the first time, her eyes aren't big at all; they're narrowed to slits as thin as paper. Moments pass, the ocean throbbing in the distance, and it's a while still before her stare loses its sharpness. When her hand falls back to her side, it's stuck in a fist, knocking against her thigh.

"It's just," she starts. Then she sighs, finally relaxing her fingers. "I thought you and I . . . I thought we connected yesterday."

"Connected?"

"Yeah. As friends."

The wind circles us, and Ruby breaks my gaze to button her coat. I cross my arms, tightening against the cold.

"We're not friends," I tell her. I try to be gentle about it, but I want to be clear: I'm not her path back to Andy, her detour from loneliness.

"We're something," she insists. "We understand each other. We were closer to Andy than anyone else." She sniffles loudly. "We feel the same loss."

We don't, though. Whatever pain Ruby feels, it's only residue from a teenage crush. It's nothing compared to the crater I will harbor inside me forever. Someday, Ruby will find another boy to love, but a twin, my twin, *Andy*, is irreplaceable. I will only grow emptier, the older I grow without him.

Ruby moves some loose pebbles on the driveway with her foot, her bottom lip curling into a pout. "You didn't change your mind, did you? About including the embroidery in the memorial?"

"No," I assure her, even though I haven't thought of it since yesterday, when I closed

300

those words — *Ruby loves Andy* — inside a drawer.

"Good," she says, punctuating the word with a choked and bitter chuckle. "It all went so wrong, you know." She shakes her head, jaw tensing. When she speaks again, she shoves the sentence through gritted teeth. "That night I tried to give it to him, everything went so terribly wrong."

Terribly wrong. Wrong. It echoes off the trees, her voice gusting around us like wind. Ruby doesn't seem to notice. She squints at her shoe, still stabbing at gravel.

"I need to get back to Grandpa," she adds. Her eyes harden, tiny and tight once again. "In the meantime, stop talking about me behind my back."

"I wasn't —" I start, but she's already turned around, rushing toward the woods. I watch her go, hands shoved into her pockets, curls billowing out behind her, until she's too far for me to distinguish her from the shadows cast by trees. I pull out my phone to check the screen.

No messages.

"Updates soon," Greta promised me earlier. It hasn't been long since we hung up, but as I wait for Elijah, arms taut across my chest, I hope for another call. I want to know what Greta would make of it —

Ruby's strange anger, prompted, it seems, by Lyle's reaction to the police; Elijah questioning Lyle only to return, again, to question Charlie.

I look at my hand, scraping at Charlie's "trademark flair" that he Sharpied across my skin. So far, it's refused my attempts to scrub it away. It lingers defiantly, a day later, this tattoo I didn't ask for. When my hand turns raw from rubbing, I turn my attention to the clouds growing thicker above me. Andy always struggled to find shapes in them. Me, I saw everything: cars, trees, deer. *Look, it's antlers,* I said to him once. He scrunched up his face, followed my finger with his eyes, then kicked at the grass, giving up too soon. *It's just moisture,* he replied. *Just water and ice.*

He was like that, always seeing what things were made of, instead of what they could be. *Who knows what's in my blood?* he asked Ruby, as if the unnatural lifestyle he wanted to escape was woven into his DNA.

When I finally hear the front door, I leap off the car. Elijah clomps down the walkway, gripping his folder tightly.

"I was looking for you," he says, stopping a few feet in front of me. "Inside."

"I figured we should talk out here. Away from . . . everyone else."

"Oh?"

"I wanted to know why you were talking to Charlie. But now I want to know what happened with Lyle. Ruby was here. She said you questioned him."

Elijah leans forward, reaching past me to drop his green folder on top of his car. "I'm sure you know I can't really say."

The wind nudges the folder open, rustling the papers inside. I try to scan them quickly, but he slaps the folder closed before anything flies away. He pulls it back toward his side, eyeing me as he tucks it under his arm.

"I told you about Lyle," I argue. "Don't I have a right to know if you think he's a suspect?"

"You know that's not how this works."

"What about Charlie then?" I try. "What were you talking to him about?"

He watches me for a few more seconds before he looks away. Shifting the folder to his other hand, he opens it to glance inside, then shuts it again before aiming his attention toward the woods.

"Will you take a walk with me?" he asks.

I blink at him. "A walk? I'm asking about Charlie."

"I understand. But there's something I want to show you." He considers my crossed arms, quivering in the cold. "It's a bit of a walk, so you might want to grab your coat."

"A walk to where?"

The corners of his mouth quirk up. "It's a surprise," he says. Then his expression eases, flattening into something more earnest. "You'll be safe, I promise. And when we get there, I'll tell you exactly what I asked your brother."

I study him, weighing his strange proposition, how he's assuring my safety when I hadn't even thought to be concerned for it. But that phrase — *exactly what I asked your brother* — hooks me more than I'd like. It feels so specific, significant, and swirling beneath the words, I hear Elijah's suspicion.

"I'll get my coat," I say.

Seventeen

We head down Breaker Lane, which ends at the beginning of the rest of the world. The road, paved with gravel, empties out onto the shore, the gray sea unfolding beyond it like a sheet of aluminum foil. Even with my mouth closed, I taste the brine of the ocean, salty as the broth in Dad's stews. The wind is thicker here, like coarse fabric rubbed against my cheeks.

Standing at the edge of Blackburn Island, it takes more effort to breathe — and it's impossible, I find, not to think of those women. Tate's dioramas flip like flash cards through my mind: the angle of Amy's leg, folded grotesquely against the hard-packed sand; Claudia's red hair, snarled with seaweed; and the slit in Jessie's dress, evidence of the rocks that battered her body as she washed onto shore.

I look to Elijah for direction. He stares at the water, gaze stretching toward a horizon filmed with fog.

"Is this what you wanted to show me?" I ask.

On the way down Breaker, all he offered was that he wanted to see if I could identify something. *Something of Andy's?* I asked. But he shook his head, glancing at his folder.

I wondered, again, at its connection to Charlie, to this destination Elijah refuses to name. I didn't tell him, then, that most of this coast is new to me, that even growing up on the island, I hardly ventured this far. Andy hated the water, and that was enough of a reason to avoid it.

It's strange, though — how he viewed the ocean as an obstacle to getting away. Dodging the foam that reaches toward my shoes, I realize that it seems like the opposite, like the water wants to suck me in, drag me out toward somewhere else. Shouldn't Andy have seen it, then, as a means of escape?

But again — those women. They confirm, I guess, that Andy was right. The fact that their bodies were returned to our shore, spit onto sand instead of carried to another coast, is proof that the ocean wants us here, contained to Blackburn Island.

"It's this way," Elijah finally answers, and he sets off walking, gesturing for me to follow.

Water rushes toward our feet as we navigate the pebbled shore. We keep to the dryer side as much as we can, but even the beach grass here is wet, the giant rocks darkened by a recent tide.

"Your brother's putting a lot of work into his museum," Elijah says after a while. "What do you think of it?"

I stop for a second, but he doesn't. He continues down the coast, oblivious to — or ignoring — my hesitation, and I step over driftwood to try to catch up.

"I'm not sure," he says when I don't answer, "that, if it were me, I'd be okay with it. Be careful there." He points to a jutting log, waiting to make sure it doesn't trip me. "Seems like it's making a spectacle, don't you think, of such a personal loss?"

When I stop this time, Elijah pauses, too. His eyes look curious, unguarded, as if he genuinely wonders what I think. And I'm struck by the word he used — *spectacle* — *which* is what I've called it, too.

"Charlie is all about spectacle," I reply. "He's an actor. He loves an audience."

"Yeah?" Elijah starts walking again. "Is he any good?"

Trailing behind him, I watch the impressions his shoes leave in the sand. It would be easy, stepping inside those prestamped spaces, using them to guide me along. Instead, I weave around the prints like rocks.

"I wouldn't know," I tell him. "I've never been to any of his shows."

"Huh," Elijah acknowledges. "So . . . you're okay with the memorial then?"

"I didn't say that."

He slows again until I step into pace beside him. I feel him watching me. "What about the rest of your family? What do they think?"

At the suspicious glance I cut his way, he puts up his hands. It's a gesture of innocence, surrender, but it forces the folder between us, a thin green barrier.

"Is that a detective question," I ask, "or a personal one?"

"I'm honestly just curious," he says. "Look." He opens one side of his jacket to reveal an inner pocket, the spiral of his notebook jutting from the top. "I'm not even writing this down."

He lets go of his coat and the notebook disappears. I pull in a mouthful of air, push it back out.

"Tate's okay with it, I guess. She's always fine with whatever Charlie does. And anyway, she's busy making her own kind of spectacle."

Elijah nods. "I saw her diorama."

"You did?"

"Just now, at the house. And the other night. During the search."

I keep my focus on the damp sand in front of us. The shore is narrowing, nudging us closer to the waves.

"It's very realistic," he adds. "The trees alone . . ." He blows out an impressed whistle.

"But is it *oddly accurate*?" I ask.

I intended a mocking edge to the question, a reference to his own phrase, but it comes out sounding sincere. I think of Tate's face in the passageway, when I asked how she knew which way to position the bodies. Her eyes sparked with something hot and raw: hurt, I think; anger for sure. But more than that, I consider now, they flashed like she was threatened.

Elijah's brow furrows.

"You said her other dioramas, the ones from Instagram, were *oddly accurate*," I continue. "I'm just wondering if this one is, too."

He thinks it over. "Ask me again tomorrow," he says, "when I see it at the museum. I'm assuming it'll be finished by then?"

"That's the plan . . ."

"Okay. Yeah, I don't know — too soon to tell. There wasn't a body in it yet."

"Well, there wasn't one in the grave, either," I say, the words sharp in my throat. "You said it was just his bones." I force a painful swallow.

"Right. But we know, roughly, the position he was buried in. We know exactly the point of impact on his skull. And as I'm sure you're aware, those are details we haven't divulged."

"Okay. So it won't be accurate then."

"We'll see," Elijah says.

Our gaze lingers. In my peripheral vision, I see the green of his folder, the grip of his hand.

"Is there a reason you asked me that?" he says. "Are you . . . concerned about something?"

"No," I say quickly. I sidestep a clump of seaweed. "Other than the fact that you still won't tell me where we're going."

He smiles a little, almost sheepish. "It's not much farther," he promises.

Beside us, the ocean roars, ruthless and wild. I turn my head to watch it, entranced by the violence of its rhythm. In a way, it reminds me of Andy — how he thrashed his ax at the trees, how he, too, had wildness in him, his eyes nearly feral each time he swung. As the ocean pulls back, its roar dulling to a fervent whisper, I swear I can hear Andy's voice: *Unnatural,* he says. *Our family is unnatural, Dahlia. We have to get out.*

"How about your mother?" Elijah asks. "How's she doing through all this?"

My scoff comes quickly. "Hard to be sure. I just found out she's a liar."

I regret the admission as soon as Elijah reacts, the mention of lying propelling him into motion. He reaches toward his inner pocket, ready to grab his notebook, but I put my hand out to stop him.

"I'm talking about her parents," I explain.

He waits for me to elaborate.

"That they died of cancer instead of murder? I know she told you when you questioned her about her sketches the other night." I scoff again at a realization. "I can't believe she told you before she told us."

Elijah's forehead wrinkles. "You didn't know?"

"Not until yesterday."

A crease deepens between his brows. "How is that possible?"

There's astonishment in the question. My mind snags on that, slow to comprehend.

"Wait," I say. We stop walking. "Did you already know . . . before she told you?"

He looks at me strangely, like I'm missing something obvious.

311

"Everyone knows," he says.

I hesitate. "Who's everyone?"

"The people on this island. That's why my father was so suspicious of your family."

I stare at him, jaw slack, until he continues.

"Your mom and her parents only lived here during the summers at first, right?"

I nod.

"But then, your mom moved here permanently, on her own, and started telling people her parents were brutally murdered."

I nod again, and in a way, it feels like I'm absorbing the story for the very first time. She didn't just lie to us. She lied to everyone she spoke to.

"She didn't think anybody would see an obituary?" Elijah says. "Everyone knew. And it freaked them out, that a person would lie about something like that."

As his words sink in, I waver between shock and embarrassment. I spent years trudging through websites for a single trace of Andy, and all that time, I never thought to check the rest of our family history. I never considered, even for a moment, that our origin story might be a lie.

Tears simmer, hot and sudden, ready to boil over onto my cheeks.

"But I didn't know!" I say. "None of us

did." A sound ripples through my throat, something between a groan and a whine. "No wonder they call our house Murder Mansion."

Those gossiping islanders. Like the wind and the ocean, their whispers have been the white noise of Blackburn Island. And yet: the snippets I'd catch — *murder, parents, that family* — while spinning through Fritz's leaf piles were never enough for me to hear the whole truth.

I grip my head on either side, squeezing my temples. "Everyone knew!" I say, because of course they did. "Out here, everyone knew. But in there" — I gesture toward the center of the island, the hill on which our house looms, gray and stony as the sky — "we had no idea. And how could we? We were so isolated. So *insulated.* God, it's so messed up. My family is so messed up."

I'm breathing heavily as Elijah looks on. I feel his eyes, soft as a breeze, skimming across my face. Our shared silence fills the space between us until I finally meet his gaze.

"I kind of used to hate you," he says quietly. "When I was a kid."

I startle at the subject change. "What?"

"I thought you had something I didn't: a

family so close you'd shut out everyone else."

I toss out a brief and bitter laugh.

"And I was mad," he adds, "that my dad paid so much attention to you all, instead of paying attention to me. But now, talking to the rest of your family, then talking to you . . . I think maybe you've always been like me. On the outskirts of it all."

He shifts almost nervously, a different man from the smug, withholding detective who baited me into this walk. "Am I right?" he asks.

I gape at him, surprised by his openness. My instinct is to tell him he's wrong, that I only felt like an outsider in my own family once Andy was gone. But then I think of Charlie and Tate, laughing behind closed doors. I think of Mom, haunting the staircase, studying the faces of her parents whose story she'd rewritten. And I think of Dad, whose stiff body language and gruff voice kept me from knowing him at all.

My entire life, I thought that Andy and I saved each other from loneliness, when really, we just built a different kind, one that felt like comfort, like safety, but in the end, was only a cocoon. And that seemed normal to me; it was just like Charlie and Tate.

But what I didn't understand, never

paused for a moment to consider, is that cocoons are inherently temporary, too tight a space in which to grow.

Andy knew that; that's why he urged me to leave with him, get away from our family, our *unnatural* life. And it kills me now, wondering what might have happened if I hadn't constantly pulled him back, hadn't held down the wings that were itching to sprout from his spine.

The ocean thuds against the sand, wrenching me away from a past I can't remake.

"I'm sorry, I shouldn't have said that," Elijah says, voice stiffer now. "That was incredibly inappropriate."

He stands straighter, clearing his throat. "To clarify, though: I didn't actually hate you, I hated my dad's obsession."

At the mention of Edmond, the hiss of *obsession,* I stand straighter, too.

"Back then, it seemed kind of . . . pathological. Almost malicious. Like he couldn't stop himself from returning to your house. Like he got off on taunting you all."

My pulse flickers. I see Edmond circling our mansion, memorizing our property, our patterns.

"And I guess I'm just saying — it's clear you're not exactly close with your family. That you're put off by what your mom did,

315

what your siblings are doing. And I relate to that. I was definitely put off by my dad. Especially since his obsessions left little time for me."

He starts walking again, and I hurry forward to fall in step beside him.

"But I've had to make peace with a lot of that," Elijah adds, "since he's been sick and all."

"How long has he been sick?" I ask, spurred on by Greta's theory, by the image of Edmond drawn back and back and back to our yard.

"It's been a while," Elijah says. "Started seven, eight years ago, I think."

Seven or eight years. Only two or three after Jessie Stanton.

"And that's when he went to the nursing home?"

Elijah's eyebrow twitches. "No. That's just when his memory started to 'turn on him.' That's how he referred to it. It only became unmanageable the last couple years or so."

Still. Even the smallest change to Edmond's mind could have been enough to disrupt him, to distract from whatever sick desire sends someone hunting for women at night.

"Was he ever violent with you?" I ask, and I see, as soon as Elijah whips his head my way, that it's a question too far.

"No," he spits. Then he stops, scrutinizing me. "Did your dad get violent with you?"

My head jerks back, whiplashed by his pivot. "Of course not."

A wave crashes onto us, soaking our shoes, the bottoms of our pants. I register my socks growing damp, suctioning to my skin, but something keeps me from moving.

Pathological, Elijah said in describing Edmond. *Malicious.*

Is it possible he, too, has considered Greta's theory — that there was more to Edmond's obsession, more to Edmond overall? Is Elijah disturbed enough by that possibility that he's forced his attention onto my father, hoping to find something that will quell his suspicions of his own?

I study his face, darker now, but find no answers. Instead, he says, "We're here."

All around us, there's nothing but the same sand, same rocks, the spot indistinguishable from the rest of the shore.

"Do you know this place?" he asks. "Do you know what it is?"

I turn my back to the water, inspecting the landscape: hard sand that yields to tall, spiky grass, and behind that, trees that shoot up, eventually blending into the woods that fill out the center of the island.

317

"No, I've never been here," I say. "Andy and I never went to the ocean."

"What about Charlie?"

I look at him, puzzled, until he opens his folder and pulls out an 8 x 10 photograph.

I recoil, thinking it's one from the shed. But Elijah waits for me to examine it.

The shot was taken low to the ground, as if the photographer were crouching in the water, the bottom of the camera licked by the waves. The angle allows for a glimpse of the landscape in the background. And in the foreground — I swallow — there's a dead woman.

She's a Blackburn victim, identifiable by the blue gown. But unlike the pictures under the shed, she isn't segmented into parts; she's photographed as a whole, her body flat upon the shore — this spot of shore, I realize, as I match its giant rocks to the ones behind the woman. Her knees are slightly bent, and her arm is flung out beside her, like she's reaching for something she'll never be able to touch.

It's Claudia Adams. The fourth victim. Her red hair gives her away.

"This was taken by one of the first officers on the scene," Elijah says, "before the public knew about the body. Except — check this out."

He jabs the upper-righthand corner of the picture, pointing at a tree that's shorter, darker, than the rest. But no — I squint closer — it's not a tree. It's a small, thin figure.

It's somebody watching.

"I asked some of the officers who were part of the investigation. They admitted they flat-out missed it. He kind of blends in."

"He?" I say.

"And most likely," Elijah continues, "they were using this photo to focus on the body itself, the area just around it. In pictures like these, we check for footsteps, other disturbances, details about the victim. There were other photos of just the surrounding area, and he wasn't in any of those."

"He?" I repeat.

"We blew it up as best we could. The quality isn't great, but — here. See for yourself."

He shuffles through the folder again and yanks out another photo. When he hands it to me, it's only a moment before recognition, sharp as a gasp, jolts through my body.

"That's Charlie," I say.

Elijah was right; the quality is terrible, shadowy and pixelated. But I know this teenage shape of him, skinny as a sapling. I know this sideways slouch.

In the photo, he's watching the scene

below him: the woman's body splayed out on the sand, her damp hair draped over her face.

"Charlie?" I say again. It comes out as a question this time.

"I think so, too," Elijah agrees. "Did he ever mention seeing one of the crime scenes, one of the women's bodies?"

I shake my head, glaring at the photo, the stick-thin shape of my older brother. Then I look at the woods above us, as thick and tangled as they are in the picture, and I try to fathom why he even would have been there.

"My first thought," Elijah says, "was maybe he took an early morning walk. Maybe he stumbled upon the commotion down here and stayed to watch the officers work. I can see that being of interest to a kid. Hell, it would've been of interest to me."

He pauses now, the moment stretching wide.

"Except — Those woods right there . . ." He thrusts his chin toward the trees. "They're really dense. Difficult to navigate. Not an easy place for a casual walk."

"What did Charlie say?" I ask. "What reason did he give for being here?"

"That's the thing. He said it's not him."

I look at Elijah in surprise. "He did?"

"He was emphatic about it. Your sister, too. And your mother . . . she was noncommittal, said she couldn't tell. To be honest, she seemed more interested in the dead body."

Behind us, the ocean races toward our feet, and at Elijah's expression — eager but careful, like he's closing in on something — my heart races, too.

"Why did you bring me here?" I ask.

His shrug is too casual. "I wanted to see if this spot meant anything to your family. If you knew its significance and could explain why Charlie would come here." He smiles with half his mouth. "Guess that was a long shot, though, since you said you're not very close with them."

But I didn't say that. Elijah did, right as he told me I was on the outskirts of my own family.

"It's just strange to me," he goes on. "Miles of shoreline around this island, acres of woods, and Charlie ended up on the one part, the one very small part, where there was a body. Before the public knew."

I take a step back, my foot splashing into water.

"If he told your sister what he saw that day, it might explain why her diorama of

Claudia Adams was so accurate." Elijah points to the photograph, the woman's waxy body. "Wouldn't really explain the others, though." He tilts his head at me. "Unless you have an idea?"

I back up farther. Satisfaction winks in his eyes — a look I've seen before, on somebody else. What was it he said about Edmond? *He got off on taunting you all.*

"I know what you're doing," I tell him. "You're going on about how you relate to me so much, how we're both on the outskirts of our families. But that isn't true. You chose to become a cop, just like your father."

His face stiffens. His features grow taut as a web waiting for a fly.

"You didn't bring me here to see if I knew this spot," I continue. "You wanted to pull me away from the house. From my family. You're trying to get me to turn on them."

"Turn on them?" He tucks the folder under his arm and reaches into his jacket pocket. Pulling out his notebook, he clicks the top of a pen that seems to have sprouted from his palm. "Turn on them about what?"

The wind picks up around us, a suffocating, gagging force. The ocean thunders like a storm.

I spin around without answering. I march

322

away from him, feet pummeling the shore. I expect to feel him close at my heels, chasing me down, taunting me into talking about things I don't have answers for. But when he calls after me, he sounds far away, like he hasn't even moved.

"Why do you think Charlie was here, Dahlia?" His words slice through the island's noise, voicing the question that's pumping through me, quickening my steps: "Why was he here?"

By the time I reach our driveway, I'm running.

Bursting through the door, I call Charlie's name, but he's not in the foyer or living room. The tables and their white cloths are topped with misshapen piles that I barely give a glance before rushing up the stairs.

I race into Charlie's room only to find it empty, and I'm struck by how tidy it is — the tightly closed drawers, the floor without clothes, the creaseless quilt on the bed. It's like the police never touched his room.

They were here, though. I remember the thud of their footsteps, Charlie's anxious gaze bolting toward Tate. And now that Elijah's caught him in a lie — that was Charlie in that photo, I'm sure it was — I know he's hiding something.

Something, I think, that's in this room.

I launch myself toward his dresser, riffling through shirts and socks, probing every drawer. I feel inside the pockets of his pants, slide my hands under his mattress. I check his bedside table, shuffle through the pages of books, and then, at the lurch of an idea, I turn to his closet.

Inside, I flick on the light switch, but the bulb flashes once before burning out. I head through the shadows toward the back, feeling for a door like the ones to the passageway, but my hands don't stutter over hinges or a knob. I crouch down, searching for a gap between the floor and a possible door. It's only once I claw against the hardwood in a fit of frustration that my nails cling to something: the thinnest groove between boards.

I pick at it. Nothing happens at first, but then the board jerks up before falling back down. I pull my phone from my pocket, turn on the flashlight, and shine it onto the floor.

There's a part of the groove, a tiny notch, that's a little wider than the rest. I can see why the officers might have missed it, especially if they were only running their eyes, not their hands, along the floor. The notch doesn't look deliberate; instead, it seems like an imperfection in the wood. But now, I squeeze my finger into it, struggling to move it around, and in a moment, half the floorboard springs open, like a tiny version of the trapdoor in the shed.

I waste no time with surprise. I stuff my hand inside it and grasp two objects, both small, cool to the touch. I pull them out and stare at my open palm, and it takes a second for my mind to catch up. Then I shake my hand violently, sending the objects clattering to the floor.

The air is trapped in my throat. I shine my light closer, needing to be sure of what I'm seeing, and now my hand rushes to my mouth.

One of the objects is a skeleton key, identical to the one that opened the door in the shed. And the other, the one that's whipped my heart into a gallop, is something I've never seen before but immediately recognize.

With trembling fingers, I pick up a dark metallic *B*.

The Blackburn Killer's branding iron.

Eighteen

I'm out of Charlie's room and down the stairs so fast, I feel like I've flown to the foyer. Voices rumble from the kitchen, and I run down the hall until I'm panting on the doorless threshold. Mom and Tate gape at me in surprise.

"Where's Charlie?" I blurt.

"I don't know," Tate says. "Last I saw, he was —"

"Charlie!"

They jump at my scream. I wait, hear nothing, and yell his name again.

"Dahlia, what —" Mom starts, but I jolt my hand up to cut her off.

Footsteps trudge from the end of the hall near the victim room. I spin around and back up until my hip hits the counter.

"This better be good," Charlie says.

"You were at one of the crime scenes," I blurt — and that slaps the smirk off his face. "And you have this." I open my palm, show him the key and the iron. Behind me, somebody sucks in a breath.

"Was it you?" I ask him. "Were you the Blackburn Killer?"

"Dahlia!" Mom says.

Charlie's face hardens. "I was *six*!" he spits, features twisting with rage. "When the first woman was killed, I was only six."

My hand shakes. The iron feels heavier the longer I hold it. The key's teeth seem to sharpen.

He's right, of course — he was far too young to be the killer.

"Then why do you have this?" I pluck the iron from my palm, stab it into the air.

At that, Charlie seems to deflate, his chest going concave as his gaze slides behind me, reaching, as always, toward Tate.

"Don't look at her!" I yell. "I'm the one asking."

He shoves his eyes to the floor.

"There . . . there must be a reasonable explanation," Mom stammers.

I glare at my brother. "Answer me!"

"Dahlia, stop," Tate says gently. She steps forward until she's standing between me and Charlie. Then she puts her hand on the sharp knob of his shoulder.

"You should tell them," she whispers.

Charlie's face appears so tortured that I

almost feel guilty — like I'm witnessing something I shouldn't.

"Tate," he whispers back. "I can't."

"You can," she replies. "Listen to what she's accusing you of. It's time, Charlie. You have to tell them."

"Tell us what?" Mom asks.

Tate squeezes his shoulder. "I'm right here."

My heart races as I watch them both. For a few charged moments, Charlie returns our sister's stare, but then he throws out an arm behind him, feeling for the wall. He lets himself fall against it and slides down until he's sitting on the floor.

Knees up, elbows on his thighs, fists against his forehead, Charlie lets out a single word: "Fuck."

My skin goes cold, waiting.

Finally, Charlie drops his hands. "I got the brand from the chest. In the room beneath the shed."

The sentence startles me, but I force myself to stay rigid. "There was nothing in that chest. I checked."

"There was nothing in it," Charlie says quietly, "because I broke into it."

I picture the splintered wood on top of the trunk. "When?" I ask.

He answers me slowly. "After Fritz found

the body . . . Andy . . . I knew it was only a matter of time before the police searched the shed. I waited until the middle of the night, when Kraft and everyone else was gone. I didn't know the combination to the lock on the chest, so I chopped it open. With Fritz's ax."

"That was *you*?" I'd been certain it was Andy, proof that he'd uncovered secrets that someone would kill to protect. But now I stutter onto another thought. "Why did you go down there? How'd you even know about the room?"

Charlie swallows. "It was just the iron in the chest that night. But that used to be . . . That's where the dresses —" He stops, his mouth moving soundlessly before he continues. "I planned to take the photographs, too. But they weren't like that, back then. Hung up like that. They used to be in the chest. And I couldn't *breathe* looking at that wall. I barely made it out without throwing up."

I feel my pulse thrumming, a taut string plucked. "Charlie," I manage. "How did you know what was in the chest?" I stare at the key overlapping the brand on my palm. "Where did you get this key?"

Charlie's gaze darts toward Tate.

"It's okay," she says softly, and there are

329

tears shimmering on her cheeks.

He closes his eyes, mouth shut tight, inhaling through his nose.

"I got it from the Blackburn Killer," he says. Beside me, Tate releases a breath. I find myself holding mine. "I got it from Dad."

"*What?* No!" Mom shouts.

I fall back against the counter, my hip stabbed by its edge.

"Why would you say that?" Mom cries. "How could you even *think* that of him?"

"Because I was there!" Charlie bellows. "I was involved with it! Always."

Silence plows through the room. I'm stuck inside it, embraced too tightly by the quiet. When sound finally surges back, it bursts from Mom's lips, her words coming out like wails.

"What does that *mean,* Charlie?"

It's a while before he answers. My heart pounds out the seconds, my head becoming so light I worry it'll float away.

"It started when I was six," he says, voice flat.

I watch his lips move.

"Dad came into my room, late one night. Yanked the blankets off me, told me we were going hunting."

Charlie knocks his fist against his fore-

330

head. Once. Twice. I flinch both times.

"I didn't question it. Even though it was dark out. Even though he didn't take the rifle. He had this bag I'd never seen before, and I . . . I went with him. I followed him to the road that leads down to the shore — which I did think was weird; he only ever hunted in the woods. But suddenly Dad stopped, and we just stood there, waiting for" — he shakes his head — "I didn't know what."

My heart keeps banging. I grip the counter to remain upright.

"Nothing happened," he says. "We waited and waited, and when I asked him what was going on, he told me to keep my mouth shut. Finally, we went back home, he sent me back to bed, and in the morning, I thought I'd . . . I thought I'd dreamed it. Until it happened again, a few nights later. The same thing: pulling me out of bed, leading me to that road. Only this time, we heard footsteps in the distance, someone's shoes on the gravel, coming up from the shore.

"Dad looked down the road and he whispered to me. Said there was a woman coming, and I had to make myself cry. I had to pretend to be lost and scared and alone so she'd stop to help me. I didn't know what he . . . But then he pinched me, hard, and I did start crying. He shoved me out into the lane and crouched back, into the bushes. And when the woman came, she . . . she looked so concerned. She asked where I lived, who my parents were, and I was so scared. I didn't understand what was happening, but something in me knew to be terrified."

He pauses, kneading his knuckles against his closed eyes. "The woman got down next to me, and she kind of . . . gathered me in her arms? And then, she was jerked away. Making these horrible noises. I didn't — I almost couldn't see . . . But it was Dad. He had a rope around her neck. He was strangling her. He was . . ."

Charlie trails off. The room feels close to airless.

"When she went limp, he didn't hesitate. He grabbed a tarp from his bag, the same kind he used for deer, and he wrapped her up, and headed back home with her in his arms. And then . . . the shed . . . He took her to the shed. He went down into that room. With the tarp. The woman in the tarp. The woman who had crouched down to see if she could help me." A choking sound grates in Charlie's throat. "I didn't understand what was happening."

332

On either side of me, Mom and Tate are crying, but my tears won't come. My eyes feel hot, itchy, and I realize now I haven't been blinking.

"He made me keep watch that night," Charlie says, "up in the shed. But through the hole, I could . . . I could see her head on the floor, the skin all purple around her eyes, like someone had punched her. I saw him wrap a blue scarf around her neck."

A blue scarf. Melinda Wharton. The only woman who wasn't discovered in the dress.

"No," Mom moans. Over and over she says it, a chorus of cries beneath Charlie's story.

"Then he wrapped her in the tarp again and carried her up from that room. And he made me follow him, again. But this time, we went down to the ocean. And we walked along the shore for a long time, even as he stumbled beneath the weight of her. Then he walked into the water, pushed her out. The whole time, I didn't say anything. But he said if anyone saw us on our way back, we'd tell them we found a woman in the ocean and were on our way to get help. He muttered something, more to himself, like, 'A man can't be a murderer if he's out with his son.'

"He told me it was *our* secret, one that no

333

one else would understand. He said, 'If you tell anyone what we did tonight, you'll be in big trouble. They'll take you away and throw you in jail, and I won't be able to stop them.' "

Mom sobs, and I feel her hand close over mine on the counter. When Charlie looks at her, his face is filled with disgust — at himself, or at Dad, I don't know.

"I was so scared," Charlie says, gaze fixed on Mom, "but I still didn't really get it. Even seeing the body, even with Dad using that word, *murderer,* even when the news about Melinda Wharton started spreading around the island — I couldn't make sense of what had happened that night. I just knew I felt terrible, all the time. Like I was cut up inside. Every day another cut."

He hangs his head. "It was two years before it happened again. I don't really remember the second woman the way I remember the first. It's all so . . . it's like seeing it through gauze. Though I did register the differences, from Melinda. Now, there was a dress. And a burn on her ankle."

He nods toward my hand, which holds the brand. Seeing it still there, I drop it immediately, as if it singed my own skin. The key falls with it, clattering to the floor. Charlie watches it, dark metal on white tile.

"Dad made me keep the key," he continues, "in a space he'd carved out in my closet. He said we'd store it there, in case Edmond Kraft ever searched his things. He said 'we' like I agreed to it. Like I wanted to be part of it. When, really, at some point, I sort of just . . . woke up to it. Woke up into this reality where I understood, definitively, what Dad had done. And by then, it was too late. I couldn't tell anyone. How could I tell? In implicating Dad, I'd be implicating myself."

Mom's hand slips off mine. She might be crying still — Tate, too — but all I can hear is Charlie's voice, a fractured melody above my percussing heart.

"A couple times, the morning after, I went down to where we'd left the body. I don't know why I wanted to see it. Maybe to know for sure what I'd done. To punish myself. One of the times, the police were already there, but I stood in the trees, watching them work. They took photos of her. Like Dad had done only hours before. And I thought about saying something. But then I heard his voice: 'They'll take you away and throw you in jail.' Because he planned it that way. He made me his partner in crime."

Charlie puts his fist to his mouth. Then

his cheeks puff out with his breath, as if he's trying not to be sick. Soon, his hand falls to his side like a dead thing lying on the tile.

My mouth is slack. It's too much to process at once. Beside me, Mom sobs out lines of denial, of horror — "No, no, oh Daniel, no" — and as my vision goes foggy, my body grows numb.

Dad.

The man who carried dead deer to our door.

The man who returned from hunting with beads of blood on his hands, who wiped them away like specks of mud.

It was always so casual, the relationship he had with death.

Locking my knees to keep from falling, my mind works to transform Dad from hunter to killer. Instead of him stalking through the woods beneath a blue sky, I see him crouching behind a bush, clothes as dark as the night itself. Instead of him aiming a rifle at the heart of a deer, I see him holding a rope and pulling it taut. Instead of him squeezing a trigger, he's squeezing a neck.

I shake my head, jolting the images to a stop. It shouldn't be so easy, blurring the lines between hunter and murderer.

My mind sputters back over Charlie's

story. It's unbearable to take it all in, to recalibrate my distant father as an actual monster, one this island has feared for decades. Despair sinks into my stomach, cold and heavy, as I think of all the women, the people, he —

My heart plummets. My legs threaten to give out. Because if I keep amending my previous theories — Dad in the shed, instead of Fritz or Lyle or even Edmond; Dad with such horrible secrets to protect — I will never escape the place where Charlie's story inevitably leads.

"But Ruby said it was Fritz," I cry out, desperate for a loophole. "She said she saw Fritz go into the shed in the middle of the night, carrying a big black bag."

"She was wrong," Charlie says dimly. "It was Dad. Fritz was never there."

I shake my head. "She said she knew it was him from his limp. The man was *limping*."

"He was carrying a dead body," Charlie mutters.

I glance at Mom, who's finally silent. I want her eyes to be pinched with disbelief, but she's staring blankly ahead, tears stalled on her cheeks.

And now I can't fight it. My mind forces other memories to the surface: times I saw

Dad walking out of the woods, hauling his dead deer home. Sometimes he'd tarp them, so all he'd have to do was drag. But for the smaller ones, a hundred pounds or so, he'd carry them in his arms. And Charlie's right. Bile creeps toward my throat, burning my esophagus, because he's right. When Dad held those deer, he never moved too steady. He stumbled more than walked. Someone watching in the dark might even say he limped.

"So when Ruby saw Andy following someone," I say, words sluggish, almost slurred, "he was really following . . . Dad. Which means, Andy must have figured out what Dad was up to, who he was, and he must have been looking for proof, or —"

I'm cut off by a humorless laugh.

"You don't get it," Charlie says, squinting at the floor. "Andy wasn't following him that night. Not in secret anyway."

My heart thumps out a warning, begging me not to ask. But my mouth disobeys. "What do you mean?"

Slowly, Charlie lifts his head. As our eyes connect, his are so pained it's like looking into open wounds. I stop myself from breathing — knowing, somehow, that his response will change me forever.

"The last woman I watched Dad kill was

338

his fourth victim. Claudia Adams. I was fourteen at the time. After that, I was too old to seem helpless. So Dad needed someone else he could use as bait. Someone he could groom to take my place."

I shake my head, raising my hands like shields. Squeezing my eyes shut, I grit my teeth against his words.

"Three years later, Amy Ragan was murdered. Dad's fifth victim," he says. "And Andy's first."

NINETEEN

Time stops as Mom gasps. We become statues, frozen in this moment. Even Tate, who flinched at Andy's name, has gone completely still. My pulse, once thrashing, is silent.

"No," I mutter.

It's a *No* of astonishment, of anguish. It's a *No* of refusal. A *No* that means *You're wrong*.

"You're lying."

"That would be nice," Charlie scoffs. "But no. I'm not. Dad told me, 'You're old enough now that the women are more likely to feel threatened than protective. Andy'll work better.' "

Something slinks into my stomach, cold but clawing. Its nails scrape against my insides, tentative for now, but still drawing blood.

"I would have known," I say, "if my twin were a murderer."

Tate inhales sharply. "Dahlia, no. They weren't murderers. Not Charlie and Andy. They were victims of Dad. Same as those women."

I turn my head to glare at her. "I hardly think those women would see it the same way."

"We were bait," Charlie says. "So, is — Is a worm what kills a fish, because it draws it to the hook? Or is it the hook that kills it? Or the man holding the rod?" He looks up at me, eyes desperate and wide. "Which is it? Because I really don't know."

"It's the man!" Tate cries.

"It doesn't matter," I say. "Andy didn't do it. I would have known. I would have *known.*"

Mom places a shaky hand on my shoulder, but I shrug it off.

"I regret it," Charlie says, "not protecting him from it. Not fighting Dad, telling him he couldn't do to Andy what he did to me. But at the same time, I was so relieved that it wasn't me anymore. That the secret wasn't just his and mine anymore; someone else had to hold it, too."

"Oh, Charlie," Mom whimpers. "He was just a boy."

"So was I," he snaps.

Mom nods, chastised, taking a step back.

I tighten my grip on the counter, ignoring the talons in my stomach, even as they dig in deeper.

"And I hated it," Charlie continues. "I couldn't *stand* knowing what Dad was doing to him. Why do you think I left, the second I got my inheritance? I couldn't be in this house. And when Tate and I finally returned home, Andy was turning sixteen — two years older than I was when Dad said I wouldn't work anymore. Jessie Stanton had just been killed, but I figured that would be the end of it. He would have told Andy, like he told me, that it was over for him now. And I wanted to see him. Andy. I wanted to know he was okay.

"But when we got here, I knew right away I was wrong. Nothing was over. I could feel it everywhere — the oppressive control Dad had over Andy. The control I'd barely escaped. And it just . . . it triggered all the — the terror, and rage, and self-hatred I'd always tried so hard to tamp down, until I was in my room, freaking out and . . . I couldn't hide it anymore. I confessed it all to Tate."

I blink at him, his last sentence slow to sink in. Then I turn toward Tate.

"You knew."

Of course she did: *You have to tell them,*

342

she said, when I confronted Charlie with the brand. And before that, she held his panicked gaze when the police were searching his room. They're so intertwined, so fastened together within their cocoon, that there's probably nothing they don't know about each other.

But this — This is more than a secret shared between siblings; it's a secret kept from everyone. From me.

"You've known," I say, "for ten years, that Dad was the Blackburn Killer." My voice quivers. "And you didn't tell anyone? You never thought to call the police?"

Tate goes to Charlie now, sinking down beside him. As she wraps him in her arms, they lean toward each other, the sides of their foreheads touching. Tate studies the floor as she speaks.

"I wanted to tell someone."

"Then why didn't you?"

"We didn't think Dad would kill again. He'd lost all his bait."

Bait. My fist clenches at the word. A sour taste pools onto my tongue.

"What if you were wrong?" I spit out. "What if he murdered another woman? That was a chance you were willing to take?"

"He didn't, though!" Tate cries. "And we didn't know how to tell anyone without

Charlie getting in trouble. He was a teenager the last time Dad dragged him along. Just a few years away from being a legal adult. We couldn't be sure he'd be safe."

From the corner of my eye, I see Mom sag against the counter. I have no strength inside me to hold her up, keep her standing. Instead, I watch her slip down until she's kneeling on the floor, head dropping into her hands, sobs muffled by her palms.

"You could have told the police about the shed," I say. "You could have said you just found it. Left Charlie out of it altogether."

Tate shakes her head. "What if Dad admitted that Charlie and Andy were part of it?"

The thing in my stomach goes still. Its claws retract, the blood it drew going dry. Now, in place of that pain, my body burns, as if struck by lightning, my bones scorched and sizzling.

"You're wrong about Andy," I say. "He would've told me."

But even as I say it, I know it's a tattered, worn-out belief, one that hardly fits anymore. In truth, there was so much he didn't tell me: about Ruby; about why he hacked at trees, why anger brewed in him sometimes, severe as a storm; about why he felt our family was *unnatural* —

I stop right there.

344

Dread gathers inside me. One by one, my memories of Andy slot into Charlie's story.

"It's true, Dahlia," he says now. "Why else do you think he had a key to the trapdoor? Dad gave him one. Just like he gave one to me."

I shake my head, still fighting it.

"And why else would the murders have stopped after Andy was gone? Dad couldn't do it without us. He *said* that once: 'I couldn't do this without you, Charlie.' Like it was something for me to be fucking proud of. Well, apparently he couldn't do it without Andy, either."

I try to stop the thoughts flying through my mind. But it's too late. They're swarming together —

Andy insisting we needed to leave

— buzzing around each other —

Andy swinging at trees like there was something inside him he couldn't get out

— flapping their furious wings —

Andy telling Ruby, "Who knows what I'd do to a kid? Who knows what's in my blood?"

Now, Mom moans so loudly on the floor, it sounds like it's happening in my head. But as I watch her crawl closer to Charlie, chugging out sobs, I realize the moan is mine this time, gushing from between my lips.

I clamp my hand over my mouth, as if I could hold back the truth: Andy's role in Jessie Stanton's murder, in the murders of Alexis Shea and Amy Ragan before her.

I think of their Honoring dates, scrambling to do the math as my stomach curdles. Andy would have been eleven when Dad killed Alexis. Only seven with Amy. *Just a boy,* like Mom said.

But with Jessie, he was days from sixteen, tipping toward adulthood, transitioning from boy to man.

"He was so disturbed that week," I say, thinking out loud. "After Jessie Stanton, he was so on edge. He wasn't even sleeping."

Now, I focus on Charlie, aiming my words at him. "He was old enough, at that point, to really understand it. So do you think . . . do you think he threatened to tell someone? And maybe Dad —"

A sob punches out of me, sudden and searing.

"Did Dad kill Andy?" I finish. "To keep him quiet?"

"No," Mom cries. "No. No. No, no."

But then Tate hangs her head. And that's when I know. She's already come to this conclusion. For ten years, she's known what Dad was. And when she learned that Andy had been killed, she didn't cry or scream or

346

stay in bed all day. She got to work on a diorama — exactly as she did for all the other victims of the Blackburn Killer.

I swing my gaze — slowly, heavily — between her and Charlie. "All week," I say, voice low, breath shallow, "you've watched me suffer, trying to figure this out. You told me to trust the family, Charlie. To trust you. And Tate. But the whole time, the two of you knew Dad killed Andy. And you said nothing."

"No!" Mom howls. "Daniel did not kill Andy! He was sick that night. He was very ill!"

Hunched on the floor, she balls up her hands like she wants to punch the tile.

"He was sick!" she repeats. "Your father was very sick! We were up all night."

The first time she mentioned this, I felt such relief that she could prove Elijah wrong. Now, I almost pity her, how hard she's working to hold this conviction, one she should already see crumbling.

"You must have fallen asleep," I suggest.

"No." Mom stamps her denial into the air. "And even if I did, I would have woken up if he left. Or . . . or when he came back."

"Like you woke up all the other nights?" Charlie snarls. An old anger, scraped up from somewhere deep, shadows his words.

Mom gapes at him, aghast. "I . . . I didn't . . ." She closes her mouth, swallowing.

"You've always been a very deep sleeper," Tate tries gently. "It has to have been Dad. Who else would have reason to hurt Andy? Who else could be so violent?"

"I wasn't asleep!" Mom yells. "Daniel was sick!"

Still on her knees, she slouches forward, digging her head into her flattened hands like somebody deep in prayer. Or, I consider instead, like somebody begging.

"Oh Charlie, why did he . . ." she starts. Sitting up, she reaches for Charlie's foot, but his leg jerks away so suddenly her palm slaps against the tile. She doesn't seem to notice. "Why did Daniel mur-murder all those women?"

Charlie chokes out a scoff. "How the fuck should I know? You think we chatted about it?"

"Please," Mom pleads. "He didn't . . . He didn't say anything?"

In Mom's question, I hear the echo of my own — *You didn't say anything to each other?* — when I asked Charlie what he and Dad spoke about while hunting.

The beauty of nature, he answered. *Appreciating nature.*

348

Now, at the memory of that response, I tremble. My insides hum with horror.

Dad killed deer, Charlie told me, to preserve their beauty before time destroyed it. And now I see the photographs — those women who will never change, never age, will only lie broken but beautiful in their ice-blue gowns — mounted on the wall like the head of a deer.

"Why?" Mom persists. "Why would he do it, Charlie?"

When Charlie answers this time, his eyes are twin torches burning into Mom. "Fuck his reasons!" he shouts. "It's never about the killer's reasons, right? Because it can never be justified. *You* taught us that. And now you want me to rationalize a psychopath's behavior? *You* married him, Mom. Why don't *you* know?"

He pauses, features pinching together. "Why didn't you *know*?" he screams.

The question reverberates once, and then it's gone. Still, it spears us all, pinning us into place with the real questions behind it: *Why didn't you see what was happening? Why didn't you save me?*

In my head, I hear them in Andy's voice.

"I don't know," Mom whispers. "I still can't believe —"

"You never paid attention to what was

349

really going on. You focused on films and newspapers and your shrine of portraits, all to hold on to your pathetic lie about your parents. You made me say their names!" he explodes. "In all those Honorings, I had to say the names of women I'd . . . And I had to hear Dad say them too! All because, what? You think there's comfort in darkness? In other people's suffering? You spent years steeping us in murder, but you don't know the first thing about it. You have no idea how hideous it looks, how disgusting it smells. You thought Dad was okay with living in the darkness you created here — but you had it all wrong; he *was* the darkness. Why the fuck didn't you know that?"

Mom's face is slack with shame. "I don't know," she says again. "I'm so sorry."

"That's not enough," Charlie huffs. "You were the adult. You loved him, and you refused to see what he was hiding right in front of you."

Mom searches Charlie's eyes, but he refuses to look at her.

"Charlie, you . . . you have to understand." Her words break as she cries. "I had no one when I came here. I'd lost everyone who meant something to me. Couldn't even keep up with friends because of the lie I was telling."

"The lie was your choice," Charlie seethes. "You could have corrected it."

"And Daniel," Mom continues, "he wanted me. He gave me a family again. He gave me you."

As Charlie scowls, face turned from her, tears creep into his eyes.

Mom stretches toward him, even as he inches away. Tate envelops him tighter now, rocking him slightly, her chin resting on top of his head. And just like that, he goes limp in her arms, like the fire he was spewing only moments ago has been extinguished.

"But you're right," Mom whispers. "I didn't know. And I'm so sorry."

Her palm hovers above Charlie's shoulder. "I'm so sorry," she repeats. "I'm so sorry, I didn't know." She touches him, and though he flinches, he doesn't lurch away. "I'm so sorry."

She buries her head in his shoulder as Charlie stares ahead, nose wrinkled, eyes brimming. The sheen of tears looks strange on him; I've never seen him cry.

"I'm so sorry, I didn't know."

The words are stifled against Charlie's shirt, but to me, they're louder than ever.

I'm so sorry. I didn't know. I didn't know, Andy. I'm sorry.

Tate reaches across Charlie to put her

hand on Mom's arm. She grips her tight, locking Charlie between them, holding him in a cage of what she thinks is comfort. Tears spill over onto Charlie's cheeks the same second they slide onto mine. Tate looks up at me, blue eyes big and imploring, ringed with red from tears of her own. Silently, she begs me to join them on the floor, to be a part of their misery, their circle of solace — but how can I? How can I possibly hug these people, each of whom kept such horrifying secrets?

"We have to tell the police," I say. "Let them know they're right about Dad."

Tate sucks in a breath as Charlie snaps his gaze up at me.

"Dahlia, no," Tate says.

"We have to. What if they arrest someone else for the murders? Like Fritz!"

"They won't arrest Fritz," she argues. "They have nothing on him because he wasn't involved."

"So someone else then. Either way, they need to know everything Charlie told us."

Charlie's reply is stony. "You'd throw me to the wolves like that? Andy, too?"

"The police will understand. Dad forced you to do it. You were only kids."

"We were teenagers, too."

"Yeah, but —"

"Dahlia." Charlie drags his hand down his face, raking away his tears. "The islanders still want to see someone go down for the murders, and the only person left with any involvement is me. I trusted you with this, I shared it with you. And now you want to take it to Kraft, just hand him the evidence he's hunting for so he can prove that his dad was right about us all along? That the Lighthouses are monsters?"

"It's not *us*, it's Dad, it's —"

"Is that what you want for Andy?" Charlie presses. "For people to remember him like that, as someone who played a role in the Blackburn Killer's crimes?"

Beside him, Mom sobs.

"Is that what you want?" Charlie repeats.

Of course it isn't.

I'd hate for that to be my brother's story, for people to view Andy's murder as a punishment he earned. I can already hear the islanders, gleeful with what they think is justice: *Well. He helped a killer. He got what he deserved.*

My eyes drift to Mom, whose tears keep falling. Her gaze sinks to the floor, heavy with everything we've learned and lost. Among it all, I hope she recognizes this devastating truth: the roots she planted on Blackburn Island, grown from the seed of a

353

single lie, have been rotting from the start.

"Dahlia?" Tate prompts.

But I don't respond. Instead, I leave my family where they sit, huddled together, waiting for my answer. I hear them calling after me, but I don't turn back.

Upstairs, I stand at the threshold of Andy's room. I hesitate for only a moment before walking toward his beanbag chair. When I flop onto it, the dust of our years apart billows around me, clouding a room, a boy, I once saw so clearly.

My whole life, I trusted him, trusted only him, and I thought he trusted me, too — enough to confide in me when someone was hurting him, when something made him feel *cut up inside,* like Charlie described.

And Charlie — if he'd just told someone, if he'd exposed Dad for the killer he was, then it never would have happened to Andy, who spent his too-brief life flashing in and out of frustration, digging his ax into trees as if, in wounding something else, he'd become woundless himself.

"Goddamnit, Charlie."

I say it out loud, even though he's too far to hear me, enshrouded by people who will ignore his sins to soothe his suffering. But as the words come out, I know they're the wrong ones. I look at Andy's bed, empty for

354

a decade now. For so long, I made myself believe he'd return to this place, or at least to me, because the alternative was too agonizing to consider. But now, glancing at floorboards that will never again creak beneath his feet, I know: it isn't Charlie I'm furious with. What Dad did — it would fuck with anyone's mind, their sense of right and wrong. In truth, I'm furious with myself. For never noticing. For not being someone Andy thought he could tell. For refusing to go all those times he said we should leave. For keeping him here, stuck in the grip of a killer, until he was killed too.

Waves of sobs crash through me, torturous and tidal.

I assumed the chest beneath the shed was split by Andy's ax, that he found the key somehow, went down to that room, but then was killed before he could show me what he'd uncovered. I assumed it because I couldn't fathom a world in which he would choose to carry such crushing secrets alone. But I didn't know him. Not his thoughts. Not his pain. Not the tenderest parts of his heart. All these years, I've been searching for, yearning for, a stranger.

Even worse: he harbored something so dark inside him, something no child should ever be near, let alone have to know.

But it's not true, is it, that he didn't try to tell me? He said our family was *unnatural,* too decked out in death — only I never wanted to listen. I wanted only to exist in the bubble of us.

Charlie, Tate, Mom — they're all downstairs, arms tangled up in one another, the space between them squeezed to almost nothing. *It's okay,* I imagine Tate saying, *we're here, Charlie, we're here.*

And I'm in a dead boy's room, the cool air my only company. I've got no one to hold me but myself.

TWENTY

The Lighthouse Memorial Museum is moving ahead as planned.

Two rooms down, Charlie tells Tate to hurry up.

"I'm putting the finishing touches on everything right now," he says. "So either you're done or it doesn't get displayed."

"I'm going as fast as I can. I lost a lot of time yesterday."

"Oh! I'm sorry if my emotional breakdown came at an inconvenient time for you. Next time, I'll try to schedule it better."

I can sense the smirk in his voice. How quickly he's returned to his usual self: sarcastic, spitting out dark humor. It doesn't even surprise me to hear that he's joking. He's the same person who chuckled through Honorings, using fake, high-pitched voices as he chanted the prayer. Only when Mom shot him a glance would he undo his smile, pretend to be reverential.

But it hits me now, like a fist to my diaphragm, that it must be how he copes. Andy hacked at trees; Charlie twists things into jokes. It steals my breath to think of it — that everything I know of Charlie might only be armor. Even his theatrics, his acting. And after what he's been through, why wouldn't he want to slip into someone else?

Still, in the wake of everything he unleashed yesterday, it seems obscene, going on as planned, opening our house to hordes of strangers.

I suppose, though, that it makes more sense — why he wants this so badly, why he needs to convince people that the Lighthouses aren't evil. After everything Dad made him do, Charlie probably believes the islanders are right about him, and he's desperate to live as if they're wrong.

"Fine, I'm done," Tate says from down the hall. "You happy?"

"Thrilled," Charlie deadpans, and I hear the two of them scurry down the stairs.

I'm lying on Andy's bed, a half-empty Tupperware of cookies beside me. In the middle of the night, I awoke on his beanbag chair, back stiff, legs sore, and a deep, throbbing hunger pushed me toward the kitchen. There, I grabbed Mom's cookies, ate two on the way back up, and walked the dark hallway back to Andy's room. Then I dove onto his bed, where I fell asleep with short-bread in my hand.

His mattress isn't comfortable. I'd forgotten about that — how he felt most at ease on solid, unyielding surfaces, so much so that he sometimes pulled his blankets off the bed and slept on the floor. Now I wonder if he was punishing himself, if he believed he didn't deserve any comfort.

My phone chimes with a text from Greta: I'm on the island. Call me when you can.

I bolt upright. Why is she here?

I'm not ready to talk to her, much less see her — not when I still don't know what I'll do about Dad. What if she's getting closer to the truth, realizing that there's something to Elijah's theory after all? I squeeze my temples, rocking on the bed. I don't want to keep Dad's secret, keep the families of his victims without closure, but maybe even more than that, I don't want Andy's murder to be dismissed as retribution.

And what if we're wrong? What if Dad really didn't kill him, just like Mom swore?

The thought worms inside me, tunneling a tiny space for hope. Because it's excruciating enough, knowing that Dad died without ever being punished for the women he murdered; it's too much to think he got away with killing Andy, too.

Mom was adamant last night about Dad's illness, screaming and howling her husband's innocence. In the moment, I wrote it off as shock, an inability to process the truth of who he was. But I do remember how green Dad looked the night of our birthday, how gray the next morning. And if Mom is right that it wasn't him, then that means Andy's killer remains at large.

Once the police learn about Dad, I imagine they'll draw the same conclusions we have, figure Andy's murderer is already dead. But if that person is still out there, I can't take the risk of confirming Elijah's suspicions. At least not yet. Not until I'm certain someone else didn't do it.

But who's left on my list of suspects? Edmond doesn't make sense anymore. If he wasn't the Blackburn Killer, then he'd have no reason to murder Andy. Same with Fritz — though, I realize with a wince, Fritz isn't innocent; he knew what Dad kept beneath the shed, and for some reason, he never said a word.

Why would he protect him like that? Why would he work so hard to save birds with broken wings, but wouldn't even try to save the island's women?

And then there's Lyle. Is it enough of a

motive, wanting to hurt the boy who hurt his granddaughter? I'm not so sure anymore. But now I think of Dad's victims, all those women who were strangers to him until he took their lives, and I remember that people have killed for far less than revenge.

I look at Greta's text. If I see her, she'll know something's changed for me. All she'll have to do is mention the Blackburn Killer, and my turbulent emotions, so close to the surface, will seep through my skin, my family's secrets puddling all around me.

Turning off my phone, I watch the screen until it blackens, a dark mirror reflecting my swollen eyes, tortured expression.

That settles it then. I won't face Greta until I have more answers.

But first: I have to face Charlie's museum.

I can hear him in the foyer, directing Tate. "No, on the credenza," he says. "I reserved it for this."

I don't want to go down there. I don't want to see the guts of our childhood laid out like organs in an autopsy. I don't want to know what Tate's diorama looks like, now that it's done. I want only, for now, to feel the stiff board of Andy's bed against my back — my own punishment, for not being who he needed me to be.

I can't stay here, though. There's been no talk of a funeral for Andy, so whatever Charlie has planned as the "Memorial" aspect of the LMM might be the only chance I have to say goodbye. And Andy deserves that; he deserves to have me finally let him go, the way I couldn't when he was here, the way I refused to when he wasn't.

I roll off his bed, wipe crumbs off my shirt, and head to my room to get dressed. I settle for the closest thing to funeral attire: black jeans and a gray sweater. When I open a drawer for socks, I find Ruby's embroidery, tucked to the side where I left it days ago. I pick it up, touching the delicate thread, tracing the flowers that encircle her handstitched confession to Andy.

Ruby's right; it should be in the memorial. If nothing else, it's proof that my brother was loved.

In the end, I'm glad he had that — someone who loved him, someone who wasn't tangled up in the brambles of our family, someone he knew would never hurt him. Most of all, I'm glad he had an escape from Dad, someone to laugh with as they wrote their notes beneath the moon.

I take the embroidery downstairs, but I don't make it past the foyer or have a chance to glance at the tables before Tate's in my way. She's stiff as a pillar, facing the credenza. When I follow her gaze, my chest tightens.

There he is: my twin, dead in the hole of the diorama. I take in the clothes she dressed him in — a tiny plaid shirt, little khaki pants, an outfit that could have been pulled and shrunk from his own dresser. Tears cling to my eyelashes. The Andy doll is facedown inside the grave, a miniature ax tossed in next to him, and there's a bright red wound oozing through the hair that Tate has glued to the back of his head. A sliver of porcelain is visible between the bloody strands, and my stomach sinks as I realize what it's meant to represent: the skull split open; the aftermath of the ax.

"Are you okay?" Tate murmurs.

I look at her. Her eyes are so blue they seem unnatural.

"How can you do these?" I ask. "Not just Andy, but — god, every doll you make is another person Dad killed. How can you bear it?"

Tate lowers her head. "It's the only way I *can* bear it," she says faintly, and it's a while before she continues. "It's like, when I'm making a diorama, I'm bringing the victim back, in some small way at least. And the whole time, I'm refusing to ignore how they died. Or who killed them."

She runs a finger along the credenza, in front of Andy's crime scene. "You said last night that I never told anyone. And on the one hand, you're right. But maybe my dioramas *were* my way of telling. Not who did it, of course. But the horror of it. The brutality." She throws up her hands. "The inhumanness."

"Instagram posts are hardly confessions," I say.

She snaps her head my way, looking at me like I'm so naïve. "That's exactly what they are. People serving up their souls for public consumption. And *my* soul" — she rips her eyes from mine, shoving them onto the diorama — "is full of dead bodies."

I startle at the comment — how gruesome it is; how it shivers with suppressed rage.

"So I kept doing it," she adds. "Extra posts, series like BehindTheCrimeScenes, just so I could keep showing more of it. My sketches. The process. And I did it because it was never enough. A finished diorama was never enough for me to convey how" — her voice grows pinched, as if her throat is shrinking — "how repulsive, excruciating, how fucking unbearable it is, what Dad did."

She shakes her head, squinting at Andy in the hole she dug for him. "But I don't know.

364

Now I'm thinking maybe . . . Maybe I won't put this one on Instagram."

I hesitate in surprise. "Why not?"

"Because you were right, he's our brother, he —" She clamps her lips together before she continues. "I want people to know him, to remember him. But why should they remember him in his worst moment, at the end?"

In the diorama, Andy's hand clings to the soil, almost like he's trying to push himself up. I tear my eyes away to watch Tate's face, how rapidly she's blinking.

"Because isn't that what I've really done with the Blackburn women? I thought I was memorializing them. I worked so hard to get every detail right — even begging Charlie, torturing him really, to tell me what he remembered of each scene — all so it could seem as real as possible. So people would remember that the women themselves were real. Human. More than just a murder. Only now, I don't know anymore. How are people supposed to see them as more than the murder when the murder is all they can see?" A tear slides down her cheek. "I guess it was all I could see."

She reaches toward the diorama, fingers hovering above Andy's body before she pulls her hand back.

"This was always how I coped with what Dad did. But I think it just kept me stuck in it. Like Charlie is. Yesterday was only the second time I've heard that story in its entirety, but he told it the exact same way I remember him telling it on your sixteenth birthday. With the same gestures, same big pauses. Almost like it was scripted that way. Like stage directions in a play."

"You're saying it seemed rehearsed? You think he's lying?"

"No," Tate is quick to reply. "I just mean, he's stuck in it. He relives it all the time. But — how could he have ever moved on from it? It's not like he can" — she raises one shoulder in a feeble shrug — "get help. Or go to therapy or anything."

"Why not?"

"Because." She scrunches her brow, like the answer is obvious. "He wouldn't be able to tell anyone why he's so messed up."

"He wouldn't have to explain it all," I suggest. "He could just tell them he was" — I search for an appropriate word — "abused."

As I say it, I know it's the correct term for what our father did to our brothers. I think of Charlie, crouched on the kitchen floor, tears slipping down his cheeks — and how I didn't go to him. Mom and Tate surrounded him with their arms, building him a safe place to fall apart, and what did I do? I ran away. I refused him even the tiniest acknowledgment of his trauma.

"No," Tate says. "It's too risky. Because what if —"

She stops, turning to the right at the sound of footsteps, Charlie coming toward us from the back hallway. He holds what looks like a checklist, focusing on the paper as he steps into the foyer. Glancing up at me, he stiffens.

"Hi," I say.

"Hey, Dolls," Charlie says, slow and timid. At first, he seems afraid I'll lash out at him. Then his face changes, as easily as sliding on a mask. His features harden, and he holds up his list. "Glad to see the two of you enjoying some sisterly bonding time. Meanwhile, I'm actually working — ever heard of it?"

His hair is slicked back, recently showered, and as he glares at us, it's as if he's scrubbed away his vulnerability, watched it swirl down the drain like dirt.

He's so good at pretending. It makes my skin prickle, makes me attempt a final appeal to call off the museum.

"This doesn't feel right, Charlie. After what you told us last night, how can we just —"

He whips a hand into the air. "To reverse course now," he says, "when everyone knows the LMM is happening, would only make us look suspicious."

"We *are* suspicious! Dad was a serial killer!"

"If this is your way of telling me you're going to the police, you might as well spit it out."

"I'm not," I admit. And at the relief that flashes across his face, I add, "Not right now, anyway. Not yet."

"Not yet," Charlie repeats, an edge to his voice. "Well, good thing, Dolls. Because we're minutes away from opening the house." He pauses. "Literally and figuratively."

He turns around, heading back the way he came. Tate sighs as he goes, dropping her eyes to my hand.

"What's that?" she asks, pointing at Ruby's embroidery, its words pressed to my thigh.

I try to exhale my frustration, forcing out a breath that's hot and long. "Just something for the museum," I say.

She tilts her head. "You're displaying something? I'm surprised you even came down for this. Especially given . . ." She waves a hand, referencing the spot where

Charlie just stood.

I stare at that spot as I answer. "I'm trying to say goodbye to Andy."

But those words together — *Andy; goodbye* — sound like a foreign language.

"So you're okay with the Honoring then?" she asks.

"What Honoring?"

"Oh. Just — it's Charlie's 'grand finale.' We're doing a public Honoring for Andy. As a demonstration, kind of?"

I gape at her. Just the thought of that — something so personal becoming so performative — makes me sputter out an indignant chuckle. "Wow. Charlie's thought of everything, huh?"

Tate crosses her arms, immediately protective. "Well, what did you think he meant by Lighthouse *Memorial* Museum?"

I shake my head. "I don't know. You're right. With our family, what else would it be?" I look at the wooden hoop dangling from my hand. I tap it against my side like a silent tambourine. "I need to find a place for this."

Tate nods, gaze still sharp. "I should go help Charlie."

I take a final glance at the diorama — the last I'll see of it before others see it, too — and as Tate walks away, a shudder of anger, or maybe just grief, passes through me. The Andy doll wears little white sneakers, the heels of which stick out from the dirt like something trying to grow.

Swallowing down the lump in my throat, I do a sweep of the rest of the foyer. Charlie's leaned our stolen doors against the walls, using them as display areas for the old watercolors and sketches from Tate's bedroom. *Behind Closed Doors,* he's labeled the series. *See what artist Tate Lighthouse created before anyone was watching.*

On the table closest to me, a card reads, *Murder documentaries, an essential element of Lorraine Lighthouse's homeschool curriculum.* Behind the card is a stack of DVDs, some whose spines are familiar to me, others I barely remember. On another card, on a different table, the typewritten font reads, *Portrait of Elizabeth Short, aka the Black Dahlia, namesake of Dahlia Lighthouse.* Tate rendered the painting in black and white from the famous photo of Elizabeth: dark curls, dark brows, dark lips. As a kid, I used to stare at it until my eyes lost focus and the painting became a Rorschach test, all those black and white blobs swimming around until they rearranged to show me myself.

He's displayed the other namesake paintings, too: Sharon in muted shades of gold; Charles in his baby chair, reaching for the only birthday cake he ever lived to see; Andrew in a suit and beard, frowning into the distance. "What a dweeb," Andy once said about the Borden painting, and that single memory fills me with a longing so strong it hurts to breathe.

As I head into the living room, I pass a table with Dad's hunting rifles, and nausea threatens to bowl me over. I have to distract myself with other exhibits until the feeling subsides.

For a while, I stand before the stubs of Honoring candles, used on each of our birthdays. Mom saved them, apparently, writing our name and age in black marker along the wax. Charlie has displayed them in chronological order, separate rows for each of our eighteen years. My cheek twitches at Andy's — shorter than the rest, stopping two candles too soon.

There are stacks of newspapers, fanned out neatly along the coffee table in the living room, and there are *Lighthouse children murder reports, as assigned by Lorraine Lighthouse,* on each of the end tables. Charlie has also displayed legal pads and pens, as if someone might be moved to write a report of their own. I recognize Andy's sharp, angular handwriting on one of the piles of stapled papers, and I zip my eyes away.

Voices burble in from outside. The windows frame a view of people gathered on the lawn, and on the perimeter of the crowd, there's a group of middle-aged women with their arms crossed, bouncing on their feet to stay warm.

Soon, they'll be in our house.

I find an empty spot beside a heap of old Honoring calendars and place Ruby's embroidery there. Using one of Charlie's pads and pens, I write, *A sixteenth birthday gift from Ruby Decker to Andy Lighthouse.* It looks amateur compared to the typewritten labels. I glance at my hand, Charlie's Sharpie mark still visible, despite how hard I've tried to wash it off. On my makeshift label, I add a line, a space, and a dot beneath the words, mimicking that sideways, lowercase *i* of Charlie's "trademark flair."

"What did you just do?"

When I turn around, Charlie's in the doorway, glowering at the embroidery from across the room. Walking toward it, he nudges me aside. Then he picks up the card I've hastily written and reads.

"What the fuck is this?" he finally says.

It's a stronger reaction than I expected, even though I knew he'd be annoyed with me for disrupting his aesthetic. Still, I explain Ruby's embroidery: how she loved Andy and he wouldn't let her; how he refused this present the last night anyone saw him; how, when she spoke of the future she wanted for them — marriage, kids — he grew angry, grew cruel.

"He said to her," I tell Charlie, " 'Who knows what I'd do to a kid? Who knows what's in my blood?' I didn't know what that meant when she first told me, but now —" I blink back tears. "He must have been thinking about Dad. Worrying that Dad's evil was something he inherited, and might inflict on someone else."

I'm surprised by Charlie's face as I speak; his mouth is ajar, his brows are furrowed, and his expression is filled with something I can't name — disgust, I think; maybe distress. When I finish, he squeezes his eyes shut, cheeks bunching with the effort, and pinches the bridge of his nose.

"What's wrong?" I ask.

Moments pass, swollen with his silence. Outside, there's a burst of laughter, the shriek of a child, a woman saying, "Soon, I think." That seems to jolt him back to life. He releases his nose, puts the card onto the table, and lets out a sigh.

"Nothing," he says.

But as a tear creeps out of the corner of his eye, one he slaps away with a furious hand, it's clear that it's something. He has that look again, that same anxiety I saw when the police searched his room.

Before I can push the issue, Tate and Mom appear in the living room. Tate has an arm around Mom's shoulder, steering her forward like she needs help just to walk, and it strikes me as strange, how quickly Tate seems to have forgiven Mom's lie. How quickly she's managed to trust her again.

I look at Charlie. He's chewing his lip, gaze lost out the window as he stares at the crowd on the lawn.

"Well," he says after a moment. "It's time, isn't it? Let's give the people what they want."

TWENTY-ONE

Thirty minutes in, I'm perched on the bottom of the stairs, watching people drift in and out. Some cock their heads to consider me, as if I'm another exhibit, while others ignore me, talking over my head about the pictures of Mom's parents.

"Get this: she tells people they were murdered," one woman says to her friend, "but actually, they died of leukemia."

I don't correct them about the type of cancer.

"That's so creepy," the friend replies.

For a while, I don't recognize anyone. There are more college students than I would have expected — mostly women — with their ponytails and timid giggles and school sweatshirts. They flock to the diorama.

My chin is propped on the heel of my hand, eyes willfully glazing over, when I hear a familiar voice.

"Hey."

I stare up at Greta — here, in my house, despite my turned-off phone, my attempt to keep her away. Her mouth is tilted into the suggestion of a smile, but her face is somber, brows knitted together.

"What are you doing here?" I ask.

She sits beside me on the stair, then folds me into a hug. My chin falls onto her shoulder, the rest of me stiff. We've never done this before, lingered in each other's arms. I want it to feel safe, feel warm, but she carries the November cold on her clothes.

"Your phone goes straight to voice mail," she says when she pulls away.

Greta gestures to the visitors milling around, some with their arms tucked tight to their sides, like they're afraid to even brush against a wall, get the dust of Murder Mansion on their skin.

"This is pretty crazy," she says. Her eyes rove the exhibits until they skid to a stop on one of the paintings. "Whoa. Is that Kitty Genovese?"

"Yeah."

"Oh my god, I love that case. Did you know that Winston Moseley, the guy who murdered her, was married with three kids? He told police he just got up in the middle

376

of the night, left his sleeping wife in bed, and drove around trying to find a woman to kill. How fucked up is that?"

I focus on the floor so my thoughts can't flick to Dad. Still, my breath is shallow. All my muscles are clenched.

"Oh! There's Linda Cook. I'm obsessed with the name for that case: the Cinderella murder."

There's a hint of giddiness in her voice, and I'm grateful that, from here, she can't see Tate's diorama — only the people who hunch over it, scrutinizing every detail.

"He could be here, you know," Greta says after a while. She leans in, speaking softly toward my ear. "The Blackburn Killer."

Beneath the foyer's chandelier, her eyes seem to shimmer, same as they do when she looks at her laptop, gaze glowing from its artificial light.

"If he did kill Andy," she continues, squeezing closer, "he'd probably get off on coming to the memorial. Really, he could be anyone here."

A baby shrieks in its mother's arms.

"Well," Greta adds, "not anyone."

I slide away an inch, pivoting so I face her directly. "Greta, why did you come?"

Her forehead furrows at the bite in my voice.

"You know how I told you I wanted to try something?" she says.

I nod.

"I went to see Lyle Decker. Asked him some questions."

"What? I thought you weren't supposed to do that."

She once told me that the first rule of being a citizen detective is to avoid interfering in real life. She could research from her computer, rifle through public documents, even track down old yearbooks like she did the other day, but she couldn't speak to suspects of an open case. To do so could jeopardize the official investigation.

"I couldn't help myself," she admits, a shiver of excitement bolting through her. "He was so close, just a ferry ride away. I had to see him."

I glance at the people in the foyer, ensuring no one's close enough to hear. "And?"

"I met Ruby," she says. "She was . . . intense. Wait — she's not here, is she?" Greta surveys the crowd.

"No," I say, and I'm actually surprised not to have seen her yet. I expected Ruby to be first in line, eager to make sure I included the embroidery.

"Okay, good," Greta says. "She did *not* like me. She wouldn't leave Lyle's side, and she was, like, shooting daggers at me out of her eyes."

"That sounds right." I remember how she glared at me in the driveway, hands bunched into fists, furious that I'd told Elijah about her grandfather. I guess I don't blame her. It's a brutal thing, having someone in your family suspected of a murder.

"Anyway, I don't think Lyle did it," Greta says, and when I stiffen, she notices. She glides her gaze over my face in a way that makes me itch.

"Why not?"

"I asked about his trespassing complaint against the police chief. He said it was just because Ruby was scared, seeing a cop in their woods. She kept asking Lyle if she was in trouble, and that made him angry. And when I asked why he forbid Ruby from going near your shed, he said Fritz walked Ruby home one day after he found her inside it, reaching for pruning shears or something. Lyle was scared she'd hurt herself."

"That's not how Ruby told the story," I say. "She said Lyle found her wandering near it."

I'm not sure why I'm arguing. I already know, with gutting certainty, that it wasn't Lyle who used the shed.

Greta shrugs. "Either way. I got the feeling that Lyle was telling the truth. He didn't seem defensive about my questions. Just annoyed."

She pauses as the front door opens. An older couple walks in, hands linked.

"And for what it's worth," she says when they walk toward the living room, "it sounds like the police already asked him all this. He kept saying, 'I told this to your colleague already.'" Mischief glints in Greta's eyes. "I didn't correct his assumption."

I take in her outfit, a dark blazer over gray slacks. She looks like every detective on TV, sharply dressed in muted colors, and I wonder if she chose these clothes for that very reason.

"So," she says, almost cheerfully, "onto the next."

"The next what?"

"Suspect." Her lips twitch, nudging toward a smile. "I've been thinking of my next move, now that Lyle's tentatively off the list, and I think I should —"

"Greta, you have to stop." Panic pinches my throat, raising the pitch of my voice. Greta's half-formed smile reshapes into a frown. Still, I don't back down. "This isn't just some case, okay? It's my brother."

She watches me before responding, and I

hope she can't hear my heart drumming. How many *next moves* will she go through, crossing off suspects one by one, until all that's left is Dad?

"I know that," she says. "Of course I know that. But you asked for my help."

"That was a mistake. I mean, look what you're doing, coming to the island without asking me first —"

"Asking you? I didn't think I needed your permission."

"— talking to people when you know you're not supposed to."

"The police already questioned him. It's not a big deal."

"It is to me!"

A woman, bending toward Tate's paintings, looks my way. I lower my voice before continuing. "I want you to leave."

Hurt blares in Greta's eyes. "But . . . it's your brother's memorial. I came here for you."

"That's not why you're here."

I couldn't help myself, she said about Lyle. And I don't expect her to, if she learns the truth about the Blackburn Killer. She's been hunting him since before we met. I can't imagine our friendship would be enough to stop her from telling the police, from blasting this news to the internet. And I'm not ready, not yet, for Andy's murder to become more of a spectacle. I'm not ready for Greta to look at me, the daughter of a serial killer, and wonder what's in my blood.

As she searches my face, I'm terrified of what she sees.

"Greta, please go." My voice is small but firm. In my lap, my hands shake. I clasp them together to hold them still.

"Are you sure?" she says after a moment.

I'm not sure of anything. But I tell her yes. Then I watch her leave, exactly as I asked.

Something strange is happening with Charlie.

I expected him to be puffed up, proud of his work, parading around to prove that — though quirky — our family is nothing to be afraid of. Instead, he's slouched in a corner of the foyer. Tate keeps trying to talk to him, pull him into the center of things, but he waves her away to wilt even further. As he glances around, gaze skipping over me on the stairs, he winces like he's in pain.

I wonder if he's realizing that all this was only a Band-Aid, that changing the islanders' minds about us won't help him change the past. From what I'm hearing, it doesn't even sound like he's swayed too many islanders. "It's all so morbid," one of them mutters at the portrait of Andrew Borden. Another, near the door, says to her friend, "We should wait outside where it's less busy. I hear they're doing a ceremony at the end."

"What kind of ceremony?" her friend asks, readjusting a toddler on her hip.

"I don't know, some witchy thing."

"Oh my god, I can't wait."

As they walk out the door, someone else steps inside. I recognize the shuffling of the person's feet as they cross the threshold. Slowly, I raise my face to his, my ankle suddenly aching where he bruised it.

"Fritz," I say.

His shoulders are slumped as he shuts out the wind, and at the sound of my voice, he looks my way, then limps toward me on the stairs. I stand up, planting my feet on the bottom step to better match his height.

"Dahlia." He bows his head, his long hair curtaining his face. "I came to pay my respects."

"Your respects," I scoff.

He nods soberly. "I'm so sorry."

"For what? For grabbing me in the shed" — I scan the foyer, checking for eavesdroppers — "or for keeping my father's secret?"

His eyes widen as he stumbles back.

"You knew," I whisper. "What was down there. And you never told."

"N-no," Fritz stammers. "No, I swear, I didn't know."

"You called them trophies," I hiss.

"Hunting trophies. Hunt-hunting trophies. That's what Mr. Lighthouse told me was down there."

I give him a scornful look. "What?"

"He always said it was his trophy room. For deer! That I should stay away from it, because he knew how much I hate" — he grimaces — "I hate hunting. All those beautiful, innocent animals . . . It disgusted me, it *pained* me, the thought of them down there."

"You told me to help you get rid of the evidence," I remind him.

"Get rid of the deer," he insists. "Mr. Lighthouse's trophies. I figured, now that he was — gone, there was no need for . . ." He trails off, shaking his head. "But I couldn't do it myself. I could barely even think of them without feeling sick. How trapped they were, down in that room, frozen in the moment of their death. I told the police all this. I had no idea about any of those photographs. About what he did down there. I'm as horrified as you."

He straightens a little, as much as his bad

leg allows. "Does this," he says, tentative, "does this mean that Mr. Lighthouse was . . ."

As the question hangs, unfinished, in the air, I look around again. Charlie's no longer in the corner — I don't see him anywhere, in fact — but in the living room, a couple laughs, whispering to each other about a murder report. Everyone else seems preoccupied with the portraits, the Honoring candles, the calendars. Some of them even take pictures.

"You really had no idea?" I ask Fritz. I let my skepticism sharpen every word.

When his gaze falters, eyes stuttering away from mine, I cross my arms. "So you did know."

"No," he says quickly. "No, it's just . . . after the police interviewed me about the shed, I remembered something. About Andy."

My heart pounds once before going still.

"He came to me," Fritz continues, "a couple days before he left — before we thought he left — and he asked me what I knew about the trapdoor. I told him the truth, what I thought was the truth. Then he said he'd been down there, and it was like he was trying to get me to admit I had, too, that I knew more than I was saying. He got so upset after a while. I'd never, *never* seen him like that, not even with his ax. He said, 'You let him! You knew and you let him!' The poor boy was sobbing so hard — but I couldn't help him. I didn't know what he was saying I let Mr. Lighthouse do."

I'm stunned by the image he's conjured: Andy *sobbing so hard*. Like Charlie, I never saw him cry, a fact I'm dumbfounded to realize. His face would scrunch and redden, his fists would squeeze the handle of his ax, but I never saw tears — and it hurts so much to picture them now. Instead, I focus on unraveling the rest of Fritz's story.

Was I right, did Andy want to tell someone what Dad had done, and was he hoping Fritz would help him? And when Fritz refused, did he believe that our groundskeeper, the gentlest man we'd known, had actually been Dad's accomplice? I can't imagine how betrayed, how utterly alone, that would have made him feel. He would have believed that no one was safe — and no one could save him.

"Until the other day," Fritz says, "I hadn't thought of that moment in such a long time. But back when it happened, I did wonder, for a little bit, if there was more to that room than I knew. And I decided, ultimately, to push that concern aside. Mr. Lighthouse was always good to me. Paid me well. And" — he pats the thigh of his bad leg — "I have bills."

Shame deepens the crease in his brow. "I wish now . . . I wish so much that I'd looked into it. But it was easier, I suppose, to pretend it hadn't happened."

I'm scowling at him, appalled that money was enough for him to ignore Andy's cries. But I can't deny that his words resonate.

It was easier, I suppose, to pretend.

I think of Charlie, strutting around here somewhere, playing the part of a grieving but otherwise unburdened man.

I think of Tate, believing her art could revive a victim, make them — and herself — a little more whole.

I think of Mom, finding solace in other people's stories, slipping inside a fiction dark enough to absorb her pitch-black pain.

And me. Did I really not know? For all those years, when my neck grew sore from my endless hunching over laptop screens, did I really not think, even for a second, that Andy might be dead? Or was it easier to search instead of suffer, to obsess instead of mourn?

"Can you forgive me, Dahlia," Fritz asks now, "for not knowing the truth, even when it was right beneath me, every single day?"

387

As he waits for my reply, I look at his hands — calloused, capable of bruising me, but the same hands that have stroked the backs of caterpillars, scattered nuts for squirrels. Growing up, I knew Fritz to be a man who believed in tenderness, in beauty. Is it any wonder, then, he didn't push to know the ugliness Dad hid?

Now, he wants me to absolve him — of his ignorance, his refusal to look deeper — but how can I, when I'm guilty of the same things?

A reporter is here. She identifies herself to someone as working for the *Blackburn Gazette*. She pauses at each exhibit, taking notes, asking islanders for quotes, and I'm relieved that, so far, she's failed to notice me on the stairs.

"I think that's *real* dirt," I hear a girl say. She's squinting at Tate's diorama.

"No way," someone responds. "Do you think it's, like, from his actual grave?"

"It *has* to be, right? Tate is so meticulous. And oh my god, is it just me or does Andy seem like he'd be . . . kind of hot?"

"Tess, he has a head wound! You can't even see his face!"

"I know, exactly. It's like: whoa, mystery man."

Tess's friend laughs and the two of them take out their phones to snap some pictures. Tess poses in front of the diorama for a selfie, tucking her fist under her chin, angling her face just right. Nausea snakes through me, but I'm finding it hard to care. Not about this, not about the toddler I saw ripping up a murder report, not even about the fact that Andy's diorama will apparently make it online, whether or not Tate posts it herself. Ever since Fritz left, I've been watching the LMM play out before me like shows I'm flipping through on TV — and none of them hold my interest.

Until I see Elijah.

He's inching between the tables in the living room, frowning at each exhibit. I sit up straighter, wondering when he got here. And how could I have missed him, if he used the front door like everyone else?

The reporter latches onto him, peppering him with questions he seems reluctant to answer. As he talks to her, he keeps glancing in my direction, and I shrink toward the wall, hoping the banister is enough to conceal me. But when he excuses himself, pulling away from the reporter to head toward the foyer, I see what he's really looking at: the diorama.

Was it only yesterday that I asked him if it

389

was as accurate as the others? He said he wouldn't know until the body was in place, and now, I wonder what he makes of Tate's choices: the doll facedown, as if Andy was rolled into the hole; the wound on the back of the head, indicating that the killer struck from behind. She'd have no reason, this time, to know any details, but I wonder how close her guesses are, if Elijah will see something suspicious in them, something that keeps his eyes narrowed on us.

I try to gauge his reaction, but his face remains neutral. A minute passes, people crowding around him to view the diorama. Finally, he pulls his notebook from his pocket, writes something down, and turns away. He breezes past the sign designating the foyer and living room as the only spaces open to visitors. Then he disappears down the back hall.

Should I follow him? I don't want him to see me, to press me on questions my haunted expression will answer. *Did you ask Charlie,* I imagine him saying, *about being at the crime scene?* But it's a risk, too, letting him walk unguarded through the house, giving his theories space to fester and spread.

Moving away from the stairs, I try to force a decision, but I only make it a few feet before a conversation stops me.

"Should we go? This is kind of boring."

I jerk my head toward the voice — a man speaking to a woman, standing at the table of Honoring candles. The woman touches the last one in Andy's row, his sixteenth, the candle he lit and blew out just hours before he was killed.

I step toward them into the living room, the word *boring* lodged like a bullet in my chest. This museum is a spectacle, a diversion, but it's appalling to call it *boring* as they linger over evidence of what we've lost.

"Boring?" the woman says. "Have a little respect. Someone was murdered here, Jack."

I relax a little, even as I keep inching toward them.

"Yeah, but . . . this is just a bunch of old movies and papers. I was expecting . . ."

"What? A confession? 'Hey, we killed the kid'?"

Jack chuckles. "Something like that."

"I'm still positive it was the Blackburn Killer," the woman replies. "Anything else is too crazy. Two murderers on the same little island? No way."

And there it is: the fear I keep returning to, the knot at the center of my tangled concerns — that when the case is closed on the Blackburn Killer, it will be closed on

Andy, too.

The further I get from the moment I learned about Dad, the less vividly I see him as Andy's murderer. And maybe I'm just fooling myself; maybe I'm pretending there's a way to absolve my own guilt. Maybe I'm desperate for his killer to be someone still breathing, still capable of suffering the punishment they've earned.

All I know is I can't let Elijah prove that Dad was the Blackburn Killer, not if he could dismiss my brother as one of his victims.

I'm about to head to the back hall to find Elijah, but a hand on my arm makes me pause.

"You're a Lighthouse, right?" the reporter asks. I stare at her hand until she lets go. "Can I ask you some questions?"

Beside me, a girl in a Rhode Island sweatshirt loudly whispers to her friend. "What's he doing? He's not getting rid of it, is he? I haven't had a chance to see it yet." I try to follow her gaze, but the reporter steps even closer.

"Ms. Lighthouse," she says, "do you have any comments about your brother?"

"What's he doing?" the girl asks again.

"Ms. Lighthouse?"

Turning toward the foyer, where the girl's

attention is pointed, I see Charlie — or the back of him, at least. He's hunched over the credenza, arm moving like he's writing something down, and I notice he's put the diorama on the floor. It's in people's way now, an easy target for trampling, and I realize that the only thing worse than seeing the diorama would be seeing it destroyed. I picture a foot crushing the doll's head, Andy's skull splintering all over again, and suddenly, I want to throw myself over his fake little body, protect it like I couldn't do for him.

But the girl's question keeps my focus on Charlie. What *is* he doing?

A few people wait behind him, trying to see whatever he's placed on the credenza. In a moment, he steps back, shoves a hand through his hair, and when he spins around, his eyes look wild with hurt.

He doesn't see me watching at him — doesn't seem to see at all, really. He walks off, out of the frame of the living room doorway, and now the people approach the credenza. I hear only chatter at first, indistinct words overlapping one another, but as I separate myself from the too-close reporter, move from the living room into the foyer, I pick out threads of sentences, register a whispered "Oh my god."

I'm standing behind a couple girls whose bodies block the new display. One of them glances back at me, then grabs her friend's arm, pulling her aside to make room. I take a final step forward, fear cementing in my stomach at those girls' expressions. Whether they know who I am or not, they're expecting a reaction.

Cautiously, my gaze drifts onto the credenza, but it takes a moment for my mind to catch up with my eyes. When it does, I suck in air so sharply, it feels like I'm inhaling broken glass.

The only way out is to never come back.

The last time I saw this note, a cry clawed out of my throat, alerting the whole house that everything was different now; everything was infinitely worse. Only days ago, I asked Charlie if he knew where it was, and I accepted it as truth when he told me he didn't.

Was he lying? Or did he find it somewhere while digging for artifacts from our past?

Looking at it again, I register for the first time that it was written in pencil. Whenever I've pictured it over the years, I've always seen the words in bold, black ink, unforgettable and permanent, but here, the graphite's been smudged by someone's touch. And in front of the paper is a white card, covered in Charlie's scrawl: *Note forged by Andy Lighthouse's killer.*

Sweat beads on my forehead, my body sweltering. I don't hear voices anymore, or whispered conversations. I hear waves, I hear wind, I hear the forces of this island trying to push in.

And now I'm leaning down, squinting at the runaway note, missing for all these years.

In a second, my eyes catch on something beneath its words. I can't tell if it's been erased, or if it's just faded over time, but it's a line underscoring the sentence.

No. It isn't just a line.

It's a sideways lowercase *i.* A twin to the one in Sharpie on my hand.

In a single motion, I snatch the note and label, snapping back up. Tears warp my vision as I whip around in search of Charlie. I find him in the living room — already staring at me. I blink until my cheeks are wet, until I see him more clearly. I shake my head through the fog of my thoughts. Is this note a reproduction, one Charlie wrote, just now, with his "trademark flair"?

But no. My thumping heart goes silent. No.

I don't want to believe it, don't even want to think it, but the way he's looking at me now . . .

Did he write it back then, the night of our birthday? Did he phrase it so we'd believe that Andy ran away? Did Charlie . . .

He keeps on staring. From across the room, he will not break my gaze. His is as glassy as the eyes of Dad's deer: pained but defeated, a dark knowledge trapped in the pupils. And now, reading the question that twists across my face, Charlie hangs his head, and he nods.

TWENTY-TWO

"GET OUT!"

Everyone goes still when I scream. The only sound is a baby's wail.

My hand, closed around the note and label, shakes at my side. The papers scratch against my palm until I shove them into my pocket.

"GET OUT! Get out of here now!"

Two roomfuls of people stare at me like fish. The only one who moves is Charlie. He sinks onto the couch in the living room, arms slack at his sides.

Footsteps rush from the back hallway, marching up behind me. "What's going on?" Elijah asks, his notebook already out.

"Get out!" I yell in his face. Then I turn to the dozen visitors still gaping at me. "All of you! Leave! Get out of here! Go!"

I stomp toward the front door, yank it open to reveal more people dotting our lawn. Their heads all turn to me at once, alert and expectant.

"What is wrong with you?" I scream at them. "Get off our property! The museum is closed!" I whirl around to the people in the house. "Get the fuck out!"

For a few seconds, nothing happens. The baby keeps howling; the eyes keep watching. Finally, Elijah steps forward. "Come on, everyone," he says, voice deep with authority. "Time to go." He waves his hands, ushering bodies toward the door.

They listen to him, confused but indignant looks plastered to their faces. One by one they walk past me into the dimming light outside, shooting me glances that drip with judgment. The reporter tries to appeal to Elijah. "Press, too?" she asks. He nods and gestures for her to leave. As the last person files out, Elijah flips a page in his notepad and pulls his pen from his pocket.

"You want to tell me what that was about?" he asks me.

I glance over his shoulder, into the living room at Charlie. He's staring blankly at the wall opposite the couch, arms limp. If I hadn't just seen him nod — that ghastly, gut-wrenching nod — I would think he was catatonic.

"Dahlia?" Mom says. She and Tate stand near the back hallway, looking from me in the foyer to Charlie on the couch.

Elijah waits — and I consider it: keeping him here to witness the confession I'm about to pry from Charlie. Afterward, he could haul him away in handcuffs, throw him in jail, get him out of my sight forever. But Elijah's pen perched above his pad feels too much like the fishy eyes of all those islanders.

"Leave," I tell him.

He looks through the living room doorway at the statue of Charlie on the couch, then slings his gaze back toward me. "I think I should —"

"Get out! The fucking spectacle is over!"

He winces at my shout, but after a moment, he nods. "I'll come back soon," he says — and it's meant, I think, as a warning.

"You do that," I mumble.

As soon as he crosses the threshold, I close the door behind him.

"What's this all about?" Tate asks, and when I turn around, she's already drifting toward Charlie in the living room, the magnet of her body pulled toward the magnet of his. She hesitates, watching his vacant expression, before sitting down beside him. "Charlie?"

I make my way to the living room, too,

stopping when I'm across from him. The coffee table squats between us, covered in old newspapers. Mom steps into the room so quietly she might as well be floating.

"Dahlia, you're scaring me," she says. But I ignore her.

"You wrote Andy's note," I say to Charlie.

Tate scoffs, but I acknowledge her for only an instant before glaring at Charlie again. "You did," I say.

Finally, he shifts his gaze from the wall to me. Chin tilted up, he opens his mouth, looks for a moment like he might deny it, but then his shoulders drop, and more than anything else, he seems exhausted.

"Yes," he says.

My heart rages as Tate gasps beside him. "Why?" she asks — and I can see from the shock on her face that this is news to her; this is something Charlie never shared.

"Yes, Charlie." My voice is remarkably hard. "Why?"

A vein bulges at his temple when he clenches his jaw. "You know why," he says quietly.

"I need to hear you say it."

He exhales slowly. "I did it to cover it up."

Now my heart bangs so violently, it feels like it might break my ribs.

"Cover what up?" Tate asks, and it's

400

almost laughable, how she still doesn't get it.

Charlie's eyes go blank. "That I killed him."

"No." Mom falls into a chair at the same second Tate gasps. "No," Mom repeats. "No, no, no" — and just like that, it's last night again, our mother uttering her syllable of denial.

Something splits open inside me, darker than the chasm I've carried since we learned of Andy's death. It's a black hole yawning wide, sucking up my last, lingering traces of light.

"What do you *mean,* Charlie?" Tate cries. "Why would you — What happened?"

I lock my knees as he begins to speak. I tighten every muscle.

"That night," he says, voice already hoarse, as if he's at the end of the story instead of the start, "part of me was relieved to have finally told someone. To have told Tate. But another part felt claustrophobic, like the past was breathing down my neck. So I went outside for air. And I heard this thunking sound. It was —"

He doesn't need to say it; I know that sound so well.

"— Andy's ax. He was railing on this tree, back in the woods a bit. He was so worked up, I-I tried to talk him down." He stares up at me. "I tried to help him, Dolls. I swear. It was the first time I'd talked to him about it, openly. He knew it had happened to me, too, but we'd never spoken about it. It was too awful to acknowledge. We were both so ashamed.

"I tried to tell him, though. Tried to convince him that this would end for him soon. In a couple years, he could leave and he'd see there was life on the other side of . . . of Dad. I told him he could be anyone he wanted to be. He could go to college, go anywhere really; he could start a family that's nothing like ours. And he stopped then. He seemed to latch onto that. I thought I'd calmed him down, that he'd be all right. But then . . ."

His Adam's apple bobs. He turns his head toward Tate, whose eyes are wide with horror — but still soft somehow. Still supportive. In her chair, Mom rocks herself back and forth.

I don't move at all.

"Then what?" Tate whispers.

"He handed me his ax. And I took it. I thought it meant he was feeling better. But then he — oh, fuck —" He rakes his hand over his face, and my stomach lurches. I steel myself for the blow I know is to come.

"He told me to kill him."

"What?"

It's not the blow I expected. It's not a blow I believe in at all.

"That can't be true," I add.

Charlie shrugs one shoulder. "He did. He told me to kill him. 'Before I do more damage,' he said. And I knew that desire. Of course I did. The desire for someone to see it. To stop it. To make him . . . not a part of it anymore."

He glances at Mom, lip curled back to bare his teeth.

"But I still tried to talk him down. I told him it's Dad who does the damage, not us. But I knew that wasn't true. Even if we never touched those women, we were culpable. And he could see that I knew it. He kept begging me to kill him. Truly *begging* me. He got down on his knees. Said he couldn't live with what he'd done. He said, 'I love her, Charlie, but anyone who dares to love me will only be ruined.' And then he said I was wrong, he couldn't have a family, could never have kids like anyone else, because all he would do is fuck them up. He had no hope anymore. That's what he kept saying. That there was no hope for him."

Charlie looks at me, and I'm a deer caught

in the headlights of his eyes. "I didn't get it at the time — what had triggered him that night; I knew Dad had killed Jessie Stanton the week before, but it seemed like more than that. Something fresh. But now — what is it, Dahlia, that he said to Ruby Decker, when she told him she loved him, when she brought up a future they could have together?"

My mouth moves without speaking, lips stitching together the silence. Then I swallow, throat huge, and mumble out the words: " 'Who knows what I'd do to a kid? Who knows what's in my blood?' "

"In my blood," Charlie repeats. "Fuck. When he said 'I love her' that night, I thought he was referring to you, Dolls. That he didn't want to ruin *you* because of what he'd done. But when you told me about that embroidery thing, I realized he must have meant Ruby. He loved *Ruby.*"

My lungs betray me, admitting no air.

"And I get how that would have undone him," Charlie continues, "having to reject someone he *loved,* just to keep them safe. Of course he felt hopeless after that, like he'd always be alone. I *know* that feeling — I've never lasted more than a month in a relationship. The second they get serious, I have to get out. Even when I'm crazy about

404

them. *Especially* when I'm crazy about them. Because how could I let anyone love me? How could I inflict my true self onto someone I care about? I swear, when someone says they love me, it only makes me hate myself more. Because I don't deserve anyone's love, not after what I've done. I don't even deserve it from my sister."

He looks at Tate when he says this, not me. She shakes her head, lips parted but wordless.

Charlie drops his head to stare at his hands. Tate grabs them with her own.

"And god, this *museum*," he says. "I was standing here, Ruby's story running through my mind, and I just couldn't . . . I couldn't do it anymore. Perform. Pretend. It's exhausting, you know. I'm always so fucking tired."

He locks his eyes onto mine.

"So I put the note out. Publicly. Immediately. So I couldn't chicken out, I couldn't go back. I knew you'd see it, and you'd know, and the whole performance would be over. Because that's always been the problem. It was *my* performance, *my* insistence on ignoring the past, on keeping it quiet, that brought Andy to the point he was at that night — that dark, impossible place where he begged me to kill him. He

405

said he didn't have the guts to do it himself because he was such a coward, he'd always been a coward, 'We're such cowards, Charlie!' "

It stuns me, how clearly I hear both my brothers in the sentence. I glance at my empty, trembling hands. Andy never told me he felt like a coward, but I knew him enough to know that he fought with trees to fight his feelings. I can picture him snarling those words.

"And suddenly," Charlie continues, "I was looking right at him, but I couldn't even see him anymore. I just saw myself. The confused and terrified kid I'd spent years trying to distance myself from — through miles, through auditions, through every role I played on every fucking stage. And it was all there that night — all that rage and shame and self-loathing, just under the surface of my skin, still leaking out of me from sobbing it all to Tate. And I couldn't stand to look at him. At *me.* So I swung the ax. And I killed him."

My legs collapse under me. My knees slam against the floor, palms slapping the wood. As tears soak my face, my shoulders shake with sobs and my stomach clenches like a fist.

My brother. My twin. My beautiful, un-

406

knowable Andy.

The pain sears me inside. When I open my mouth to howl, my breath scalds my tongue.

"And I buried him," Charlie says above my sobs. Above Mom's sobs, too. Above Tate's. We are three broken women, at the mercy of a story from a broken man. He doesn't cry at all.

"And I wrote the note. And the next day, I got the hell out, and I've never come back until now."

I press my forehead to the floor. My chest convulses as I cry, my throat already raw. Behind my closed eyes, I'm seeing the boy in the credenza, the one who held my hand and shushed me in the dark; I'm seeing how his tongue touched his upper lip when he carved his name into wood, when he claimed a little something of his awful world for himself; I'm seeing him crash into his beanbag chair, seeing him stand by my bed, pulling me from a nightmare I didn't know I was in; I'm seeing him smooth down his hair, seeing it spring back up, seeing both of us laugh at his untamable parts.

I want to latch my fingers onto his. I want to tug him free of our father's grip. And I want to go back and know him — really fucking know him — and tell him that, even

407

in that knowing, I love him, I love his untamable parts.

I stay on the floor as long as I need to. A long time. A really long time. Sobs threaten to tear me apart, to crack me open like an earthquake does the ground. But my body is relentless; it keeps me together, trapping my agony inside me — a sharp, ricocheting thing.

When I finally drag my arms off the wood, lift my head to look at my family, I see that I'm the only one left crying. Mom's gaze is wet and haunted and fixed on Charlie, but her tears have paused for now. Charlie keeps his eyes on his lap, folding and unfolding his hands, glaring at his own fingers like he wishes they belonged to somebody else. Tate is watching our brother so fiercely I imagine he can feel her stare like a windburn on his cheek. Her lips are pushed to the side, like she's deciding on something, and even before she speaks, I know that what she says will make me sick.

"We'll keep it a secret," she tells him.

And there it is, a tidal wave of nausea, about to take me down. "We'll *what*?"

"He's suffered enough," she says, whipping her head toward me. "And you heard what he said: he was only giving Andy what he wanted — a way out. Right?"

She looks at Mom, who's frozen in her chair. "I . . ." Mom says, but when seconds pass and she doesn't continue, fury rockets through me, blasting through my grief.

"You can't possibly agree with her," I seethe. "He *killed* Andy. He killed your son!"

"He says . . . he says Andy wanted that," Mom murmurs.

"Andy wanted *help*! Or that's what he needed, at least. Not an ax in his fucking skull!"

"I know. I know. And that's my fault. I kept it . . ." Mom bows her head. "I kept it too dark in here to see the real darkness. I should have noticed. I should have protected you all so much better than I did." Her breath shivers as she exhales. "I'm so sorry, Charlie. I'm sorry I didn't know." She lifts her eyes to him. "I didn't protect you then, but I can protect you now. Tate's right, you've suffered enough." She clasps a hand over her mouth, triggering her tears. "My god, how you've suffered!"

Tate nods eagerly, watching Mom. Then she pivots toward me. "Please, Dahlia."

"You're crazy," I fume. "What do you think is going to happen? The police are closing in on Dad. Elijah was here today, nosing around the house, and it's only a matter of time before they find definitive proof that Dad was the Blackburn Killer. And once they do, they'll —"

"They still won't know about Charlie," Tate says. "Or Andy. And we don't have to tell them. We can play dumb, pretend we had no idea about Dad. We can let them assume it was always him, alone out there, and that he murdered Andy, too."

No. No way. Charlie took my brother from me, he *killed him,* instead of getting him help. He never spoke up, for all the years it happened to him, and that was the problem, that's what made Andy the person he became: someone without hope. And now they want me to keep quiet, too?

I'm already shaking my head as I look at Charlie, but his expression stops me. He still isn't crying, but there's anguish on his face so jagged it seems like it would cut me if I touched him. Gone is his confident swagger, his condescending smirk. All that's left is pain. And I know — despite my fury, I do understand — that it's pain that's always been there, that the swagger and smirk have been masks to protect the tortured boy beneath. I know, now, that it was like that for Andy, too, that even when he screwed up his face to hack at trees, his hardened features were just a cover for his raw and chronic suffering.

And if Andy really wanted to be gone . . .

No. I clench my jaw, rejecting the thought, pressing my teeth together as it tries to creep back.

If Andy was truly begging Charlie to end his suffering . . .

"How do I know you're telling the truth?" I sob at Charlie. "You've lied for years, and even when you confessed last night, you still held something back."

Charlie nods, glaring at the coffee table. Then he looks at me. "You're going to have to take my word for it," he says. "Is that going to be enough?"

For me, it never has been — not even with Andy, the one person in this world I told myself I trusted. I never took him at his word when he said there was something wrong in our house. And look how that turned out. I made him my entire world, and I still didn't know enough about him to save him; I still didn't trust it was true when he told me we needed to leave.

And now here's Charlie, asking me to believe him, to trust that the gaping hurt in his eyes is a symptom of truth-telling.

But it could all be an act. Another role he's learned to play.

"Please, Dahlia?" Tate says again — only this time, it's a question instead of a statement, a desperate plea. When I look at her, I see it all over her face: the fierce and painful love she has for Charlie, a love that's us-against-the-world even though he's made this world so hard.

My sobs slow as I consider her. How much did Tate have to bleed for her dioramas, knowing that her brother had been a part of their gruesome story, knowing that she could make the story smaller, make it bite-size, but she could not make it gone? How much bitterness has Tate swallowed down over the years, just to keep the sweetness of her relationship with Charlie?

I think of my own coping mechanisms — my incessant searching, my conviction that my twin and I knew each other's minds — and now, taking in my sister's tear-streaked face, it's like I'm seeing her for the first time. We're so similar, it turns out: loving someone who's shattered, holding them so tightly, as if our arms could keep them whole. And I know, I *know,* that if the roles were reversed, if Andy had been the one to kill Charlie, if it had been *his* hands on the ax, *his* swings that ended my other brother's life, I wouldn't have told a soul. It wouldn't have been right, maybe — but it would have been love.

Everyone's waiting for me to answer.

Mom's fingers push against her lips, eyes set on mine. Tate leans forward, begging me without any words. And Charlie — I try to read his face: how his cheeks seem hollowed out; how his jaw juts back and forth. I could choose to see it as something he's rehearsed, an expression he's crafted to appear vulnerable, ashamed, tortured by years of trauma. Or I could choose to see it as truth. I could choose to believe my brother — the only one I have left.

"I'm sorry, Dahlia," he says, and his voice is so small, cowering at the back of his throat. "I'm sorry to all of you. Mom, Tate. And fuck, Andy, I —" The sentence cuts off, snipped like a string, and he shakes his head, leaving it dangling.

"But Dahlia," he continues, "I know what I took from you. I know your loss is different. And I'm always sorry. I'm always so fucking disgusted."

I picture what could happen next: Elijah coming back, hauling Charlie off to a sealed-up room, just like the one beneath the shed. Could I really do that, send him back there, even if the punishment would fit the crime? Is that what I want for my brother — to relive the worst of his life, to be stuck in a cell with the ghost of our father, to grip the bars and forever feel the handle of the ax?

Who would that benefit? Who would that save?

"He wanted to die?" I ask Charlie. "You swear to me — no more lies, no more confessions after this: Andy begged you to kill him?"

It won't be enough to make it okay. But I need to be sure.

Charlie's head sinks toward his chest. Moments pass, the room strangled of its air. Then, blinking out a tear that races down his face, he nods.

"And you didn't *intend* to do it?" I press. "You didn't kill him because . . . because he wanted to tell someone about Dad, and you wanted to keep your involvement a secret?"

He snaps his head up. "I wouldn't have done that. I didn't even *see* Andy anymore. I only saw myself. And I wanted to . . . I wanted to kill that part of myself. The crying, begging, hopeless part. But not Andy. I never wanted to hurt him."

"But you did," I say. "You hurt him instead of helping him."

He looks like I've hit him, eyes round and sad like a little boy's. Still, he nods again. "I know," he says.

I nod, too.

I couldn't save Andy. I didn't see his

whacks against trees the way I should have: as a cry for help, as proof that he needed more than I alone could give him. But as I stare at Charlie, at all the pain kept caged inside him, I see that I have the chance to save someone else.

Finally, belief sinks into me, spreading across my bones. I marvel at the weight of it: heavier and lighter than I thought it would be.

And though it hurts like hell to say it, the words like barbed wire on my tongue, I force them out: "I won't tell."

Tate and Mom exhale in relief, but I thrust a hand into the air. "On one condition."

Tate narrows her eyes. "What condition?"

"Charlie needs help," I say. "Look at him."

His expression hasn't softened — no sagging of his features that would mean he's letting go. It's all inside him still: shame, self-loathing, immeasurable misery. He's taut with it right now, limbs tense, face almost gnarled.

"It isn't over for him," I say, "just because he told us what happened. He'll still be performing, out in the world, with everyone else, and it will continue to devour him. And then who knows what he'll do — kill someone else, maybe?"

415

"I'd never," Charlie insists. "I never wanted to hurt Andy, I swear. I don't want to hurt *anyone,* not ever again."

"Not on purpose," I say. "But you kept everything inside you, all bottled up, for so long. It's no wonder it exploded out of you like that. And now who knows what could happen the next time someone triggers you, like Andy did that night."

"So . . ." Tate draws out the syllable. "What are you suggesting?"

I wipe a hand across my cheek, feel the tears that spill, even as I speak. "Actually, you suggested it. Therapy."

"You told her I should go to therapy?" Charlie asks Tate.

"No! I told her" — she glares at me — "it's *not an option.*"

"It's going to have to be. He needs to see a therapist. And not just him! We all do! We —"

I stop, squeezing my eyes shut, trying to dam up my tears. I wait until I'm no longer crying, and then I open my eyes to begin again.

"We've been so isolated, all our lives. Everyone thinks they know us, but *nobody* does. Tate, you said yourself, it's hard for you to make friends. And it is for me, too! But even worse than that" — I think of

416

Greta, the hurt warping her face as I told her to go — "I've pushed away the only one I have. And I don't think that's normal. We're not normal."

"I'm sorry," Mom murmurs. "I did that to you all, I'm so sorry."

"See?" I say. "This is what I mean. Yeah, Mom, you fucked up. Actually, 'fucked up' doesn't begin to cover it. But what is your plan to move on from that? Are you going to apologize the rest of your life? I don't want that for you. And Tate, I want you to have friends, not just followers. We need people in our lives. Not just gossipers. Not just ghosts."

I look out toward the foyer, at the shrine of Mom's parents hanging above the stairs. It strikes me now: How different, really, are those picture frames from my laptop screen? For years, she and I have kept them pinned in place, the people we've lost, but we've really only pinned ourselves.

"We've all done things we can't take back," I say. "And I don't know how to keep those things from eating us alive. We need help. Outside help. Andy never had that, and then he —" I fight back a sob. "Charlie needs help, Tate. More than any of us can give him."

"But he can't tell the therapist what happened to him," Tate argues. "He'll go to prison if he does."

"I'm not saying he has to tell them. But he needs to learn how to deal with his emotions. All the performing, the pretending — that's what Dad conditioned him to do. And look what it's done to him. He still keeps everything inside, and it's nearly killing him. Even today — you saw what he was like during the museum. He seemed like he was in physical pain."

Tate squints, still skeptical. Mom opens her mouth, closes it again, while Charlie stares at me.

"Either you get help," I say, speaking only to him, "or I go to the police and tell them everything. That's my condition. That's the only way I can live with this. The only way I *will* live with this. You need to get yourself the help you didn't get for Andy."

For a while, he only looks at me, eyes tracing patterns across my face. I expect him to break our gaze, to turn toward Tate, see what she thinks he should do. But his focus remains on me. I watch his stare darken, his brows draw together. And now I see the Charlie I've always known: the guarded one, the one with all the masks.

Before I know what I'm doing, I stand up, lean across the table between us, and place my palm against the side of his face. At first, it feels hard beneath my fingers, as if I'm touching only bone — but then his breath hitches and he lifts his hand, cradling mine as I cup his cheek. For a few moments, we hold each other like that, his skin foreign to me, but familiar, too.

"Dolls," he whispers, so tenderly it makes my throat swell.

"Will you do it?" I ask him. "Will you let someone help you?"

He sighs deeply and it somehow changes his eyes. They brighten a little — just a little — like a night sky inching toward dawn. Then, still pressing my hand to his face, my brother sighs again and nods against my palm.

TWENTY-THREE

The doorbell rings early the next morning, when we're all still bleary, eating cookies in the kitchen. Charlie startles at the sound, jumpier than the rest of us, but Tate strokes his back as Mom leaves to answer the door.

When she returns, she's trailed by Elijah.

"I have an update," he says, "regarding the investigation."

I force myself not to look at Charlie.

"But first," Elijah adds, "I understand you found the runaway note."

My heart gives a panicked kick. "Who told you that?" I manage.

His gaze, falling on me, feels like a spotlight. "A reporter from the *Blackburn Gazette* saw you grab something in the foyer, right before you started yelling. I asked around, and more than one person claims to have seen the note." He waits a beat. "Anyone care to explain?"

"I found it," Charlie says, shrugging as he

420

stands from his stool. It only takes him a second to transform for this performance, stretching from slumped to straight. But I recognize the effort it's taking. His lines are clunky on his tongue. "Yesterday morning. I was doing one last sweep for artifacts. And I came across it, in my parents' closet. Mixed up with a bunch of my dad's things."

Elijah's eyes spark at that.

"We searched this house," he says. "Why didn't we find it in your dad's things?"

When Charlie hesitates, I'm surprised to find myself answering for him, my voice sounding steadier than I feel. "You told me the other day that the note wasn't part of your search. You said it would be like finding a needle in a haystack."

Elijah watches me so intensely I wonder if he can see my pulse, throbbing in my neck. "I did say that, didn't I?"

"And Dahlia freaked out," Charlie says, relaxing into his role, "when she saw I'd decided to display it." He affects a derisive chuckle, one that scuffs a bit too hard. "She's like that. *So* dramatic. Telling me what a *spectacle* I was making it."

Elijah's focus remains on me. "Is that right?" he asks. My blood pumps faster, and when I only nod, he continues. "And where is the note now?"

I run a hand over my back pocket. I'm still in yesterday's jeans, the ones I shoved the note into, needing it gone, out of sight, away.

"Right here," I say. I pull it out and extend it toward Elijah, along with Charlie's label. "I wasn't trying to hide it from you. It was just — an emotional night for us, and I forgot about it."

Reaching into his own pocket, Elijah removes a plastic bag. He holds it open so I can drop the paper into it. I hesitate when I see the mark that revealed it all, Charlie's "trademark flair," but I bank on it meaning nothing to Elijah, who never saw Charlie's first draft of artifact cards. I let go of the note, and he tucks the bag inside his coat.

"Will you be able to tell who wrote it?" Tate asks. "And know who killed our brother?"

Her voice is shaky with unease, but from the way Elijah responds, it seems he interprets it as a timid sort of hope.

"To be honest, that's doubtful," he says, "considering the fact that we're talking about a possible forgery. But we should be able to determine, at least, whether or not Andy wrote it."

"What was your update?" Mom asks. She folds her arms across her sweatshirt, trying

422

to reposition her anxiety as impatience.

Elijah clears his throat, shifts his feet — preparing for something. "We recovered a partial fingerprint from one of the photographs beneath the shed. It appears whoever originally handled them was very careful." His eyes sweep across us all. "But not careful enough. The print is a match for Daniel."

My stunned silence is genuine. Even now, I haven't gotten used to it, the fact that Dad was a killer. I'm shocked to hear Elijah say it, shocked that he figured it out so fast when I've lived for twenty-six years, never seeing the truth.

"What does that — What does that mean?" Mom asks.

"It means," Elijah says, "that later today, we're going to announce to the press that Daniel Lighthouse was the Blackburn Killer."

Mom's moans come quickly, the same horrified sounds she's been making for days.

Unlike Charlie, who gives a scoff of anger, and Tate, who gasps like she's gulping for breath, I don't think Mom is acting. Tears wet her cheeks, her hand trembles against her mouth, and I see her still trying to process it all, still trying to detach her love from a man who never deserved it.

"Are . . . are you sure?" Tate asks. "How can you even tell with a print so old?"

"Actually, it's fairly new. Our best guess is that it's only a couple weeks old."

"A couple weeks!" Mom cries. "But the murders stopped years ago!"

"Be that as it may," Elijah replies, "it seems that Daniel still visited that room." He hesitates, as if reluctant to continue. "Likely as a way to relive his kills."

My body floods with cold. Mom yelps out another cry.

Squinting at Elijah, Charlie takes a step toward him. "How do we know you didn't plant that print on the photo? For days now, our father's been a sitting duck in the morgue."

I stare at my brother. His bravado no longer sounds forced; his performance of outrage, disbelief, is wholly convincing. It frightens me a little, how well he's committing to the fiction.

Ignoring the accusation, Elijah slides his attention onto me. "I understand this is devastating news," he says, and I'm not sure what he sees on my face, but as he takes me in, concern softens his expression. His eyes become gentle with empathy, something his father never offered.

"I have some more questions for all of

you," he continues. "But first, I want to give you the opportunity to tell me . . . whatever you might want to tell me."

"Like what?" Tate asks, her face pale.

"Anything you might have seen. Anything you might know. Information that could add to the evidence we have against your father. If you do know something, it would be in your best interest to tell me now."

Again, his gaze touches mine.

Do I want to tell him? There's still time. I could go back on my word.

Charlie's confession clicks on in my mind, a filmstrip stuttering into motion, and I watch it play out in the shadowy colors of Andy's final night: my brothers face each other, breathing hard, hurting from the same wounds, but only one of them survives. And is it fair that it's Charlie, when he had longer to process what Dad did, and to try to make it right?

No. Of course it isn't fair. Andy's bones in the ground will never be fair.

But we made plans last night, the four of us. At the dining room table, over plates of pasta that Mom had undercooked, we decided we're going to get off this island, spend some time together away from the house. It was Mom's idea. "No Honorings," she promised. "No murder stories. Just us."

At first, it made me feel prickly, thinking of us trying to pretend we were a family like that: one who vacations together, staying up late with wine and games, laughing until we ache.

"It's not a vacation," Mom disagreed. "It's a chance to know one another. Away from all this. We can fight. We can scream and cry. The three of you can yell at me until you can't speak, I don't care, I deserve that. Just as long as we're together for a while. Somewhere safe."

"Somewhere safe," Charlie repeated, eyes cast away from Mom. "I think that's the most motherly thing you've ever said."

Mom shifted in her chair, looking both pleased and apologetic.

Chewing thoughtfully, Tate watched Charlie. "I think we should do it," she said. Then she turned to me. "But you have to come, too, Dahlia. It's not a family vacation — or a family . . . chance-to-know-each-other — if we're not all there."

"I don't think I —"

"Come on," she insisted. "Let's be sisters."

I searched her expression for mockery, for meanness, for acknowledgment that the comment was absurd — we've always been sisters, even if just in name — but her face was wide open, hopeful as a child's. Her eyes sparkled in the overhead light, bright as the ocean from movies, blue waves glittering with sun. Turns out, it's hard to resist the pull of a look like that, one meant to draw you in instead of keep you out.

So I agreed. Against the itch on my skin, the sickness swimming inside me, I agreed to leave with them. And it's true, there's still time; I could tell Elijah everything. He could read Charlie his rights, haul him out to his car. But I don't want Charlie — or any of us — to leave like that. Not in handcuffs. Not in a police cruiser with the lights flashing like there's a criminal inside. I want us all to walk out the door of this house on our own, to look back if we have to, and know that whatever we did to each other inside, we made it out of there together. Alive.

Now, Charlie's mask begins to slip. He glares at Elijah, working hard to seem defiant, but it's clear he can't hold it much longer. Already his eyes are darkening, tears seeping forward, ready to trickle down his cheeks. Before Elijah can catch it — the shame, the agony, the secrets my brothers both had to carry — I distract him with a question. I commit to the fiction, too.

"Do you think my father killed Andy? Do you think that Andy found out who he was, and then my dad killed him to protect his secret?"

It's the same theory I've been throwing at him for days — that the Blackburn Killer murdered my twin — but knowing now that it isn't true makes it so much harder to say.

I think the lie will always be a thorn in my throat. I think I'll have to choose to swallow it again and again.

When Elijah responds, there's a hint of sympathy in his voice, maybe even a clot of his own pain. Dad and Edmond don't compare, of course, but Elijah, too, has been hurt by his father, a man whose behavior he never understood.

"We don't have proof of that at this time," he answers. "But it's possible."

It's what I was fishing for him to tell me. Still, I avoid his eyes.

I know this fiction won't fix us, won't heal what's broken and lost. But right now, glancing at Charlie, I find him looking the same as yesterday, when he held my hand to his face, when we saw in each other the same desire to undo our brother's wounds. And it makes me sure — as sure as I'll ever be, at least — that keeping his secret is the best thing to do.

Not the right thing. I will never believe it's right. But I can believe in doing what's best for my family, and I can wish that right and best weren't at such terrible odds.

In the end, Elijah doesn't question us for long. I think he senses our exhaustion, our devastation, hanging like fog in the air. He promises, though, to follow up soon.

I walk him to the door, an uneasy quiet stretching between us.

"One more thing," he says as I reach for the knob. "Did you ever ask Charlie about the crime scene photo?"

I keep my expression steady — no twitch or blink that he can read.

"I did," I say.

He watches me expectantly.

"And I think I was wrong," I add, resisting the urge to clear my throat, "about it being him."

"Really," Elijah says, and now he reaches inside his jacket to pull out a copy of the photograph. He unfolds it carefully, like he's setting up a trap. "This isn't him?"

He points to that skinny figure tucked within the woods.

All I can see this time is how small Charlie looks. How vulnerable. How alone. He leans to the left like a tree about to fall, and I wish I could reach inside the photo, help to hold him up.

Bending closer, I pretend to scrutinize the

image. Then I straighten and shake my head.

"It was cloudy and dark the day you showed me. But in this light" — I gesture to the chandelier — "I can see it better. It isn't him."

Elijah opens his mouth to speak, then closes it again. I rush to fill his silence.

"Anything else? I'd like to get back to my family." I open the door for him to leave, and a cold breeze shoves into the house. "As I'm sure you can imagine, we have a lot to process."

Elijah searches my face before turning his attention toward the back hall. He waits a moment, as if hoping Charlie will hurry out to tell him the truth, then returns his gaze to me.

"That's it," he says, "for now," and he tucks the photo back into his coat, where I hope I never see it again.

Greta is quick to forgive me. I call her in the afternoon, but as soon as I apologize, she heaps the blame onto herself.

"You were right," she says. "My obsession with the Blackburn Killer gave me tunnel vision, and I lost sight of how deeply this affects you. It was insensitive, acting all excited to talk to suspects."

"No, you don't understand," I reply. "I

430

wasn't pushing you away because you were out of line. I was pushing you away because I was scared for you to learn the truth."

I'm standing in the backyard, facing the family plot, the wind growing louder as I wait for Greta to respond.

"What truth?" she says.

She deserves to hear it from me, not from some headline on the news. Still, the fear kicks in — that she'll see my family as nothing more than facts for all her folders.

I take a breath, let the salty air sting my lungs, and I tell her anyway.

"I found out a couple days ago," I say, "that my dad really was the Blackburn Killer."

I wince within her silence, waiting for the barrage of questions, the giddy spring to her voice. But in a moment, she groans, like the revelation pains her.

"Shit," she says. "I'm so sorry. You must be going through hell. What can I do for you?"

Tears rush to my eyes, hot with gratitude and relief. I look at the sky, almost silver today, its clouds shiny with a light that tries to break through. Then I look into the woods, at the dirt where Charlie buried Andy, where he wanted to bury a part of himself, and I cry even harder.

431

"Hey," Greta says softly. "Talk to me."

I think I will. When I see her again, I think I might tell her everything — what my father did to my brothers, what they did to each other, what I've chosen to do for them — and I want to believe that she'll keep our secret. That even as I walled myself off from anyone but Andy, even as I searched for him each day until I could hardly see, I still found something true, something real, something I didn't know the value of until now.

"Thank you," I tell her.

"For what?"

"Just for —" A sob cuts through my sentence, but I push myself to finish it. "For being a friend."

Later, when I'm off the phone with Greta, I find my family transforming the house. Tate boxes the museum's exhibits, Charlie returns the doors to their rightful hinges, and Mom dismantles the victim room.

I watch her for a moment, through the open doorway. She sits with a shredder on the floor between her legs, feeding it newspapers two pages at a time. For so long, those newspapers were my textbooks. Their gruesome stories taught me the lessons I clung to for years — that no one can be trusted; that there's safety in seclusion; that

432

if you keep away from others, you keep yourself from harm. And yet I've learned in recent days that all those lessons were wrong.

Around the room, trash bags are swollen with paper strips, and still, the shelves are only half empty. It's a fool's errand; destroying the stories won't bring back the dead. But already, the room looks bigger, brighter, the paperless shelves revealing themselves to be painted a gleaming white.

Sensing me, Mom lifts her head. She gives me half a smile, eyes watery but resolute, before returning to her chosen task.

My task is to take the stuff from the museum down to the driveway. Not all of it — the murder reports get thrown away — but we've decided to offer the rest of it to the islanders.

"Should we . . . donate it?" Tate asked at first.

"Put it all outside," Charlie said. "It'll be gone by the end of the day."

Turning around after plopping the last box on the curb, I'm stopped by a glimpse of a girl in the trees. Ruby's been Watching again, and as she slips out of the woods to walk toward me, her big eyes look a little smaller, the edges pinched with sadness.

"You're leaving, aren't you?" she asks.

"Soon," I tell her.

She nods, gaze drifting away.

"I was surprised," I say, "not to see you yesterday. I put your embroidery on display, like you asked."

She shrugs one shoulder. "I didn't think I was welcome. You kept sending people to question us."

"Right," I say, and I don't correct her about Greta. "Sorry about that."

"Besides," she adds, "I wouldn't feel Andy in there." She nods toward the house. "I feel him out back, in the woods, where we spent our time together."

She bites her lip, trying to keep it from trembling. She catches me watching and attempts a weary smile.

"Well, goodbye," she says, thrusting out her hand.

It's a strange, too-formal gesture, but I return it anyway.

As she pumps my arm, I'm surprised by the swell of regret inside me. Here is a girl who loved my brother — even with his anger, his tornadic moods — and I wish I knew what drew him toward her all those nights, what the two of them laughed about, if Ruby ever saw him cry.

I love her, Andy said to Charlie, *but anyone who dares to love me will only be ruined.*

He was wrong about that. Ruby wasn't ruined. She's intense and she's odd, but she's part of our story now. Without her memories of Andy, the key she offered without a clue of everything it would ultimately unlock, I'm not sure I'd have ever learned the truth.

So no. She isn't ruined. In a way, she helped to save us.

"He did love you," I tell her now.

"Andy?" she asks, apprehensive. Then her wariness dissolves as her eyes swell with hope. "How do you know? You said he never talked about me."

"Trust me," I say — and that's all it takes. Light beams across Ruby's face, even as the sky stays gray.

The next morning, our bags are by the door. We wait for Mom in the foyer, listening to the house groan in the wind.

"It's complaining that we're leaving," Tate says.

"Let it," Charlie scoffs.

We've managed to avoid the news so far, turned away the persistent reporters. But last night, voices frothed up from the street like waves, trying to drown us with their anger, their disgust, their *how could they not have knowns*. None of us blame them. Actually, it's a relief, that the islanders, the victims' families, finally have the answer they've always deserved.

When Mom appears, she seems haggard, overwhelmed, her hands lost in the sleeves of her oversize sweater, its pockets deep and sagging.

"Sorry," she says. "That was Fritz on the phone, clarifying our arrangement. He'll keep an eye on things while I'm gone."

At Fritz's name, I feel a twitch of discomfort, one I know is misplaced. I wonder when I'll stop associating him with the room beneath the shed, when I'll think of him again without flashing to his fearful grip on my ankle, when my body will accept the truth my mind already knows: Dad was the dangerous one among us. Only Dad.

"Oh," Mom says. She reaches into her pockets, pulls out four slim candles and a lighter. "I thought we could . . ." she starts, but when she sees our faces, she stops. "What is it?"

"You said no Honorings," Charlie says.

"There won't be, once we leave. I just thought — well, we have to do *something* for Andy, don't we? And how else can we . . . But no. No, you're right." She opens her palm to stare at the lighter. "I just don't know another way."

She isn't wrong. Right now, there's no grave we can visit, no ashes in an urn. Any other family would plan a service, scour a funeral home's brochures. But we're not another family. We will try to be, I think, in the future we'll head toward when we walk out the door, but for now, we're still just us. And this is what we know of honoring someone. This is how we remember the dead.

Tate and I glance at each other, and between us, Charlie rolls his eyes. "Fine," he says, sighing. He grabs the candles from Mom and passes them out.

Something sour squats on the back of my tongue, a taste so potent I could gag. But as Mom tries to light her candle with a shaking hand, I force myself to swallow. In a moment, the flame catches, and from there, it's muscle memory. Mom touches her wick to Tate's, who touches hers to Charlie's, and the circle's complete when he passes the flame to me. Above the shared light of our candles, his gaze meets mine.

"You want to start?" he asks.

I inhale deeply, wondering if there's any part of Andy that lingers in the air, if the cells he left behind could have lasted this long, survived the grime of all these years. He'd think it was stupid, me wishing for that, wanting so badly to breathe him in. But at my core, there's a longing for Andy I know I'll never lose. I feel it as I watch the flame, as I let his name fall from my lips like a tear from an eye.

"Andrew Lighthouse," I say.

Then Charlie, voice foggy: "Andrew Lighthouse."

Then Tate, quiet but controlled: "Andrew Lighthouse."

And, finally, like we always did, we end with Mom. "Andrew Lighthouse," she whispers.

We don't need to look at one another to see when to speak. We know the rhythm of this moment, the space between the final utterance of his name and the first word of our prayer.

"We can't restore your life," we say together, "but we strive to restore your memory with this breath."

And as we blow out the candles, smoke spiraling up to obscure the air, I see him for a second, still just a boy. He opens the door of the credenza, urging me to follow him into the dark. *Come on, Dahlia,* he says, voice all squeaky, his beckoning hand so small. My throat hardens, the image wobbles in front of me, and when I feel a tentative palm against my back, I blink to find my brother gone.

"You okay?" Charlie asks me.

"Are you?" I ask back.

He shrugs. I shrug. It's the best we can do.

We grab our bags, pass through the front door, let Mom lock up behind us. When we're halfway down the driveway, I do what Andy never got the chance to: I look back at the house one last time — its gray stone, its walls that kept our secrets — and I turn away from it, knowing what Charlie's note said was true: the only way out is to never come back.

We're going to walk to the ferry, accept the islanders' gasps, their circling whispers, the way their eyes press on us as palpably as hands. Then we'll stand with our backs to the wind as the boat chugs us toward its perpetual destination: away.

Charlie, Tate, and Mom have booked rooms in a hotel on the mainland, one with a view of water instead of woods. We can't go far or the police might think we're flee-ing, like we have something else to hide, but we'll take some time to live among one another, to figure all this out. Meanwhile, Mom will decide if she'll return to our haunted house or, like the rest of us, leave it behind for good.

Tonight, I'll walk toward my tiny apartment, down the street from their hotel. Greta will be waiting for me in the café, face lit by her laptop on the counter, the scent of fresh muffins in the air. When I come through the door, she'll open her arms to me, and instead of merely tolerating her embrace, like I did at the museum, I will savor it this time. I will be sure to hold on tight.

Beyond that, I don't know. Maybe even after my family scatters — Charlie and Tate to New York, Mom to wherever — I'll stay in that room above the café, the one I chose because it was close to the boat that would take me back if news ever came of Andy's return.

But maybe not. I've got no need to wait for him now. I can go anywhere.

The world is cruel, yes — my mother taught me that; my whole family did — but it's enormous, too. And there's got to be some space, some people in it, for me.

ACKNOWLEDGMENTS

Once again, I must begin by thanking you, the reader. Thank you for investing your time in this story, these characters, this strange and unsettling family. Special thanks to the bookstagrammers, bloggers, librarians, and booksellers who passionately — and tirelessly — strive to connect readers with books. I'm sure I speak on behalf of all authors when I say that the work you do is invaluable to us.

Thank you to the best of all agents, Sharon Pelletier, whose storytelling instincts and editorial feedback are unparalleled — except by my editor, Kaitlin Olson, whose insightful suggestions and questions always open up new layers of my own story to me. Book by book, these smart, kickass women have made me a better writer, and I am so lucky to have this opportunity to work with them.

Thank you so much to everyone at Atria

Books, especially Megan Rudloff, Isabel DaSilva, and @AtriaMysteryBus master-mind David Brown, all of whom are behind-the-scenes literary rock stars. Thank you to editorial assistant Jade Hui, copyeditor Laurie McGee, and huge thanks as well to designer Kelli McAdams and art director Jimmy Iacobelli for creating what is truly the cover of my dreams.

A grateful tip of the hat to the late Frances Glessner Lee, whose "Nutshell Studies of Unexplained Deaths" inspired Tate's crime scene dioramas. I first learned about Lee in Rachel Monroe's excellent book, *Savage Appetites: Four True Stories of Women, Crime, and Obsession,* which also informed many of the ideas about true crime that I explored in this novel.

Much gratitude to Georgia Hardstark and Karen Kilgariff, the hosts of the podcast *My Favorite Murder,* without which I would have never found my way to writing this book. Georgia and Karen continually create a safe space for weirdos like me who have a fasci-nation with murder, and they never lose sight of the fact that it's the victims, not the killers, that deserve to be remembered.

Thank you to the incredible writers who have supported me over the last couple years, whether it be through blurbing my books, helping me brainstorm, or just offering me a space in which to scream and/or rejoice. Special thanks to Amina Akhtar, Andrea Bartz, Samantha Downing, Meghan Evans, Layne Fargo, Wendy Heard, Christina McDonald, Mindy Mejia, Megan Miranda, Maureen O'Brien, Daniela Petrova, and Wendy Walker.

Thank you to my friends for your continual support and enthusiasm; for group texts that make me laugh and keep me sane; for perfectly timed Taylor Swift gifs; for promoting my books to your book clubs; and, to two of you in particular, for choosing my book as the "one book you'll read all year."

Thank you to my very supportive family (aunts! uncles! cousins!), and thanks in particular to my brother-in-law, Greg, who always has thoughtful words to say about my stories; my sister, Kate, who uses her adorable dogs to help spread the word about my books; and to my parents, who, three books in, continue to be my most excited cheerleaders.

Finally, thank you to my dog, Maisy, for all the cuteness and cuddles (which are essential to my writing process), and to my husband, Marc, who is the most helpful and hilarious human on earth, and who ultimately inspired this book. He first suggested

The Family Plot as a title for a different novel I was working on, one that stubbornly refused to be named. "No, that doesn't work at all," I told him, "but that is a *great* title." Then I scrapped that other novel and wrote this one instead.

ABOUT THE AUTHOR

Megan Collins is the author of *Behind the Red Door* and *The Winter Sister*. She is the managing editor of *3Elements Review* and taught creative writing for many years at both the high school and college level. She lives in Connecticut, where she obsesses over dogs, true crime, miniatures, and cake.

The employees of Thorndike Press hope you have enjoyed this Large Print book. All our Thorndike, Wheeler, and Kennebec Large Print titles are designed for easy reading, and all our books are made to last. Other Thorndike Press Large Print books are available at your library, through selected bookstores, or directly from us.

For information about titles, please call:
(800) 223-1244

or visit our website at:
gale.com/thorndike

To share your comments, please write:
Publisher
Thorndike Press
10 Water St., Suite 310
Waterville, ME 04901